# Second Chances

# Second Chances

Linda Chadwick

Bonneville Books
Springville, Utah

This is a work of fiction. The characters, names, incidents, places, and dialogue are products of the author's imagination, and are not to be construed as real.

ISBN 13: 978-1-59955-304-7

Published by Bonneville Books, an imprint of Cedar Fort, Inc.
2373 W. 700 S., Springville, UT 84663
Distributed by Cedar Fort, Inc., www.cedarfort.com

Library of Congress Cataloging-in-Publication Data

Chadwick, Linda, 1969-
  Second chances / Linda Chadwick.
    p. cm.
  ISBN 978-1-59955-304-7 (acid-free paper)
  1. Single fathers--Fiction. 2. Problem families--Fiction. 3. Mormon families--Fiction I. Title.
  PS3603.H3325S43 2009
  813'.6--dc22

                                        2009015788

Cover design by Angela D. Olsen
Cover design © 2009 by Lyle Mortimer

Printed in the United States of America

10  9  8  7  6  5  4  3  2  1

Printed on acid-free paper

# Dedication

To my five children, Eric, Amber, Tyler, Courtney, and Sarah for their loving support. To my husband of twenty-two years who encouraged me to follow my dream and never stopped believing in me. I love you all.

# Acknowledgments

Special thanks to Jennifer Shelly and Amy Carpenter for taking the time to read my manuscript and for the much-welcomed advice they had to offer. Thanks to my editor, Heather Holm, for all of her hard work in making *Second Chances* the best it could be. I appreciate you all!

# Chapter 1

The alarm clock beeped annoyingly and brought Larry out of the dreamland he was enjoying. Blinking a couple of times, he glanced over at the red numbers glaring at him. They were taunting him to get out of bed and face his obligations.

He reached out from beneath the floral comforter and shut off the terrible noise. He pulled the covers up again, wishing he could find his way back to the unconscious state he had just left. It was a place where he felt safe—somewhere he could set his own rules to life, love, happiness, and anything else he wanted to control. He knew it wasn't a place he could stay and hide, because it wasn't real. Reality was what was waiting for him on the other side of the bedroom door.

He looked around the dark room and sleepily thought how hard it was to get out of bed when even the sun hadn't shown its face yet. But then, it was only the first week of March. The sun would be coming up earlier in a few months, and then the snow would finally melt away, the flowers would start to bloom, and the warm spring weather would have everyone wearing short sleeves and riding their bikes. Of course, living in Fairview, Utah, the winter weather could last well into the springtime. He remembered years ago when it snowed on Memorial Day, which sent them home early from their camping trip and put a damper on all the holiday activities. It didn't bother him, really. He had a lot of work to do and had spent the rest of the day at the office.

Memories of family flooded his mind, sending throbbing pain through the front part of his head. It was the kind of pain that feels like every vessel in your head is playing Hacky Sack with your brain. He let out a soft, painful groan and reached up with one hand to massage his forehead. He didn't need a headache to start the day, especially on a Monday morning, and especially on this *particular* Monday morning.

On a typical Monday morning, he would have hit the snooze button at least three times before finally pulling his tired, weak body out of bed and taking a quick five-minute shower. He would put on his blue or grey pinstriped suit, his black leather dress shoes, and rush downstairs for breakfast.

There he would find his beautiful wife, Barbara. Her silky, long, brown hair would be pulled back into a ponytail, and she would be wearing her favorite blue cotton bathrobe with matching slippers—the ones he'd bought her for Christmas two years previously. Her stunning brown eyes would shine as she cheerfully greeted him with a warm smile and a kiss good morning. Waiting for him on the kitchen counter would be two pieces of buttered wheat toast, a glass of orange juice, and the morning newspaper. Without much time to spare, he would gulp down the juice, grab the toast to eat on his way, and stick the paper under one arm. Feeling rushed and overwhelmed, he would give Barbara a quick kiss good-bye and be off to work. This was how most of his mornings went.

But this Monday morning would be different. He wouldn't need to put on one of his pinstriped suits, because he wouldn't be going to the office. There would be no buttered toast, no orange juice, and no morning paper waiting for him on the kitchen counter, because this Monday morning his wife would not be there waiting for him.

It had been six months since Barbara first started feeling sick. She assured everyone that she was all right and continued to take care of the children and the house while Larry worked extra long hours to ensure his promotion at the office. Until her severe pain started, he really had no idea how sick she was. Eventually the pain reached a point where she could no longer ignore it and went to the doctor to see what was wrong.

The doctor ordered several tests, including x-rays, blood tests, and an ultrasound. He told them he would call when the results came back, probably in one or two days. They were shocked when the next day they got a call from the doctor who wanted Barbara to have a CT scan of her pancreas. The urgency in the doctor's voice left them with an unsettling feeling of panic.

They looked helplessly into each other's terrified eyes as they waited anxiously in the doctor's office for the results of the ultrasound. Neither of them knew what to say, and both of them were silently praying for the best, but preparing for the worst.

Finally the doctor came in holding a folder in his hands. Inside were the results of the ultrasound: Barbara had cancer of the pancreas. There were several small tumors throughout her pancreas. The cancer was advanced and had also spread to her liver and kidneys. Surgery was not an option. Chemotherapy would shrink the tumors but not prolong her life, which could be anywhere from four to six months. The doctor gave her prescription medication to help with the pain, but that was all he could do for her.

Out of nowhere, their lives had suddenly hit a brick wall. They had nowhere to go and no options to consider. What they were being told was hard to comprehend: four to six months left with each other, four to six months to do all the things they'd planned, and four to six months to get Barbara's affairs in order.

Larry recalled the unspeakable rage he felt that day. He demanded that the doctor do something—anything to try and save her. But after all the talking, all the arguing, and all the anger, the answer was still the same—Barbara was going to die. He became outraged with Barbara as well, accusing her of not seeing the doctor when she first felt sick. Why couldn't she for once put her needs before someone else's? Barbara felt terrible and apologized to him all the way home. Before long he was weeping like a baby in her arms and pleading with her not to die.

The sadness and despair of losing Barbara burned inside him like an uncontrollable wildfire. He still harbored a great deal of anger—more anger than he would ever admit. He was the one who had all the answers, the one she turned to for support, but when she really needed to count on him, he was helpless. How could he live with himself knowing he'd let her down when she needed him the most?

Larry rolled over and ran his hand across Barbara's side of the bed. She had slept beside him for the last nineteen years, stealing the covers, putting her cold feet against his warm legs, and affectionately kissing him good night. She was not just a wife and mother but was also his best friend. How could he ever learn to live without her? He didn't deserve being a widower at forty-two, and he didn't deserve being left alone to raise three children by himself.

The pain in his head tightened, forcing him to climb out of bed and go to the medicine cabinet in search of Tylenol. Standing in front of the bathroom mirror he could see some gray starting to show in his chestnut brown hair, as well as in his mustache. He had to admit that the years were finally catching up with him. He looked a little closer and found a small bald spot starting to show on top of his head. He sighed heavily, threw some cold water on his face, and rubbed his hazy green eyes. It was useless to worry about his looks anymore. He knew if Barbara were standing next to him, she would tell him that grey hair meant maturity and the bald spot was attractive. She could always make him feel young and handsome no matter what the circumstances.

He went to the dresser and pulled out his favorite pair of old blue jeans, the ones Barbara said he should get rid of, and his Dale Earnheart Jr. sweater he bought three years ago at the NASCAR race in Las Vegas, Nevada. It was one of the last times he and Barbara spent alone together. After that, the demands at the office increased and their time together decreased. Time with Barbara narrowed down to a kiss in the morning and a five-minute chat at night. It seemed there were just not enough hours in the day and he was wearing himself thin trying to divide his time between work and home.

Larry shook his head, trying to shake out all the memories, the sorrow, and the regrets. He opened the bedroom door and paused. Hesitant to step out into the hallway, he took a deep breath. Today was the start of a new life; a life without his beloved wife, a life where he would need to be the father and the mother, and a life he wasn't sure he could succeed in.

Anxiety almost overwhelmed him when he thought of taking on Barbara's role. He wondered how the children would respond, or if he could even connect with them, and it terrified him. Nevertheless, he would keep his fears and anxieties under wraps, putting on the appearance of the strong, all-knowing parent.

"Good grief Larry, they're only kids!" he told himself sternly as he took one step out the door. He looked down the hall at the other bedroom and saw light coming from beneath the door. It was his youngest daughter Katie's room. She wasn't the one he needed to worry about, so he headed downstairs.

The first door on the right was his oldest daughter Jody's room. The door was closed, so he gave it a soft tap and waited for an answer. When there was none, he opened the door and peeked in.

"Jody, get up! Do you know what time it is? You'll be late for school," he said loudly, ready for an argument if that's what it took to get her out of bed. There was a small groan from under the heap of blankets, but no movement.

He looked around her room, realizing how fast she'd grown up. When she was younger they were inseparable, but as time went on they had drifted apart. He really didn't know much about her life anymore. She would be seventeen on April 14, and she definitely wasn't his little girl anymore. Instead of the butterflies and flowers that used to decorate the walls of her room, they were now covered in posters of people he didn't recognize. A fuzzy pink chair and a table with a phone on it stood in one corner of the room. In the other corner there was a wood desk with an iPod, books, and a picture of her and her mother.

When there was still no movement from the twin-size bed, he reached down with both hands and shook the heap of blankets. "Jody, I mean it, it's time to get up," he said again in a firmer voice.

She threw the blankets off and sat straight up in bed. "Okay, dad! Don't have a heart attack! I'm awake!" she grunted irritably. Her short brown hair was messy from a restless night's sleep, and her glossy brown eyes were glaring up at him. She was the spitting image of her mother, right down to the wrinkle in her forehead when she was mad.

"Breakfast in thirty minutes," he said, a little agitated that she was still in bed. She gave another grunt and threw the covers back over her head. Larry closed the door and headed down the hall.

The next room was Christopher's, his only son. The door had a large, yellow sign that read, "Caution do not enter" in big black letters. He knocked on the door, and after a few seconds he heard a faint, "Come in." The walls were covered in posters of skateboarders and different styles of guitars. In the corner of the room was a TV with a Nintendo game cube hooked up and several games on the floor. There was also a guitar and amplifier sitting in the other corner.

"Are you about ready for school?" Larry asked, sounding more like a drill sergeant than a father.

Chris was sitting on the side of his bed and putting on his camouflage skater shoes. His naturally curly brown hair was getting a little long and hung over one eye. He was wearing a black T-shirt that had, "Ask me if I care" written on the front, and his baggy blue jeans were ripped on one knee. Still, at about five-foot-six, he was a handsome young man. He had his father's green eyes and his mother's fair complexion. He would

5

be sixteen on August 31 and was a sophomore at North Sanpete High School.

Larry had pushed him to try out for the freshman football team as soon as he entered high school, mainly because Larry had been the star quarterback of his own high school team. He was sure Chris would love football as much as he did, but Chris didn't even make it though the season. Barbara said it was because it was Larry's dream and not Chris's, and they needed to support Chris in what he wanted to do. Larry knew his son's passion was skateboarding, but he thought it was a waste of time, not a sport.

"I'm ready," Chris snapped without looking up.

"Are you really going to school dressed like that?" Larry asked, referring to the ripped blue jeans.

"What's wrong with the way I'm dressed? It's not the seventies anymore," Chris said, smirking.

"Well, all right. Breakfast will be ready in thirty minutes." He decided to let that argument go for now.

He shut the door and returned upstairs to Katie's room. This enthusiastic eight-year-old was in the second grade at Fairview Elementary and loved to go to school. She was their last child and the apple of his eye.

Larry and Barbara had not expected to have another child, but Katie surprised them. Katie had a rough start in life when she was born six weeks early. Barbara slipped on a patch of ice one cold day in January. She went right to the hospital when she felt the contractions begin, but they were unable to stop them. A few hours later, on January 9, 1999, Katie Ann Porter was born. She weighed only four and a half pounds, and the doctors put her in an incubator to help her breathe.

Katie was a fighter and continued to improve daily. After only three weeks in the newborn intensive care unit, she came home. She had always been a little smaller than most kids her age, but that didn't stop her from keeping up with them. She loved to play soccer and ride her scooter alongside Chris on his skateboard.

Larry reached the top of the stairs, and sure enough, her door was open. She was dressed and brushing her long brown curls. Her room was decorated in pink—pink walls with a border of butterflies and flowers. A Barbie house stood in one corner of her room, and on the other side was a white bookshelf filled with all kinds of books. By her bed was a doll cradle that held two dolls side by side with a blanket over them. She had already made her bed and sat her favorite teddy bear on top. On her door was a large yellow sticker that said "Katie's room." She was definitely still his little girl.

"Almost ready, sweetie?" he said, gleaming proudly. She turned around, saw her dad standing in the doorway, and ran into his arms.

"Hi, daddy. I've been ready for ten minutes now," she announced with pride.

"Good, then you can help me with breakfast. Hop on." He turned his back to her and put out both arms.

"Hurray!" Katie squealed with excitement and jumped on his back for a piggy back ride to the kitchen.

Breakfast consisted of frozen waffles, brown and serve sausage links, and juice. Larry was pleased with his accomplishment. After all, Barbara was the one who did all the cooking. He was much too busy to be bothered with it. However, there was a time when he and Barbara took turns cooking, and he loved it. They even turned it into a competition, trying to find the best recipes to outdo the other. But the demands of work took over once again, which put the responsibility back on Barbara.

He placed the food on the oval dining room table and went to the stairs. He yelled, "Breakfast!"

"I'm starving to death. Can we please eat without them? Please, please, please?" Katie pleaded with folded hands.

"Okay, Katie, go ahead."

Chris was the first one upstairs. He plopped down on the chair and looked over the food. "I'm not very hungry," he sighed.

Larry was insulted. "Now look, I made this whole breakfast so you wouldn't go to school hungry. You need to eat something," he stated crossly.

Chris didn't respond. He got up and walked over to the refrigerator and took out a gallon of chocolate milk. He popped the cap off and took a long swig right out of the jug. He opened the kitchen cupboard, removed a package of chocolate chip cookies, and stuffed four of them in the pocket of his blue Levi jacket. Then he picked up his backpack and skateboard from off the floor and headed for the back door.

"That's what you're eating for breakfast?" Larry asked irritably.

"Yup," Chris said, not turning to look at his father. "Tell Jody to hurry up. I'll be in the car." He walked out, slamming the door behind him.

"What's that all about?" Larry asked Katie, who was scarfing down a waffle. She shrugged her shoulders and went right on eating.

Jody walked over to the kitchen table and looked over the meal with the same expression as Chris. "I don't eat meat," she said.

"Since when?" Larry asked, getting frustrated with them all.

"Since I was like, five. I'm not hungry anyway," she said, heading for the back door.

"What is it with kids and breakfast anyway?" Larry said throwing his hands up in the air.

Jody picked up her backpack and left without saying good-bye. Larry looked at his plate and decided he wasn't hungry anymore either.

"I don't want to miss the bus. See you tonight," Katie said with a smile. She kissed him on the cheek, picked up her pink princess backpack, and was out the door.

Larry got up and cleared the table. He threw all the dishes into the sink and decided to worry about them later. He walked over to the den to get started with work.

Well, actually, the den was now his office. Starting today he would be working only two days at the office and the rest of the week he would spend working from home. He'd been an accountant with J.J. Jensen for twelve years. He loved his work but realized someone would need to be at home with the children. That's when he proposed working two days in the office and three days at home. Since his company was based in Provo, he would actually be saving time and money.

It was funny now that he thought about it. Barbara asked him once if he could work from home so he could spend more time with the family. At the time he thought the whole idea was crazy and told her there was no way the company would go for that. It was true he spent a lot of time at the office, but he made good money and they'd always had nice things, such as this beautiful three-story home with a three-car garage. And he was finally able to buy that brand new Ford double cab diesel pickup truck he'd always wanted. Best of all, Barbara was able to stay at home and raise the kids just like they'd planned.

Everything in his life was perfect—his job, his family. Things were going good, and then Barbara got sick and everything changed.

He picked up their wedding picture and cradled it in his hands. He admired Barbara's beauty and remembered their special day. They were married September 28, 1988, in the Manti Utah Temple, for time and all eternity. So many memories that used to make him smile now only added salt to the open wound.

Larry and Barbara met while attending college at Brigham Young University. He had just returned from serving a two-year mission in South Dakota and was majoring in accounting. Needing a little extra money, he got a job at the bookstore on campus. Barbara was already working there and taking classes in agriculture.

He knew from the moment he saw her that she was the one for him, and after three tries, she finally consented to go on a date with him. Larry knew just from talking to her at the bookstore that with her outgoing personality, dinner and a movie just wouldn't cut it. So he took her to the fun dome for their first date. After several hours of miniature golf, go carts, and rollerblading, they were hooked on each other. They spent every waking hour together for the next four months, until the day he popped the question.

Larry knelt down on one knee, and with a ring in one hand and a single red rose in the other, he asked her to marry him. He thought for sure his heart was going to explode right out of his chest. Barbara meant the world to him, and he couldn't imagine living without her. Then she said yes, and his life was never the same.

Now, as he stood there in his cold, empty house, nothing seemed right. He didn't care about his expensive truck sitting in the garage, and the home that was once warm and inviting felt more like a prison. He missed Barbara so much that it felt as if his heart had shattered into pieces.

He wiped away a tear and returned the picture to the fireplace mantel. He wondered how he was going to get through this when she was a part of everything around him. Pictures of the family hung on the wall. The red and white afghan she crocheted for him so he wouldn't get cold while watching Monday night football hung across the back of the couch. Her favorite rocking chair sat in the corner of the room, and the book she was reading was still sitting on the end table beside it.

Emotion overcame him as he sat down at his desk, and he felt utterly alone. It seemed that even his Heavenly Father had deserted him. Larry had done everything he was supposed to—the priesthood blessings, the fasting and prayer, and the faith that Barbara would overcome her cancer. But the miracle never came, and now Larry was left alone to live his life without her. He was angry with the Lord for that. Why did he have to take her away? What good is it to have faith if in the end you still lose the one you love? Questions without answers hung in the back of his mind and fed the fire that burned inside him. He turned on the computer and tried to lose himself in work.

He was deep in thought when the phone rang and almost knocked him off his chair. He looked up at the clock hanging above his desk: 11:25 a.m. He picked up the receiver.

"Hello, Porter residence."

"Hello, is this Mr. Porter?" the woman asked politely.

"Yes, this is Larry Porter."

"My name is Margaret Thompson. I'm the principal at North Sanpete High School." There was a slight irritation in her voice as she spoke. "Your son Christopher has been involved in a fight at school. I'd like you to come to my office so we can talk."

The minute he hung up the phone he could feel the tension building. He picked up his keys and rushed out to the truck.

As he walked down the hallway toward the office, Larry could see Chris sitting in a chair slumped over. He tried to keep his cool but thought how stupid Chris was to do something like that. The family had enough to deal with right now.

Chris looked up when Larry entered the office, and Larry noticed that his son had a black eye and cut lip. Larry took a deep, stay-in-control breath and shot Christopher a disappointed look. A tall, blond-haired woman behind the desk stood up to greet him.

"Are you Mr. Porter?" she asked with a bright smile.

"Yes I am," he answered. Chris put his head back down and fiddled with his hands.

"I'm Clair, the secretary. I'm sorry to hear about your wife," she said sympathetically. "Mrs. Thompson is expecting you. Go right in." She pointed to a door with a plaque that read, "Margaret Thompson, Principal."

As Larry walked away, he irritably wished that people would stop saying how sorry they were. No one could be sorrier than he was. And to make matters worse, when you live in a small town like Fairview, word gets around to everyone. People he didn't even know were at Barbara's funeral.

He opened the door to find a stocky, redheaded woman sitting behind a large wooden desk. She had several pictures of her family sitting on her desk, and on the wall behind her hung four wood plaques, all indicating she had completed different courses in education. She stood up and reached out her small, plump hand.

"I'm Margaret Thompson the Principal. I'm sorry to hear about your wife. I'm sure this must be hard on the whole family." She shook his hand and gestured toward one of the chairs in front her desk. "Please, have a seat."

"Thank you," Larry mumbled, biting his tongue.

"I'm sorry to call you in like this, but we have a no tolerance policy for fighting at this school," she stated bluntly. "From what I understand, Christopher was offended by something another student said, so Christopher hit him. Regardless of what the student said, Christopher threw the first punch, and therefore will be suspended. Our usual policy is a one-week suspension; however, under the circumstances, I have only suspended him for the rest of the day. He will also have after school detention for one week. Does this sound like a fair punishment to you?" She finally stopped talking long enough for Larry to answer.

"Yes, that sounds fair." He didn't feel he had any say in the matter anyway. She was blunt and to the point and left no room for argument.

"Mr. Porter, I'm very concerned about Christopher and the way he seems to be lashing out at others. Do you have him in any kind of counseling?" Larry noticed the deep concern in her voice.

"The kids have been with Barbara's mother for the last week. They just got home yesterday, so I really haven't had much time to do anything," Larry responded. He was baffled by her forwardness and felt backed into a tight corner.

"We have a great counselor here at school. His name is Mark Petersen. If you'd like, I could set up a time for Christopher to come in and meet with him."

"All right, that would be fine." Larry would agree to anything right now. He just wanted to get Chris home and find out what was going through his head. It wasn't like him to start a fight. What was he thinking?

"Good then. I'll get that set up." She smiled, obviously pleased with herself. "Again, I'm sorry for your loss. If there is anything we can do, please let us know." She shook his hand again and escorted him to the door. He could see why she was the principle. She had controlled the whole conversation and led him in the direction she wanted him to go.

Chris was still slumped in the chair with his head down. Larry grabbed him by the arm. "Let's go," he huffed as he pulled him up from the chair and directed him toward the door. Chris yanked his arm away and stormed off to the car. He stayed a safe distance in front of his father.

The ride home was quiet. Larry was trying to think of something to say without losing his temper. Chris sat close to the door, his elbow on the armrest and his head resting on his hand. He wasn't interested in hearing anything his father had to say.

Chris wanted everyone to think he was tough, but no one knew how much he was hurting inside. He and his mother held a special bond that no one would ever understand. She took the time to really talk to him and help him solve his problems and achieve his goals. His father wouldn't even give him the time of day, let alone his own personal attention. His mother always knew when he'd had a bad day and would bring cookies to his room where they would sit and talk about life. She also went with him to the father and son campout when his father was away on yet another business trip. She was the coolest dad there, even winning the three-legged race. Chris knew his father would never care for him the way his mother did. And now she was gone, leaving him feeling isolated and alone.

As they pulled into the driveway, Larry's disposition softened. He turned to look at Chris. "Do you want to tell me what happened?" he asked calmly.

Chris shrugged his shoulders as if he really didn't care. "The kid made me mad, so I punched him. Then he hit me back and the whole thing just blew up," he said, scoffing. He appeared to have no remorse for what he had done.

"Don't act like this was no big deal, Christopher! If circumstances were any different, you would have been suspended from school for a week!" Larry's voice rose with anger over his son's nonchalance.

Chris rolled his eyes. Who did Larry think he was to be lecturing *him*? This was coming from the father who had never been around and who didn't have a clue what was going on with his own family.

"Well then, it's a good thing that circumstances weren't different," Chris snarled sarcastically. He pulled up on the handle of the truck door just as his father grabbed him by the arm to prevent him from leaving.

"Just a minute! I'm not through!" Larry said harshly. "What was going through your head that would make you punch somebody in the face?"

"Wouldn't you like to know," Chris grumbled. He pulled free from his father's grip and exited the truck with a loud slam of the door.

Larry angrily slammed both fists into the steering wheel. He was frustrated and confused. This was not like Chris. He was always the quiet one, the passionate one, and the shy one. What had gotten into him, and why was he shutting him out?

Larry slammed his fists into the steering wheel again. "Our son won't talk to me, Barb!" he shouted. "What am I supposed to do with him?" Letting off more steam, he slammed his fists into the steering wheel again and again.

After taking a few deep breaths, he got out of the truck and slowly walked into the house. As soon as he opened the door he could hear Chris's stereo blasting from the basement. There would be no talking to him now. He threw down the keys and headed back to the den, determined to get some work done.

It was all quiet when he heard the back door bang shut. He looked up at the clock. It was 3:35 p.m. He heard an uplifting little voice. "Dad, are you home?" Katie called from the kitchen.

"In the den, Katie," he called back. Three seconds later she was on his lap and telling him all about her day at school. To him it was like a breath of fresh air. In her eyes, he could do no wrong, and he liked that feeling for a change.

# Chapter 2

"Time for dinner," Larry yelled from the kitchen. The members of the ward had offered to bring dinner in for them, but Larry had refused. They had already done enough. The counter was full of goodies, and he thought it was about time for him to do the cooking. He whipped up a gourmet meal of hamburgers and potato chips.

Katie was the first one to the table and offered to say the prayer. After three calls downstairs, Chris finally came up from his room. He was silent and kept his eyes on the floor as he took a seat at the dinner table. Larry didn't want to stir things up again, so neither of them said a word.

"Oh, my gosh! Did someone beat you up?" Katie exclaimed, catching a glimpse of Chris's black eye.

Chris smiled at Katie. "You should see the other guy," he teased, knowing that Katie's curiosity was getting the best of her.

"Did you punch him?" she pried, wide-eyed and intrigued.

Larry approached the table and interrupted before any more could be said. "Let's not talk about it at the dinner table." Katie gave her father a disappointed frown.

"Where's Jody? Shouldn't she be home from school by now?" Larry asked Chris. He was usually late getting home from the office, so this unfamiliar territory. However, he was sure school would be over by now.

"Well, high school gets out at two thirty, so she's probably at somebody's house," Chris said with an "I don't really care where she's at" sound in his voice. It was now 6:15 p.m., and Larry was starting to get worried.

"Does she do this often? You know, being sixteen with a driver's license doesn't give her the right to do whatever she wants." He didn't want her to have a car in the first place, but Barbara thought it would give her a sense of responsibility.

"She's usually home in time for dinner," replied Chris, reaching for the bag of potato chips. He was in no mood for small talk.

"Well, let's go ahead and eat; I'm sure she'll be along shortly." *And she'll have some explaining to do as well,* he thought irritably.

Larry was sitting in his recliner reading *Sports Illustrated* and keeping an eye on the clock when Katie came in holding her favorite teddy bear, the one with the pink dress and a matching bow. She sat down on the arm of his chair. Her precious smile had vanished and was replaced by a troubled look.

"What's the matter, honey?" he asked softly. He put his magazine down so he could give her his full attention.

She rested her head gently on his shoulder and let out a sigh. "Do you miss mommy?" she asked sadly.

Her question brought tears to his eyes, and he fought to keep them from falling. He wanted to be strong for her and not show his emotions, but the thought of his little girl missing her mother was like having a dagger run through his heart. He knew the time would come when the kids would want to talk about their mother, but he was hoping for more time to prepare. In his own warped sense of thinking, he figured that if he just didn't talk about Barbara, maybe it wouldn't hurt so much.

He looked down into Katie's innocent brown eyes. "Yes, I miss her very much," he whispered in her ear. "But she will always be with us, watching over us. Do you know that?"

"That's what mommy told me when she got sick." Katie sat up straight so she could look her father in the eye. Her face was gleaming with excitement as she remembered something important. "One day before mommy died, she gave me this teddy bear. We named her Peggy. She said it was my special bear, and when I felt sad and missed her, I could hug Peggy and it would be like hugging her. She put her picture by my bed so I could always see her."

A more serious look came into Katie's eyes as she remembered something else. "She told me she didn't want me to feel sad." She paused

15

for a moment, and then she leaned over, put her hand up to Larry's ear, and whispered, "But sometimes I still do."

Larry could no longer hold back the tears. They were streaming down both cheeks. "I feel sad too, Katie," he said, admiring her strength.

Katie realized how sad her father was and wrapped both arms around his neck. "Don't cry, daddy." Her voice was filled with concern. "Mommy's waiting in heaven for us. We learned in Primary that we could be together forever. Mommy said it's because you took her to the temple to be married, so we'll see her again someday." He tightly held his little girl in his arms. She had more faith at eight years old than he would ever have in his lifetime.

"Daddy, I can't breathe," Katie squealed as she tried to break free of his tight hold.

"Then we'll keep Peggy close by and give her lots of hugs until we see mommy again," he said, releasing Katie from his grip and wiping away his tears. "Now, you go take your bath, and later I'll read you a story." He gave her a reassuring smile to let her know that everything would be all right.

"Okay, but as soon as Jody comes home we need to have family prayer, cause I promised mommy I wouldn't let you forget," she said, shaking her finger at him.

"Oh, well, if you promised mommy, then we definitely should do it."

Katie went upstairs to take her bath and Larry went to the phone to call the police. Just as he picked up the phone, the back door opened.

"Do you know what time it is?" He yelled, slamming down the receiver. He was so enraged that he could barely speak. "I have been worried sick!" He could feel his face getting warm as his anger grew with every word spoken.

"I was at my friend Jessica's house. We were listening to music and lost track of time," Jody said, unconcerned. "Gee, you don't need to blow a gasket," she added. Jody knew her father would be mad, but this was ridiculous. After all, she was almost seventeen years old.

"You lost track of time? It's almost eight o'clock! School has been out for five hours! In all that time you couldn't even call and let someone know where you were?" His voice grew louder as his anger intensified. "How irresponsible!"

"I didn't think about it!" she yelled back, her hands planted firmly on her hips. "And don't act like you care where I've been! You were never home long enough to care before!"

"I was at work earning a living. Is this how you acted with your mother?"

"Don't talk to me about my mother! You know nothing about me and mom!" she snapped. Her father knew nothing about her life, and she meant to keep it that way.

"I know she would never let you get away with something like this!" he shouted, pointing his finger at her. "You're grounded, young lady!"

"So, you think you can play the parent just because mom isn't here anymore?" She stood up tall so he would know that he didn't intimidate her. "Well, I have news for you! I only have one parent, and she's dead!" She ran downstairs and slammed her bedroom door, knocking the pictures off the wall.

Larry took a deep breath. He braced himself against the counter and ran his hand though his hair. "What's happening to my family?" he whispered, baffled by the day's events.

Katie came downstairs in her pink bathrobe and peeked around the corner. "Is everything okay with Jody?

"Yes, honey, everything's fine. We just had a fight." He walked over to her, bent down on one knee, and gave her a kiss on the forehead. "Nothing to worry about."

"Can we still have family prayer tonight?"

"Sure, but we'll let her calm down first. Go brush your teeth and get into your pajamas. Maybe then we can get her to come upstairs."

Jody threw herself on her bed and buried her face in the pillow. "I hate him! I hate him!" she cried. "He will never be a father to me!"

He had never been there for her—not like a father should be. Now that her mother was gone, he thought he could make up for all the damage he'd done. Well, that wasn't going to happen. She held too much resentment and anger to ever allow him back into her life.

She pulled herself off the bed and walked over to her dresser. She picked up the picture of her and her mother. With tears of sorrow streaming down her face, she looked down at their smiling faces. "I miss you so much," she sobbed uncontrollably. "I wish you were here. Why did you have to die?"

The picture was taken at the mother daughter dinner the previous October. Memories of that night filled Jody's mind. She knew how much pain her mother was in and had begged her not to go, but Barbara knew how important the night was to her daughter, and she refused to let anything keep her from going.

"Why did I only think of myself, when I knew how sick you were?" she cried, touching her mother's face. She'd been so caught up in school, with track meets, social club, and friends that she hadn't realized how sick her mother was. Now she was miserable and feeling selfish and angry with herself.

Jody lay back down on her bed and tightly clutched the picture to her chest. She remembered all the wonderful times they'd spent together, and she wished there could have been many more.

Larry went downstairs to try to talk to Jody but got no response from knocking and pleading at her door. He walked down the hall to try to talk to Chris about the fight. Chris opened the door but stood in the door way.

"I want to talk to you about the fight," Larry calmly stated. "The principal is setting up an appointment for you to see the school counselor tomorrow. She thinks it might help with your anger."

Chris let out a snort. "You adults always think you have all the answers. Well, I heard you yelling at Jody tonight. Are you going to go see a shrink for your anger?" he said bitingly, his voice full of vengeance and sarcasm.

"We're not talking about me. Besides, I had every right to be mad. She had me worried sick," Larry complained, trying to justify his behavior.

"Whatever. I'll go see the counselor if it makes everybody happy," Chris said, rolling his eyes. He closed the door and locked it before Larry could say any more. It ended up being just Larry and Katie having family prayer together.

As Larry collapsed into bed that night, he wondered how Barbara had managed everything so well. He was physically and emotionally exhausted. He wondered how she got everything to run so smoothly. She never complained and never got angry, and she always held things together. She was a much stronger woman than he had given her credit for.

He looked at her picture sitting on the nightstand, and now, more than ever before, he felt a great appreciation for his wife. He just wished she were lying beside him so he could tell her so.

# Chapter 3

Larry woke early on Friday morning. He awakened even before his alarm clock started beeping. The week had been overwhelming. Chris had given him the silent treatment the entire week, and Jody only wanted to fight. This was much worse than anything he had ever dealt with at the office.

After a quick shower he went to the kitchen to make a nice breakfast. He found it was much easier to let the kids get up on their own than to call them every morning. The last several days, however, he just plain didn't want to get out of bed. He had no desire to do anything. He felt discouraged about life and depressed about his future. Nothing seemed important anymore—not his job, not the house, not even his own life. He was beginning to wonder if he would ever feel optimistic again.

There wasn't a day that went by that Barbara didn't tell him she loved him. Even when he was away on business, she would call him and let him know she was thinking of him. It wasn't so easy for him to show his emotions. It was in the beginning, but as his life became more complicated, he just plain forgot to say those three most important words. He would say them every day, if he could just have her back.

Guilt was starting to eat at him for not holding up his end of the bargain. He'd promised Barbara he would be there for the kids, and he knew she would be disappointed in him for lying around feeling sorry for himself, so here he was, standing in front of the stove, cooking up a wonderful breakfast for the kids.

Katie came running down the stairs. "Something smells good," she exclaimed. The table was piled high with scrambled eggs, hash browns, and golden pancakes. "Wow, you made all this yourself?" she asked in puzzlement, as though he had a gourmet chef hiding in the closet.

"Of course I did. Did you think your father couldn't cook?" he asked with a smile.

Katie piled her plate full of food. "I love pancakes. You should make them every day," she announced, drenching her pancakes with syrup.

"Katie, that's quite enough syrup for two pancakes," Larry laughed.

"But daddy, that's the best part," she said with wide eyes and a quivering lower lip. She was making sure she got her point across. She had him wrapped around her little finger and didn't even know it!

Larry was amazed when both Jody and Chris made an appearance at the breakfast table. Chris flopped down in the chair next to Katie and piled three pancakes on his plate. He leaned over and whispered in her ear, "I agree with you on the syrup thing." His words made her giggle, and he grinned.

Katie loved her big brother and liked to spend time with him. They would play everything from Candy Land to sword fighting. She would play the princess who was held captive in a tall castle, and he would be the knight in shining armor who rescued her. It soon became her favorite game. Chris didn't mind if it made her smile. He still spent time with his own friends but made sure he left time open for Katie.

Jody pushed the pancakes around on her plate trying to make everyone think she was eating. She wasn't buying into this whole picture perfect family routine. In fact, she was positive it wouldn't be much longer before her father went back to his old ways. Until then, she was not going to play into his outstanding parent charade.

"Why aren't you eating anything, Jody? Isn't this like the breakfast your mother used to make for you?" Larry asked lightheartedly.

Without looking up from her plate, Jody raised one eyebrow. "Well, if you had been around more in the mornings to help mom, then you would know what she made us for breakfast." She was going to make sure he knew she was still mad.

Larry was already feeling guilty for not spending enough time with Barbara before she passed away, so Jody definitely hit a sore spot. Emotionally overwhelmed and at the end of his rope, he bolted up from his chair, throwing it over backward, and paced both hands on the table.

"I am sick and tired of your attitude, young lady!" he shouted, his face turning bright red. "I had a job I had to be at every morning. Your mother knew that. She appreciated all the hard work I did for this family. I sacrificed so you could have nice things—like those designer jeans you're wearing, and those expensive shoes on your feet. Who do you think paid for them? Not your mother! She was at home trying to raise you ungrateful children!" The anger and rage over losing Barbara had been building up inside him for some time now. Although he knew his anger was being directed at the wrong person, he was powerless to control it. "Everything I've done has been for this family!" he shouted.

Infuriated with her father and emotionally distraught over the loss of her mother, Jody brazenly stood up to confront her father. With the years of resentment bubbling up inside her, she glared at him through hate-filled eyes. She'd deeply buried any love she had for him so that only anger and hurt remained. She was yelling so loudly that Katie stopped eating and covered her ears.

"Do you honestly think that's what mattered most to mom? The money? She never spent any of it on herself! She wanted you to be home with us! I heard her crying in her room one night when you were working late. She was crying because you were never home with her! So don't talk to me about sacrifice! Mom made more sacrifices than you'll ever make!"

Jody grabbed her backpack and headed for the door.

"Just a minute, young lady!" Larry snapped. "We're not finished!"

With one hand on the doorknob, Jody turned around. She spoke calmly but bluntly. "You know deep down that if you'd been around more you would've seen her getting sick and done something about it before it was too late." She was placing the blame where she thought it belonged—on her father.

"Don't go twisting this to make it look like it was my fault! Your mother knew she was sick, and she refused to see a doctor! It wouldn't have mattered if I was working or not!"

"Well, it doesn't matter now anyway, because all your money and all my designer jeans aren't going to bring her back!" She opened the door and slammed it behind her.

Larry turned to look at his other children and realized what an awful scene he had made. Katie had her hands over her ears and was crying. He bent down and put his arms around her. "It's okay, Katie. Don't cry. Jody's just mad at me right now. Everything will be all right." He spoke softly to her, trying his best to comfort her.

"No it won't be all right! Our family will never be the same now that mommy's gone!" she sobbed.

Chris picked up his skateboard and backpack. "I better go before she leaves me," he said calmly. He was dealing with his own anger and resentment. Although he agreed with Jody, he didn't want anything to do with this fight.

Larry drove Katie to school in an attempt to dry her tears. He assured her as she got out of the truck that everyone was just sad right now, and things would get better soon. Even as he said it, he wondered who he was trying to convince—Katie or himself?

On his way home, Larry decided he'd better go to the grocery store. It was something he'd been dreading all week. Barbara had always taken care of the grocery shopping and all the cooking. He had to face the fact that Jody had a point—he wasn't around much of the time. He didn't know what Barbara brought home from the store or what she cooked. Most the time he came home late from work and found his plate wrapped in foil and sitting in the refrigerator. The house was dark and all was quiet. He would warm his dinner in the microwave and work on one of his accounts while he was eating. After he finished, he would quietly go upstairs, change out of his clothes, kiss Barb on the forehead, and go to sleep. All this shopping and cooking was new to him, but the cupboards were almost bare, so it was a task he had to deal with.

He grabbed a shopping cart with a wobbling wheel and started down the first aisle. *Now where is the produce section?* he thought. If Jody didn't want to eat meat, then he'd make sure she had plenty of other food. As he went up and down the aisles, he became confused about what to buy, and increasingly appalled at the high prices.

Waiting impatiently in the check-out line, he picked up a magazine and started flipping through the pages. He heard an unfamiliar voice behind him.

"Excuse me sir, are you Mr. Porter?"

He turned to see an elderly woman in a red flowered shirt. Her gray hair seemed to sparkle in the bright lights of the store.

"Yes, yes, I am," he answered, puzzled by the stranger's sudden appearance.

"I thought so. You look just like the picture Barbara showed us. I'm Ellen Wright. I knew your wife from the senior citizens' center. We were saddened to learn of her passing. She was a wonderful lady and a great asset to our community. She's the reason we still have our center."

He was confused. He didn't want to be rude, but he really didn't know what she was talking about. "How did you know my wife?" he asked politely.

"From the senior citizens' center. She volunteered there three mornings a week, right up until the time she got sick. She went to the city meetings and fought to keep our center from getting torn down and turned into a shopping mall. She stood up to a board of six men and one woman. She was fantastic! She never backed down until she got the answer she wanted. She had spunk, that's for sure," Ellen said, laughing. "Didn't you know any of this?" she asked, surprised.

He vaguely recalled something Barb said about wanting to volunteer somewhere now that Katie was going to school. He had no idea how she spent her days or that she had taken on such a big role in the community. It surprised him, and he didn't know how to respond. After all, he was gone all the time, so how *could* he have known?

"Well, I'm sorry for your loss. She was an amazing lady and will be missed greatly."

"Thank you," he mumbled.

How could he not know all the wonderful things Barb had done? Sure they talked, but most of the time he was busy working and gave her only half of his attention. She probably told him about it and he didn't listen. How could he have been so stupid and inconsiderate? Why did it take losing her to make him realize how exceptional she was?

He drove home slowly, his mind on the woman at the store. Barbara was an amazing woman and an amazing wife and mother. Without question, she'd supported him in everything he did.

After he finished college and got his degree, he was employed with a reputable bank in Provo. It was a great nine to five job that left him time for family and fun. But the pay wasn't good enough for him, so he went in search of bigger and better things. That's when he was hired on with J.J. Jensen's. Barbara told him money wasn't everything, but he wouldn't listen. She supported him in his decision, but she was skeptical about it. He immediately wanted to move his family to Fairview. He loved the area and the Manti Temple. They debated back and forth for months before Barbara finally gave in.

As Larry pulled around the corner of the cul-de-sac where he lived, he saw a blue Honda accord parked in the driveway. He knew the car well. It was Maggie, Barbara's mother. Maggie and Barbara's father, Bob, lived in Provo, so they were able to see them often. Actually, Maggie and Bob were more like his own parents.

Larry's parents, Bruce and Betty Porter, lived in Sacramento, California, where Larry had grown up. They were not members of The Church of Jesus Christ of Latter-day Saints, so when Larry wanted to serve a mission for the Church, problems immediately began to arise.

Larry's best friend Doug was a member of the Church and often invited Larry to attend meetings with him. Larry went a few times but didn't really take an interest in it until he went to Utah with Doug's family to see the Mormon Miracle Pageant in Manti, Utah. That's where he learned about Joseph Smith and the Book of Mormon. He became curious about the Church and wanted to know more. Doug invited him to his house to talk to the LDS missionaries, and after just three of the discussions, Larry knew he wanted to be baptized.

He explained to his mom and dad how he felt when he read the Book of Mormon. He knew it was the true church and wanted to be baptized. At the time, his parents thought their son was just going through a phase. After all, he was only sixteen, and they were sure he'd outgrow it, so they consented to let him be baptized.

On November 8, 1982, Larry was baptized and confirmed a member of The Church of Jesus Christ of Latter-day Saints. His testimony grew stronger throughout the next couple of years. When he turned eighteen he told his parents that he wanted to serve an LDS mission for two years. They were outraged! How could he take two years off of college to go around preaching something that in their eyes was not true? If he did this, he would not be welcomed back into their home.

Larry was devastated by their reaction and went to his bishop for advice. The bishop told him to go home and pray about it before making a final decision. Larry spent the next week praying and searching the scriptures for answers. By the end of the week, he knew without a doubt he was to serve a mission for the Lord no matter what the sacrifice.

After his two-year mission to South Dakota, he returned home to find his things waiting for him in the garage. He moved in with Doug's family for a while and then moved to Provo, Utah, to attend Brigham Young University. After a few years, his parents gradually started to talk to him again, but they never came to Utah to see him, not even for Barbara's funeral. After he and Barb were married, Maggie became like his mother. He felt close to her and was comfortable talking to her about anything.

He still kept in touch with his younger brother, Allen. Allen never joined the Church, but Larry hadn't given up on him yet. He was still in California with his wife and two boys, Toby and Mathew. He would come to Utah twice a year to visit, and Larry tried to make it out to California to see Allen and his family when he could.

"Hi mom," Larry said as he came into the house and kissed her on the cheek.

Her short, once dark brown hair was now nearly all gray, but at sixty-two years of age, she was in top physical condition and still ran a mile or more each morning.

"I'm so glad to see you. The laundry hasn't been done all week, the dishes are piled in the sink, and I've still got a ton of work to do on an account. Can you stay and help?" It wasn't really a question. He knew she would do anything for him.

She stared him down like a mean old grizzly bear. It was just the way Barbara looked at him when she was angry.

"Larry, the kids have been home less than a week, and already things are in turmoil. I can't always be here to pick up after you," she said firmly. "You have children that are old enough to help out around here. These children need some responsibility; otherwise they'll walk all over you. Barbara gave each one a chore to do, and they couldn't go anywhere until that chore was done."

Larry was shocked at her reaction. She'd never questioned helping him before. She had to know he couldn't do this all on his own. He walked over and took a seat at the kitchen table, slumping down in the chair.

"Okay Maggie, I can give them chores to do. That's simple enough, but how do I make them follow through? Right now I can't get Chris to even talk to me, and Jody only yells at me. I have no control over what these kids are doing, and it's driving me crazy!" He threw his hands in the air to make his point. He didn't mean to throw all this at her, but he could really use her advice right now.

Maggie walked over to the table and sat down across from him. Her face was warm and caring. "Have you talked to your bishop?"

"I don't think I want to see him. I haven't been to Church in over two months. I don't feel worthy to seek his counsel," Larry said looking at the floor. He was too ashamed to look her in the eye.

"Larry, that's what he's there for. You can't go through this alone. You need his wise counsel and your Heavenly Father's spirit to comfort you."

"I'm not worthy of that either," Larry said, embarrassed. He focused his eyes on the chip in the tile floor. He rested his head in his hands, wishing she hadn't brought up the subject of religion. It wasn't that he didn't trust her and her opinion. It was because he was afraid of disappointing her. Since she was so much like a mother to him that he longed for her approval, not only in his actions as a father to her grandchildren, but also in his accomplishments as an individual.

"You need to kneel in prayer for renewed strength to get through each day," she said with a strong sense of conviction. He didn't have the heart to tell her that he hadn't prayed since Barbara passed away. It was partially due to him not believing in prayer anymore, and partly because he was angry with the Lord for taking Barbara away.

"I don't know if I believe in that anymore," he admitted. "I had faith that Heavenly Father would send us a miracle, and that miracle never came. How can I have faith in a God who deserted me when I needed him the most?" Larry had been questioning everything lately that he had previously believed in.

"Heavenly Father hasn't deserted you! He's *always* been there for you! Your miracle was not in him saving your wife. Your miracle is having Barbara as your wife for all eternity. You need to have faith that the Lord needed her for a greater purpose and that you'll be with her again."

"I just don't know what to believe anymore!" Larry exclaimed tearfully. "I thought my faith would pull her though, and it didn't, so how do I find that faith again?"

"Larry, you had faith when you were baptized and when you served a mission. You had faith when you took Barbara to the temple. You need to find that faith again. Not just for you, but for your children also. Your children need you now more than ever, so don't make the same mistake you made with Barbara," she said, placing her hand on top of his.

"What mistake?" he asked hesitantly, not really wanting to hear the answer.

"Larry, I love you like my own son, but you took her for granted. You thought she would always be around, and after you made your millions, you would retire and spend all your time with her. But she got sick, and now you're left to live out your life without her. Don't take your kids for granted too. You're a wonderful provider—there's no question about that, but you need to work on your parenting skills. The good thing is that you still have time to change things—to become the kind of father your kids need and that Barbara would be proud of." Maggie had tears in her eyes as she spoke sincerely from her heart.

Larry knew that what she said was true, and he couldn't stop the tears from flowing. "Did Barbara ever tell you she was unhappy?"

"She tried to tell *you*."

Larry sighed heavily. "I think it's too late for Jody and Chris. They hate me," he said with regret.

"That's not true, they're just hurting inside. Give them some time to come around. Be there for them, but don't push them. It might be a good idea for all of you to see a counselor together."

"I don't want to go tell all my personal life to some stranger," he said, and then he laughed. "That's funny. I told Chris just a few days ago he had to go see a counselor."

"Well, a part of you must believe it could help then."

"I guess. I'll think about it," Larry said, thinking that *he* would not be the one going to a counselor.

Larry sat at his desk twiddling his pen. He wasn't really thinking about work. Instead, he was thinking about what Maggie had said. Dinner was done, Katie made sure they had family prayer, and now all the kids were quiet. Chris and Katie were playing checkers, and Jody was doing her homework. He thought that now would be a good time to get some work done, but Maggie's statement weighed heavily on his mind. All of it was true. He was a terrible father and husband. Only now was it becoming painfully clear.

Somewhere on his way up the career ladder he had become obsessed with money. Every waking moment was spent trying to better his career or make more money, which had ultimately taken him away from his family. He thought it was partly to do with how poor his family was when he was growing up. They struggled to acquire everything they had, and he swore it would not happen to his own family. When the first paychecks started coming in from J.J. Jensen's, it gave him the most remarkable feeling of power and independence. He yearned for bigger and better, no matter what the cost.

Instead of taking his son fishing, he was in a board meeting. Instead of taking his girls for ice cream, he was calculating numbers. Instead of being home with his beautiful wife, spending quality time with her and loving her every minute of everyday, he was off on a business trip doing an audit. He did take Barbara for granted. He assumed she would always be there for him. Their dream was to have a second honeymoon in Hawaii, but every time they tried to plan for it, work got in the way. He thought Hawaii would always be there and they would eventually go one day. But that day never came.

How could he change things now to make the situation better with the kids? Chris and Jody had already made up their minds about him. He was also certain that Jody blamed him for Barbara's death. How could he change that? Could they ever forgive him for not being there and become a family again? Or was it just too late?

# Chapter 4

Sitting in the back seat of a police car was not the way Jody intended to end her night. She wasn't really sure what time of the night it was, but she guessed it was after midnight since it was about ten-thirty when she hauled her suitcase out her bedroom window.

After two weeks of fighting with her father, she decided to pack up her things and leave home. She wasn't even sure where to go. She had no money and no plan, and she was certain that if she took the car her father would report it stolen. She called her friend Jessica who helped her find a place to stay until she could figure out what to do.

Jody knew anything was better than living with her father another minute. He was on her case all the time. Just this morning they had a huge fight over what she was wearing to school. Sure, it was true, she did a lot of things just to make him mad, but she was going to make it very clear to him that they would never have the kind of relationship she and her mother had. He chose his work over his family a long time ago, and she was going to make sure he never forgot it.

She missed her mother immensely and needed her now more than ever. It devastated her to think that her mother wouldn't be there for her graduation, her wedding, or even the birth of her first child. Jody was angry, but she wasn't really sure why or at whom she was angry. She wondered if maybe she was just angry at the whole world and the circumstances she was in. All she knew was that she wanted her mother back, and there was no way her lame-brained father was going to take her mother's place.

Jody's mother was the one who had helped her get started in track and field. Her mother had believed in her more than she believed in herself. She supported her in everything she did and was the kind of mother that all of her friends envied. She did everything from shopping at the mall on Saturday afternoon, to spending the afternoon doing facials. Her mother always made time for her.

She was also the perfect example of how you should live your life. She taught Jody to pray and to stand up for what she believed in. Jody saw strength in her mother and felt of her strong testimony. She was indeed the perfect role model.

After climbing out her bedroom window, she and Jessica caught the bus, which took them to the west side of town. Jessica was strong and outgoing—not at all like Jody who was timid and shy. She was not afraid to stand up to people and never let them push her around. She had short, jet-black hair and blue eyes and wore three earrings in each ear and one in her nose. Sure, she was a little rough around the edges and not at all like her other friends, but Jessica made her feel good about herself. Jody would forget her problems when she was with Jessica.

When they arrived at the rundown trailer park, Jody wondered if she'd made the right decision. The mobile home had pieces of siding hanging off, and there was trash all over the yard. Windows were broken out on each side of the trailer, and cigarette butts lined the walkway. It looked like something you would see on a TV reality show called "Fix my trailer." The steps wobbled almost as much as her legs were wobbling as she made her way to the old wooden front door. Jessica gave a knock, and after a minute, the door opened.

Standing in the doorway was a boy dressed in old blue jeans and a white tank top. For a minute Jody thought she would lose her dinner. She knew her face looked as sick as she felt. She assumed that Jessica's friends were girls. The thought never crossed her mind that she would be staying with a boy.

"Hi, this is Jody, the one who needs a place to stay," Jessica said, pointing a finger at Jody.

"Jody, this is my friend Cody." With a squeak of the door, he let them pass. There was a second boy sitting inside smoking a cigarette. He was wearing old blue jeans and no shirt. He had tattoos down both arms, and Jody could see that the one who answered the door also had a tattoo of a dragon on his left shoulder.

"This is my other friend Jake," Jessica said, pointing to the other boy.

"Have a seat," Cody smiled, gesturing toward the cluttered sofa.

Jody left her suitcase by the door and made her way over to the sofa. She moved some laundry and sat down. She could feel the springs of the old blue couch beneath her. Empty beer cans littered the coffee table as well as the floor. The trailer gave off a nauseating smell of stale cigarette smoke and alcohol, which only added to Jody's already sick stomach.

Pulling her Levi jacket tightly closed, she sat down and crossed her legs. She was already extremely uneasy about the whole situation when Cody suddenly staggered over and flopped down on the sofa beside her. She folded her arms and scooted close to the edge.

"Want a smoke?"

"No thank you," she said politely. She could feel the anxiety rising within her.

"How about a beer?" he asked, picking up a can. He flipped open the top and handed it to her.

"Oh no, I'm not thirsty," her voice croaked shyly.

"Jody, you don't want to be rude. Take the beer," Jessica snarled from a across the room. She was already drinking one, which took Jody by surprise. She had no idea her new friend drank.

"Okay, thank you." Her hands were trembling as she took the beer. She felt awkward and out of place. She figured she would just hold it and pretend to take a drink now and then so she would not offend anybody.

As they sat there and talked about cars, sports, and their criminal records, Cody inched his way closer and closer to Jody, making her feel jittery and uncomfortable. Originally she had thought he was good looking, with his sandy-blond hair and his baby blue eyes. But when he put his arm around her shoulder, he gave off a horrible odor of beer and cigarettes, which quickly changed her mind. Besides, his closeness gave her an unsettling feeling in the pit of her stomach; a sensation that nagged at her, letting her know she was in the wrong place. She knew right then she needed to get out—and quick. She was usually discreet around strangers and didn't want to cause a scene, so she turned away, clutching the side of the couch with one arm.

"I think you should sleep in my room tonight. What do you say?" Cody said, smirking. He slurred his words as he reached over and tried to grab her leg.

Somewhere deep inside, Jody found her inner strength. She used both hands to firmly push him away. She jumped up from the sofa and yelled, "Get off me, you slime! I'm not sleeping in your room!"

"If you want a place to stay, you'll sleep where I tell you to sleep," he snapped arrogantly and shot up off the sofa.

Jody turned and headed for the door. Her legs were trembling beneath her, but she was determined to make her escape. "Come on, Jessica, we're leaving!" she insisted indignantly. She grabbed her suitcase and reached for the doorknob.

"These are my friends, Jody. Where do you get off acting like that?" Jessica demanded angrily.

"Jessica, I'm your friend too! Didn't you hear what he said to me?" How could Jessica turn on her like this?

"Cody's a nice guy," she said, winking at him. "You two make a cute couple."

With a smirk on his face, Cody approached her and grabbed her by the shirt. He pulled her close and said, "Come on, let's have some fun!"

Jody was not about to go down without a fight. She used her suitcase to give him a piercing blow to the groin. In agony, he let out a yelp and dropped to the floor, which gave Jody a chance to get out the door and down the wobbly stairs.

Jessica and Jake were yelling at her from the porch, but she didn't stop running. She kept on going, dragging her suitcase behind her and wondering how she'd gotten into this mess. She knew her mother would have never have approved of Jessica—and for good reason. She'd trusted Jessica to help her and be her friend, but she was not the person Jody thought she was.

Jody didn't dare look behind her for fear they were following her. Her adrenaline was pumping, which kept her weak knees from buckling beneath her. Her hand was tightly gripping her suitcase, and she could feel the perspiration on her forehead. Out of breath and exhausted, she slowed down to a fast pace walk. She suddenly heard a car pull up behind her, and she stopped walking and nervously looked over her shoulder. It was a police car.

Larry was having another restless night. He wondered if he would ever get used to sleeping alone. He was just about to doze off when he heard the phone on his nightstand ring. He glanced at the clock. It was

2:26 a.m. *Who could be calling at this time of night?* he thought drowsily.

He turned on the lamp next to the phone and picked up the receiver. "Hello," his voice squeaked out, barely making a sound. He cleared his throat and tried again. "Hello," he said again in a louder voice.

"Hello sir, sorry to wake you," a voice answered in a very business-like manner. "This is Officer Brady from the Fairview police department. We have your daughter here at the station."

"My daughter is downstairs asleep in her bed. Are you sure you have the right number?" he asked, dazed and confused.

"Well, let me put her on the phone for you."

After a pause he heard sniffling and crying into the phone. "Dad, it's me, Jody. Can you come get me?" she sobbed.

"Jody! What happened? Are you all right? Are you hurt?" Larry sat straight up in bed. His heart was pounding as he imaged the worst.

"I'm okay," she said between sobs. "Can you please come get me?" she pleaded.

The officer took the phone back. "She's all right—just a little shook up. We found her over on the west side of town. Seems she had a little run-in with some kids that were drinking and—"

"She's been drinking?" Larry abruptly interrupted.

"No sir, it doesn't appear that she's had any alcohol tonight. Apparently, one of the boys she was with came on a little strong and she ran off. We picked her up down the road a ways. From the looks of her luggage, I'd say she didn't plan on coming home for a *lo-o-n-n-g* time. If you ask me—"

"Excuse me, officer," Larry interrupted irritably. "Can I come pick up my daughter now?"

"Yes, come right down. We'll have her waiting for you." Larry quickly hung up the phone. He pulled on his blue jeans and a T-shirt and headed for the station.

Traffic was light at 3 a.m. in the morning, so Larry made good time. As he drove, he wondered how he could reach his daughter and break down the walls that she'd put up between them. He knew there needed to be some changes, but what? What could he possible say or do to make her change her mind about him? She needed to know that through a slow process, he was making changes—changes that he should have made years ago.

When Larry opened the door to the police station, he found Jody sitting in a chair with her head in her hands. Across the room sat a metal desk piled high with papers. A cup of coffee and a doughnut sat next to a nameplate that said "Officer Brady" on it. The station was quiet and no one seemed to be around.

Larry went to Jody and put his arms around her, not knowing how she would respond to his affection. Surprisingly, she wrapped her arms around him, squeezing him tightly and sobbing into his shoulder.

"Its okay, honey. I'm here now," he whispered. "Everything is going to be all right." He kept his concerns to himself, only imagining what could have happened to her tonight.

A large bald man with a beer belly came around the corner. "You must be Mr. Porter," he grunted.

"Yes, can I take my daughter home now?"

"Sure can. Just sign this paper stating that we have released her to you, and you're free to go."

"Is she in trouble for something?" he asked following the large, annoying man over to his desk.

"We do have a curfew here in town. She was out past midnight, so that makes her in violation. However, under the circumstances, we only gave her a warning and not a citation."

"Thank you. I'm sure you won't be seeing her again." Larry signed the papers and picked up Jody's suitcase sitting beside the chair. He took a deep breath and started for the door, hoping that Jody would follow his lead.

"Have a good night," the officer said, taking a bite a doughnut.

"Same to you," Larry smiled. He was happy to finally get away from this obnoxious man. Larry threw the suitcase in the back of the truck and climbed into the driver's seat. He watched Jody for any indication that she wanted to talk, but she was rubbing her red, swollen eyes and staring out the window. Larry started the engine and pulled out of the parking lot.

They'd drove about ten minutes without either of them saying a word, when Jody finally broke the silence. "Aren't you going to ask me where I was going with my suitcase? Or what happened to me?" she asked.

"Well, I am curious about where you were going, and worried about what happened to you tonight. I'm sad to think things are so bad for you at home that you would rather be out on the streets. I also know things are tense between us right now, and I don't want to argue anymore," he gently replied.

"Aren't you worried I'll try to run away again?" This new approach he used was a little strange. She thought for sure that she would be grounded for the rest of her teenage years.

"Oh, don't get me wrong. I'm definitely worried!" He pulled into the driveway and turned off the engine. "I love you more than you will ever know, but I've come to realize that you're not a little girl anymore, and I can't control you. You're going to have to make your own choices in life—good or bad. I'm here to help guide you in those choices, if you'll let me." She sat motionless, keeping her eyes on the floor. She could feel emotions inside her starting to stir. Emotions she wasn't ready to deal with yet.

"I know I've made a lot of mistakes and I haven't always been there for you. But I'd really like to try this father thing again if you'll let me. Who knows, maybe this time I'll get it right," he smiled, really looking at his daughter for the first time in years. How beautiful she was, and how grown up she looked. He regretted missing out on so much of her life. "When you're ready to talk about tonight, or anything else, I'm ready to listen. And I promise there will be no more yelling."

Jody turned to look at her dad for the first time through their entire conversation. She nodded her head yes, afraid that if she spoke, she may start crying again. She pulled up on the handle of the door and paused. Looking back at her father, she softly said, "Thanks for coming to get me."

Larry carried the suitcase into the house and handed it to Jody. "I hope you'll unpack," he said, smiling.

Jody shot him a half smile and headed to her room. She knew she was home to stay. Happy to be home, she dropped her suitcase on the floor and flopped down on her bed. The night brought back memories—memories she thought she'd hidden. Her mind flashed back to the time when she was eight. She had tried to run away then too. She packed up all her toys, made a peanut butter and jelly sandwich, and locked herself in her clubhouse in the back yard. Soon her father was knocking on the door, pleading with her to come out. When she refused, he went into the house and brought out two sleeping bags. They slept side by side in the clubhouse. It was the best night of her life.

Larry got back into bed feeling satisfied with the way things had gone. *Well,* he thought, *I may not have won the war, but I did come a little closer to victory tonight.* He looked over at Barbara's picture. It was smiling at him as if to say that Barbara was pleased with his efforts.

"Thanks Barb. I think I understand now how to reach her. I love you sweetie," he said, softly touching Barbara's face. "Good night."

# Chapter 5

Chris stuffed the three books he was carrying into his backpack and then stuffed the back pack into his locker. He picked up his skateboard and headed out the back door of the school. Although it was only ten o'clock in the morning, he decided to skip class and go blow off some steam at the skate park.

Skateboarding was his outlet—his escape from reality and the harsh circumstances of the real world. With the wind blowing in his face and the adrenaline rush he felt every time he hit a jump, it was the best medicine ever. It was a nice 58 degrees out—perfect skateboarding weather. It was the first day of April and the tulips were already starting to bloom.

Chris planted both feet on his skateboard, stuck both hands into the pockets of his Levi jeans, and started off down the sidewalk. He knew that because it was early in the day there would be no one at the skate park to bother him. He preferred to be alone. Nobody understood how he was feeling, not even that stupid counselor he was seeing. As far as the counselor knew, Chris was doing great. But the truth was that he was miserable without his mother. It felt like someone had just taken his whole world and put it into a blender.

Everything around him had changed. It was as if life had suddenly directed him into unfamiliar territory, and it terrified him. He couldn't make sense of all the feelings that were flushing through him—anger, hate, and despair. Some days it seemed impossible to live without his mother. She was the only one he could talk to when life got crazy. He couldn't talk to his father, Jody seemed distant and distracted much of the time, and the counselor at school made him feel like a mental case. Without his mother, he felt alone against the world, and nobody could help him.

He turned the corner and just like he thought, there was not a soul in sight. He whizzed down the first slope and felt the cool breeze against his skin. An adrenaline rush hit him as he plummeted down one side and up the next. There was no one to answer to here—not his father telling him what to do or a counselor asking stupid questions. It was just him, the skateboard, and the concrete. He felt the tension ease with every hill. With every jump he felt a sense of freedom—a release from the world and all its burdens. He was enjoying himself so much that he hadn't noticed the three boys getting out of an old beat-up Chevy truck.

"Hey, you!" Chris heard one of them shout. He stopped dead in his tracks.

They looked rough with their shaved heads and their tattoos. The one that walked in front of the others wore black baggy pants and a white T-shirt. He had blue eyes and had an earring in his bottom lip. A tattoo of a snake wrapped around a knife covered his left arm.

An intense fury was in his eyes as he looked at Chris. Chris stood motionless. He knew it was too late to run, and no one was around to hear him scream. His pulse raced and he began to perspire. He clutched his skateboard tightly in his right hand and prepared for almost anything.

"Do you know who I am?" the one with the tattoo asked. He was eyeballing Chris up and down.

"No," Chris replied, barely getting the words past his lips. Pacing like a wild animal before the kill, the boy was now circling him. Chris stood perfectly still but stayed on his guard.

"Well, I know you. You're the one who broke my little brother's nose."

*He must be talking about Jeff,* Chris thought, panicking. Jeff was the kid he'd fought with at school. When he said something about Chris's old lady kicking the bucket, Chris had lost it and punched him in the nose.

"Well, it's time to pay the piper," the bully said with confidence. He walked up to Chris, stood only inches away, and eyed him like he was his prize game.

Chris wasn't about to wait for his next move. He took a deep breath and lifted his skateboard high in the air. With all his strength, he swung the skateboard at the boy's head. It hit him on the side of his face and knocked him to the ground. Chris threw the skateboard to the pavement and began to run as fast as his legs would take him. He heard Jeff's brother yell, "Get him."

One of the other boys grabbed the back of Chris's T-shirt and yanked him backward, which stopped him from running any further. He turned around just in time to feel the stinging blow of something hard hitting the front part of his head. Shaken and disoriented, he fell to his knees. The ringing in his ears echoed through his cloudy mind as the ground suddenly started to spin. He felt the warm blood gush down his face as blinked to keep it out of his eyes. It was obvious he was no match for these three boys. They knew what they were doing and had probably done it before.

Another hard, agonizing blow to his right arm sent him to the ground. Chris cried out in pain and grabbed his arm. All three of the boys started kicking him in the chest and stomach and were yelling for him to get up and fight like a man. Chris tried to roll away to avoid the devastating blows, but he found himself surrounded by the constant pounding of feet. The pain in his chest was unbearable, and he thought for sure he would stop breathing.

Another piercing kick was delivered to his side, followed by two more to his stomach, and Chris's body went limp. Excruciating pain ran through his abdomen, and he lay helpless.

"How does it feel, huh?" one of them chuckled. He could hear them laughing and taunting him, but his vision was a blur. The blood from his head wound now covered his face, which made it hard to see. He curled into a ball and covered his head with his arms for protection. He wondered if they would kill him, and he thought about his mother. He felt himself drifting off into unconsciousness, and his body felt lifeless and weak.

Mocking his painful groans, one of the boys picked Chris up by his shirt. Another forceful blow was delivered to the back of his head, which sent him into utter darkness.

Larry had been sitting around this huge oval conference table listening to people argue for two hours. He wished they would come to an agreement on the merger and end it already.

J.J. Jensen's was debating whether or not to merge with Benson and Associates. He really didn't care one way or the other. He would continue his same routine, working three days at home and two days in the office. He was here just as a formality.

His mind drifted off and he thought about home. Things had calmed down some since the late night trip to the police station. Jody still refused to talk about it, and he didn't want to push her. The counselor at the school said Chris was doing well, though he kept to himself much of the time. Katie was her usual cheerful self and kept busy with piano lessons and school. Things were going well, maybe a little too well. He felt as if a dark cloud was lurking just around the corner.

Larry was totally consumed in his own personal thoughts, when Glenda, the secretary, popped her head in the door. "Excuse me, Mr. Porter. You have an emergency phone call on line four," she said, her lipstick glimmering in the lights.

Startled by the interruption, he leapt from his chair and politely excused himself from the room. He exited out the side door and irritably wondered which kid was in trouble this time. He picked up the receiver on Glenda's desk. "Hello."

"This is the emergency room at Sanpete Valley Hospital. We have your son Christopher here; he's been in an accident." Feeling his pulse start to race, Larry reached out with one hand and steadied himself against the desk.

"Is he all right?" he gasped, trying to stay calm.

"He's all right, but you'll need to come to the hospital."

Larry could feel his breakfast creeping up his throat and had to swallow hard to keep it down. He hung up the phone and made it to Fairview from Provo in less than forty-five minutes. He streamlined through the doors of the emergency room and straight to the nurses' station. A heavyset woman who was talking on the phone was sitting behind the desk, and she barely acknowledged Larry. He was panic-stricken and sweating profusely.

"Excuse me miss, I'm looking for my son, Christopher Porter? Can you tell me where he is?" Larry asked anxiously.

"Please, have a seat. Someone will be right with you." She gave Larry a half smile and went right on talking.

"Can I go to his room?" Larry asked impatiently.

"They're just bringing him back from x-ray. If you'll just have a seat, there's a police officer here to talk to you," she answered harshly and pointed a stubby finger at some blue plaid chairs sitting in the corner.

"Why are the police here? What's happened to him?" Larry snapped impatiently. He wanted answers and he wanted them now. He was ready to reach across the desk and strangle her with the phone cord if she didn't answer him right away. Just then a police officer came around the corner. He was holding a note pad in his hands.

"Hello, I'm Officer Shelly. If you'll take a seat over here, we can talk," he said, smiling politely. He was a young man in his mid-twenties, with dark brown hair and green eyes.

"Is my son all right? They're not telling me anything." They sat down and the officer pulled out his pen.

"Your son was attacked by three boys this morning at the skate park. Detective Ben Carlson was on his way home when he witnessed the attack and immediately called for backup. Thanks to his quick response, we were able to apprehend the boys just moments later, and they're now in our custody."

"You're not telling me about my son. Is he all right?" Larry asked loudly. He was frustrated and tired of getting a run around.

"They took him to x-ray a little while ago. They should have him back to his room shortly. He was unconscious when we found him, but came around on the way to the hospital and was able to give us some information. Now, can you give me any reason why these boys would want to harm your son?" he asked, concerned but with a business-like tone.

"Of course not! My son is a good kid!"

The nurse behind the desk stood up and approached Larry. "You can see your son now," she said, smiling. Her tone was much friendlier this time.

With a pleading look on his face, Larry glanced at the officer. "We can talk later," he said. "Go to your son."

"Thank you." Larry stood up and shook the officer's hand. He followed the nurse through two big doors. She escorted him to Christopher's room and opened the door so he could enter. "The doctor will be in shortly," she said, quietly closing the door as she left.

Chris was lying on the bed with his eyes shut. He was wearing a hospital gown with a blanket covering his legs. Monitors were hooked up to his chest and an oxygen mask covered his nose and mouth. He had an IV in his left hand, and his right arm was in a splint. His hair was matted in blood and there was a white bandage wrapped around his head. The blood from his cut was still oozing out, which was turning the bandage red in one spot. His right eye was swollen and badly bruised, and he had another cut down his right cheek. The color had left his face, causing his skin to look milky and pale.

Larry took a deep breath and exhaled it slowly. He cautiously approached the bed and sat down next to Chris. He gently touched his son's arm just above the IV. Chris's skin was cold and clammy, which sent a chill down Larry's spine.

"Chris, its dad. Can you hear me?" he whispered softly. Chris opened his left eye slightly and looked over at Larry. "Hi, you don't look so good," Larry said with a smile. Chris nodded in agreement. "Don't worry, the doctor will have you fixed up and back on your skateboard in no time." He meant it to be funny, but he saw Chris cringe when he said the word skateboard.

The doctor finally came into the room. He was carrying a clipboard and was a lot younger than Larry. He had dark hair and glasses and was wearing a long white doctor's jacket. Larry guessed him to be about thirty or so. He introduced himself as Dr. Woolstenhulm and shook hands with Larry.

"The CT scan shows he has a slight concussion from the blow to the head, and we'll need to stitch up that laceration on his forehead.

"His right arm is broken, but the growth plate looks good, so we'll just keep it in a splint for a few days until the swelling goes down. Then we'll put a cast on it.

"He also has two fractured ribs. There's not much we can do for that. We could put a wrap around him to support them for a couple of days. However, I'm a little concerned about his eye. There's some bleeding going on, so I've called in an ophthalmologist to take a look at it. We should know more after that."

"Thank you, doctor. Can I stay with him?"

"Of course. I'll be back in a few minutes to stitch up his forehead. We gave him something for the pain, so he may seem a little groggy." He left the room and left the door slightly ajar.

Chris had been trying to stay awake to listen to the doctor. He opened his good eye, and with concern on his face, he looked at his father.

"It's okay, Chris. I'm staying with you," Larry assured him. "Are you in pain?"

Chris reached up and pulled the oxygen mask off so he could talk. "I can't see out of my eye," he mumbled.

"There's a specialist coming to look at it, but don't worry, I'm sure everything is okay."

Chris pulled the mask off again. "I'm really sleepy," he said, slurring his words.

"Yeah, the doctor gave you some medicine for the pain, and it makes you feel that way. I'll be right here with you, so go ahead and sleep," Larry said, gently rubbing the top of Chris's head.

It took forty-two stitches to close up the laceration on Chris's forehead. The doctor said the stitches would dissolve in a couple of weeks. He also put a wrap around Chris's mid-section to support his ribs, which was the most painful for Chris.

Chris had barely caught his breath when the ophthalmologist came in to check his eye. She was dressed in black dress pants and a blue satin button-up shirt. She had jet-black hair and wore tiny, black glasses. Larry thought she looked more like a lawyer than an ophthalmologist. She introduced herself as Dr. Whitman and proceeded to check Chris's eye. She brought out a special microscope called a slit lamp to look inside the structure of his eye.

"Well, what he has is called hyphema. When someone gets hit really hard in the eye, it causes bleeding. It can be cleared up with some eye drops, and you'll have to wear a patch over your eye for four or five days. At that time we'll recheck the eye and make sure everything is okay, but you'll need to get plenty of bed rest." She wrote out a prescription and handed it to Larry.

"Thank you, doctor, we appreciate the good news."

"You're welcome. Make sure he stays in bed for the next week. I don't want any more injuries to the eye." She patted Chris on the foot, and with a smile, she left the room, her flower-scented perfume still lingering behind her.

"See, I told you there was nothing to worry about," Larry commented.

Chris nodded. He was feeling too exhausted to say much of anything. He closed his eyes and let his sore body relax, and he soon drifted off into a deep slumber.

As Larry sat beside the bed and watched his son sleep, he noticed how much Chris resembled him at his age. He remembered the day they'd brought Chris home from the hospital. At nine pounds and ten ounces, he was quite a chunk! Barbara was in labor for ten hours before the doctors finally took him by C-section. When Chris finally made his appearance, he was a beautiful baby, with lots of dark hair.

Larry was ecstatic to have a son—a son he could teach to play sports, go fishing, and do all the things a father and son should do. He bought him his first football when he was only three months old.

When Chris was a baby, Larry would watch him sleeping in his crib and wonder what life had in store for them. He thought of all the things he'd always wanted to do if he had a son, and he began to make plans.

*But look at us now*, he thought, stroking Chris's thick, dark hair. They'd drifted so far apart that he didn't even know his own son. He bent over and softly kissed the top of Chris's head, and he realized for the first time just how unimportant his job really was. Why didn't he realize this when Barb was alive, when they could have been a family?

His mistakes and poor choices in life were screaming out at him, making him wish he could crawl under a rock and hide rather than face them head-on. How did he let himself get so far off track? He wasn't always like this. There was a time when his family took precedence over everything else in his life. But somehow the tides had changed, throwing him off course and leading him into dark waters.

He slid down in his chair, placing his head in his hands, wondering how he was going to reconnect with his children after all the damage he'd done. He knew now he'd let himself get so involved with work that he couldn't see anything else. Only now that Barbara was gone was he able to see the destructive path he'd left behind.

"I think we'd better keep him overnight, just for observation," Dr. Woolstenhulm said as he entered the room. "They have a room ready for him upstairs, so someone will be down shortly to get him."

"Thank you for all you've done, doctor," Larry said, standing to shake the doctor's hand.

When the doctor left the room, Larry slipped outside to make a quick phone call to Maggie and let her know about the attack. He asked her to stay the night with the other kids so he could stay with Chris.

When he got back to the room, they were ready to move Chris upstairs. Before long, Chris was in his own room fast asleep.

Larry waited until he knew Chris was settled in okay before he went to get a bite to eat and something to drink. Two LDS missionaries greeted him as he stepped into the elevator. He smiled politely but kept silent, hoping to deter what was sure to come next. He found his way to the back corner of the elevator and looked at the floor to avoid eye contact.

"Good evening," one of the missionaries said, smiling as he held out his hand. "I'm Elder Nash, and this is Elder Lauritzen." Larry hid his true feelings and shook their hands. After all, it wasn't their fault he felt the way he did. "Do you have family here in the hospital?" Elder Lauritzen asked.

"Yes, my son." Larry hoped to avoid the next question and watched the numbers on the elevator as it slowly climbed to the third floor.

"Would you like us to give your son a priesthood blessing?"

Larry exited the elevator and started a fast-paced walk. The missionaries were not deterred and kept up the pace as Larry hurried down the hall. When they reached Chris's room, Larry reluctantly agreed to the blessing, but he wanted no part in it. Before Barbara passed away he would have been the first to give Chris a priesthood blessing. Before her death he had perfect faith in prayer, believing that through the priesthood anything was possible, but now he was left with uncertainty and doubt.

Larry stood at the back of the room. His arms were folded, his head was bowed, but his heart was stiff. He listened to the missionaries bless Chris with the strength to overcome this brutal attack and for him to make a full recovery. It was like taking a step back in time, only it was Barbara lying in the hospital bed and he was the one giving the blessing. He had used almost those same words, but the Lord wasn't listening. He felt as if the Lord had pulled away just when he needed him the most.

When they were finished with the blessing, Elder Lauritzen handed a Book of Mormon to Larry and asked him to read some of it that night.

"I already told you I'm a member of the Church," Larry snapped irritably.

"I understand, but I have a strong feeling that I need to leave this with you tonight. Humor me, please?" the young missionary said, smiling convincingly. Larry remembered that he was once a missionary too, so he reluctantly took the book from the missionary's hands and thanked them for the blessing.

Larry sat down in the blue leather recliner in the corner of the room. He held the book in his hands and remembered what Maggie had said about finding his faith. He wondered if his faith was gone forever.

He slid his fingers across the words "Book of Mormon." Not long ago he had leaned on this book for support and comfort, and now it scared him to death to hold it in his hands. He sighed heavily and opened the book to somewhere in the middle. He had begun to read in Alma when he came across a verse that grabbed his attention. It was Alma 22:16.

"But Aaron said unto him: If thou desirest this thing, if thou wilt bow down before God, yea, if thou wilt repent of all thy sins, and will bow down before God, and call on his name in faith, believing that ye shall receive, then shalt thou receive the hope which thou desirest."

Hope was the key word. All he had right now in his life was hope. He decided to study a little more on the subject of hope, since that's what he was relying on these days.

He flipped through the pages, skimming over the verses one by one until he came to Moroni 7: 40–42.

"And again, my beloved brethren, I would speak unto you concerning hope. How is it that ye can attain unto faith, save ye shall have hope? And what is it that ye shall hope for? Behold I say unto you that ye shall have hope through the atonement of Christ and the power of his resurrection, to be raised unto life eternal, and this because of your faith in him according to the promise. Wherefore, if a man have faith he must needs have hope; for without faith there cannot be any hope."

Larry closed the book and rested his head back against the recliner. He pondered the scripture. Without faith there cannot be any hope. Right now he had no faith and very little hope. All he felt was anger and resentment for not being able to save his wife's life. And now, as his son lay in a hospital bed, he couldn't even muster up enough faith to know that Chris would be all right.

Besides having no faith, Larry was full of doubt—doubt that his children would ever allow him back into their lives, doubt that he could fulfill his role as a father, and doubt that he would ever be able to regain his testimony and lead his family down the path of righteousness.

He felt more discouraged than ever before. How was he going to pull it all together and live up to the expectations Barbara had left behind if he had no faith in the future?

# Chapter 6

The sun peeked through the beige mini blinds hanging in the window of Chris's hospital room. Larry was asleep in the soft leather recliner when the light hit him in the face and woke him. He hadn't slept soundly anyway. Chris woke up in terrible pain around 3 a.m., so the nurse gave him more medication in his IV. It helped some, but he was still restless most of the night. He was also running a fever, which concerned the nurses. Larry was up with him most of the night, caressing his head and reassuring him that he would be all right. It reminded Larry of when Barbara was sick.

Barbara was in so much pain toward the end. The medication the doctors gave her only took the edge off of it and didn't get rid of it. Larry would sit up with her at night, hold her hand, and caress her head. They talked about the past and all the fun times they had together. It seemed to help take her mind off the pain. There were so many times he had to go for a walk to regain his strength. It tore him apart to see her suffer. He would have taken the pain from her in a heartbeat if he could. Just like now, with Christopher, he would take the pain away if he could. It's a hard thing to watch your children suffer.

Larry stood up and stretched his arms, which resulted in a lot of cracking and popping noises going down his spine. The recliner wasn't the most comfortable place to sleep. Chris's eyes were closed, and he was resting peacefully, so Larry went into the bathroom to splash some cool water on his face. When he came out, the nurse was checking Chris's pulse. She was a pretty girl with long, dark hair pulled back in a French braid. She couldn't have been over twenty-five. Larry wondered if everyone was getting younger or if he was just getting old.

"Good morning! I'm Rachel. I'll be Chris's nurse today," she buzzed cheerfully.

"Nice to meet you. I'm Larry, Chris's father. How's he doing?" He walked around to the other side of the bed to get a better look.

"Well, his lungs sound good. Let's check his temperature," she said, pulling out a thermometer.

Chris let out an irritable groan when she stuck the thermometer in his ear. "Good morning, sleepy head. Your fever's down this morning. Are you having any pain?"

"My ribs really hurt, and my eye throbs," he complained as he rubbed the wrap that was around his mid-section. "Can I have some more medicine?"

"I'll check with the doctor, but I don't think that'll be a problem. He'll be in to see you in a few hours, but he did say you could start with a clear diet this morning. How does orange Jell-O and apple juice sound to you?" she teased.

"Yum," Chris replied, unenthused.

"Good, then I'll be back with your Jell-O in a few minutes," she said laughing as she closed the door behind her.

Chris looked at his dad. "Thanks for staying with me last night. You didn't have to."

"I know, but I wanted to. Besides, Grandma Maggie stayed with Jody and Katie, who are both very worried about you, I might add." Chris tried to reposition himself in the bed, which brought tears to his eyes. Larry got him under the arms and helped pull him to a sitting position. "Can I get you anything?"

"Yeah, some new ribs," Chris said, making them both chuckle, which made Chris's ribs hurt even worse.

Rachel came in carrying a tray with Jell-O, two cartons of apple juice, and a blueberry muffin. She sat the Jell-O and one carton of apple juice on the small table beside the bed, and then slid it up in front of Chris.

"The only way you're going to get better is if you regain your strength. After you finish, I'll be back in to give you some pain medication." She turned and offered Larry the tray with the other carton of apple juice and the muffin. "I know you haven't eaten anything either," she said to him.

"Thank you, I'm starving," Larry said, taking the tray.

"I'll be back later, so enjoy your breakfast." She was like a whisk of fresh air with her optimism and her bubbly personality.

Chris took a few bites and a small drink of juice. He turned pale and pushed the rest of it away. "I'm too sick to eat," he grunted. He rested his head back on his pillow and took small, short breaths to ease the pain. He didn't want Jell-O; he just wanted something for the pain.

"It's all right, there's no rush. You can try again in a little while." Larry rose from the chair and moved the table away.

A few minutes later Rachel came back like she'd promised and injected more medicine into Chris's IV. "There now, that should take the edge off a bit." It wasn't long before Chris was resting comfortably again.

Larry was flipping through television channels when the door opened. "Hello, I'm Dr. Baker, Chris's pediatrician." He reached out and shook Larry's hand before Larry could even stand up.

"I've been going over all of the blood tests and x-rays, and everything looks really good. He should make a full recovery."

"I'm relieved to hear that. Thank you, doctor," Larry said. "However, his ribs are still really bothering him. Is there anything you can do for him?"

"Unfortunately, that's going to be the most painful part of his recovery. It could take up to six weeks for the ribs to heal and there's not much we can do. He'll need to stay in bed as much as possible for the next week, but then I want him up and walking. He should be able to return to school by then. We also need to take that wrap off before he goes home. It doesn't help in the recovery and will restrict his breathing, which can lead to pneumonia. What I want him do is take ten deep breaths every hour for the first few days to help keep his lungs clear." He talked as he listened to Chris's lungs and heart, and then he pulled out his notepad and began to write.

"I'll also send you home with a prescription for Lortab—that's a pain medication—and also penicillin to help with any infection." He was writing as fast as he was talking, sending the impression that he was rushed.

"So, he can go home today?" Larry asked, surprised.

"We'll need to follow up with him in a week and get a cast on his arm, but I see no reason to keep him here any longer. If he gets worse or has any bleeding, we'll want to see him right away. The nurse will go over all of that with you before you leave. Do you have any questions?" He handed Larry the prescriptions and started walking toward the door.

"No, I think you answered all of them," Larry replied. He wanted to get out of there. He hated the hospital due to the fact that Barbara spent much of the last two months of her life there. It was gloomy and depressing to him.

Rachel came in and went over the discharge instructions, checked Chris's vitals once more, and removed the IV.

Chris's body felt heavy and weak as he pulled himself out of bed and began to get dressed. He painfully felt every achy muscle in his body, especially his ribs. Flashbacks of the brutal attack emerged, sending a cold chill down his spine.

Rachel brought a wheelchair in for the ride to the car. Chris reluctantly sat down after Rachel told him she would tie him to the seat if he didn't. They thanked Rachel for everything and headed for home, with Chris feeling every bump and pothole in the road.

Once home, Chris collapsed into bed, exhausted from the agonizing ride. Larry gave him a pill for the pain and a heating pad for his ribs. The pill relaxed him enough that he was able to sleep for the next several hours.

"Chris, are you home?" Katie yelled excitedly as she ran down the stairs. She was so happy to see her brother—*alive*. She thought for sure she would never see him again. "Are you okay?" she asked as she gently and cautiously sat down on the edge of the bed.

"Yeah, I'm fine. It just hurts a little," Chris said, trying to show his tough side.

"Well, you look like Popeye the sailor man," she laughed, referring to the patch on his eye.

Chris smiled. "I think it makes me look like a mean pirate," he said with a growl in his voice.

Katie laughed at her brother's poor impression of a pirate. From the den, Larry heard Katie talking to her brother and went downstairs to intervene. When he reached the door he couldn't help but delay his intrusion as he listened to what Katie had to say to her brother.

"I drew you a picture while you were in the hospital. Can I give it to you now?" she asked, gleaming. Chris nodded his head and Katie proudly presented him with a folded piece of paper from the front pocket of her overalls. "I hope you like it."

Chris smiled as he unfolded the paper. He noticed the confident look on Katie's face.

Written on the top of the page in big, red letters were the words, "I Love Chris." Below the words she'd drawn a house with four people standing in front. Chris instantly knew who he was because she had drawn bandages all over him. Then Jody was next, holding her cell phone in her hand. She'd put her father in the middle, holding his briefcase, and Katie was beside him wearing a big pink bow in her hair. Chris was amused at the detail she'd so carefully put into each family member.

"Well, do you like it?" she asked cheerfully.

"It's a true masterpiece Katie. I love it!" He smiled and pulled her into a hug. "But I have one question. Who is this person above the house?"

"Duh! That's mommy! She's our guardian angel now." Katie had drawn her mother wearing a long, yellow and gold dress with bright beams shooting out from her radiant spirit. Chris could see she had spent more time drawing her mother than any other member of the family. "If you ever feel sad, you can look at the picture and remember that mommy loves you," Katie said with confidence.

Chris fought back the tears. He knew how much thought and love had gone into the picture. "Thank you Katie. I will put it on my wall so I can remember that."

Larry was fighting back the tears as well. He could sense that Chris was tiring and decided it was time to intervene. "Katie, it's time to leave Chris alone so he can get some rest," he gently said from the doorway.

"Okay, daddy," Katie said, sighing. "I hope you get better real soon so you can take me to the park to play," she said to Chris.

"Me too," Chris replied, rubbing his sore ribs.

"I'll leave the door cracked a little, so if you need anything, just ring the bell I gave you," Larry instructed Chris. "Don't try to yell, because it will only hurt."

Chris nodded. Since they took the wrap off around his mid-section, it even hurt to breathe. It was like getting kicked all over again.

He lay back and tried to go to sleep, but every time he closed his eyes he saw Jeff's brothers face, taunting him, laughing at him, and looking at him with pure hatred. With his left hand he gently felt the bandage that covered his stitches and remembered the unexpected blow that knocked him to the ground. It sent a jolt of terror though him even now.

Larry sat down and basked in the silence of the house. Dinner was over and the dishes were done. Chris was resting peacefully, and Jody had gone to a school dance.

Katie was also gone. Maggie and Bob had come to see Chris and ended up taking her with them for the weekend. Maggie thought it would be a good idea for Katie to get away from all the commotion. Besides, they would be leaving at the end of the month for a one-year mission to Australia, and Larry wanted Katie to spend time with them. They were going to postpone it after Barbara's death but decided she would have wanted them to go ahead with their plans.

Hoping to take his mind off the events of the day, Larry turned on the lamp beside his recliner and looked for something to read. He needed a moment of peace to collect his thoughts. The last few days had been overwhelming, and his nerves were raw. He worried about Chris getting better, about Jody still being angry with him over the loss of her mother, and Katie trying to make sure everyone was happy. The stress and worry were taking a toll on him, leaving him mentally distraught.

Suddenly, out of the stillness of the house came a horrifying scream from the basement. Larry threw down his newspaper and bolted for the stairs, taking them two at a time. He reached Chris's room and swung open the door. Chris was in bed tossing and turning and yelling in his sleep. "Stop it! Get off me!"

Larry sat down on the edge of the bed and shook him gently. "Chris, wake up," he said loudly.

Chris sat straight up in bed and threw punches with his one good arm. "Get away from me!" he blurted out again.

Larry grabbed Chris's arm, just in time to stop him from punching Larry in the jaw. "Chris, wake up! It's dad!" he shouted.

Chris stopped punching and opened his good eye. Frightened and confused, he looked around the room. Sweat dripped from his scared, pale face, and his body trembled from the disturbing images in his mind. Larry wrapped his arms around him and comforted him. "It's okay now. It was only a dream," he whispered.

Chris realized he'd been having a nightmare and angrily pushed his father away. "I'm fine, just leave me alone!"

"Chris, it's okay to be scared. What happened to you was an awful thing, and it would help you to talk about it."

"There's nothing to talk about! I'm fine! Just get out and leave me

52

alone!" Chris yelled. His voice was filled with fear and embarrassment.

"I want to help you through this. Talk to me!" Larry touched Chris's shoulder and spoke gently to him.

"Don't touch me!" Chris shouted angrily, pushing his hand away. "Get out of my room!"

Larry didn't want to fight, so he left the room. He was concerned and frustrated. He knew that sooner or later Chris would need to talk about the attack—if not with him, then with the police. The officer from the hospital had called twice asking to talk to Chris. He said they could only hold the boys for forty-eight hours, so Chris would need to go down and make a positive ID on them tomorrow. But Larry could see that now was not the time to talk to him about it.

Larry closed the door and headed back upstairs. He was angry, frustrated, and hurt. His emotions were running away with him, and he felt powerless to control them. He wanted to tell his son that he'd changed; that he wasn't the same person he used to be. Chris could talk to him, lean on him, and trust him. But instead, Chris kept silent behind his wall of anger and resentment.

Larry knew that if Barbara were still there, she would know exactly what to do. He realized that Chris and Barb shared a special bond between them that at times sparked jealousy in him. One night he came home from work and found them in the driveway playing basketball together. He was angry with Barbara for taking his place. He should have been the one playing basketball. She invited him to join the game, but instead of making lifelong memories with his wife and son, he released his jealous anger at them. He stormed into the house and lost himself in his work. That's when he decided to let Barb play with the kids so he could work harder to get ahead in his career. It made sense to him at the time, but now he could see how childish and selfish it was.

The thought of how much precious time with his family he'd lost and the wedge he'd driven between them was like a burning poison running though his veins. His frustration built until he could no longer contain it. He forcefully punched his fist into the wall, leaving a mark of anger behind. How could he have been so stupid, so selfish? He'd thought Barbara was trying to take his place, but instead, she was only trying to fill the void he'd left behind. Now he was trying to reconnect with his son, and his son wanted nothing to do with him. Maybe it was too little, too late.

He looked at his family's picture hanging on the wall. *Why did Heavenly Father take her away? It wasn't fair!* He needed her there with him to help him though this.

"I want you back Barb!" he cried in a selfish rage. "It's not fair!" He picked up the glass of water he'd been drinking and hurled it across the room at the fireplace, just missing the pictures and shattering the glass into tiny pieces. "Why did you leave me? I can't do this on my own! You should be here with me!" he raved resentfully.

He picked up the lamp that was sitting on the end table, jerked the cord right out of the wall, and threw the lamp across the room into the bookshelf. It shattered the white porcelain base and knocked the books off the shelf. Larry's heart was beating hard and fast, and his entire body shook as his animosity grew stronger.

He was angry with Barbara for leaving him, and angry that she'd left him to raise their children by himself. How could she have let this happen? She'd ruined their family, their plans, and dowsed his hopes for a bright future.

He walked over to the mantel and picked up her picture. The sight of her face quickly diminished his anger. He knew it wasn't her fault that she got sick. If it was anybody's fault, it was his, just like Jody had said.

"I'm sorry honey," he whispered, softly touching her face. Tears flowed as he felt the anger leave his body and he began to relax. "I miss you so much! I wish I could hold you in my arms. I love you Barb," he cried, heartbroken and miserable. He fell to his knees, clutching her picture to his chest and weeping uncontrollably.

He had taken her for granted, and now it was too late. If only he could turn back the clock and start over again. He would fix things, make everything better, and be the kind of husband that Barbara deserved.

He heard the back door slam and he swiftly got to his feet. He quickly put the picture back on the mantel. He wiped away the tears and turned just in time to see Jody staggering through the kitchen. She was drunk!

# Chapter 7

$\mathcal{C}$hris looked at his surroundings and thought how much it resembled something out of the movies. The officer told him they would have to release the three boys if he didn't make a positive ID. So there he sat, behind a one-way mirror, waiting to see his attackers again.

Chris was sitting at the front of the room with an officer from the hospital, and his father was standing in the back with a plainclothes detective. Chris was still not feeling well, and he wasn't sure if it was his ribs that hurt or the thought of seeing his attackers again. His stomach was in knots, and he was sure he looked as sick as he felt. It was a good thing his father was in the back of the room. He didn't want to have to listen to him tell him again that he was doing the right thing.

Chris wasn't even going to come. He wanted to let the whole thing go since he thought it would just stir up more trouble. But his dad insisted, saying that if he didn't put them behind bars for what they'd done, they would hurt someone else. As much as he hated the thought of seeing them again, he didn't want anyone else to go through what he'd gone through. His biggest concern however, was that their friends would come and finish the job.

The door on the other side of the mirror opened and six men walked in wearing handcuffs and shackles. They were dressed in orange jumpsuits and carried cardboard signs with numbers on them. The officer instructed Chris to carefully look at each one of the men before making a final decision. He needed to be absolutely positive which ones attacked him.

Chris knew right away which three they where, but he carefully looked at each one, taking time to remember their faces. Number two was Jeff's brother—Chris knew that without a doubt. It was a face that would haunt his thoughts forever. He remembered looking into his cold, unfeeling eyes just before he rammed his skateboard into his head. He could see the black and blue mark it had left on his cheek. Numbers four and five were the other two boys. He got a good look at them as they got out of the truck.

Larry stood quietly in the back of the room. His arms were folded as he agitatedly shifted his weight from one foot to the other. He had to hold himself back from breaking the mirror and tearing the boys apart for what they'd done to his son.

Chris gave the numbers to the officer and asked to be excused. He was feeling sick to his stomach. He stood up from his chair and felt a little lightheaded. Suddenly, he heard someone yelling. He turned to see Jeff's brother shaking his handcuffed fists at the mirror.

"Come out here and face me like a man, you wimp!" he shouted furiously. "I'm not through with you! Just you wait!" He was still yelling when two officers ushered him out the door.

Larry came up and put his hand on Chris's shoulder. "You're doing the right thing," he reassured him. Chris pushed his father's hand away and started for the door. He could feel the room move around him.

"Don't worry, Chris, he can't see you," said the plainclothed officer.

"He may not be able to see me, but he knows I'm here," Chris said calmly, fighting back the fear.

He left the room and quickly found a water fountain. He took a long drink and let the cool water sooth his dry, scratchy throat. Then he sat down in the first chair he came to. His palms were sweaty and he could feel his heart race. He slid down in the chair and rested his head back against the wall. He took a deep, cleansing breath, relieved to be out of that room and away from Jeff's brother.

"That was a pretty tough thing to do, what you just did in there."

Chris looked up to see a tall man in his mid-twenties. He was about six feet two inches and had sandy blond hair and blue eyes. He had a muscular build and was wearing khaki pants with a striped shirt that buttoned up the front. Chris noticed a badge hanging from his belt.

"What do you mean?"

"Well, facing the boys who did this to you. That was really brave. A lot of kids, including some adults, wouldn't have done it."

The man sat down in the chair next to Chris, rested his elbows on his knees, and looked directly into Chris's strained, pale face.

"I don't know how brave I am. I'm still shaking."

"That's nothing. I've know grown men who have wet their pants right there in the chair." He was smiling at Chris like he'd known him his whole life.

"You're kidding! They were that scared?"

"I'm telling the truth. They took one look at the men behind the mirror and lost it."

Chris laughed at the thought and felt a little better about the situation.

"But you know," the man continued, "it wouldn't hurt to talk to someone about what happened."

"I've already heard that from my dad," Chris said sullenly.

"He's right, you know. I've seen a lot of cases like yours come through here, and the ones who are able to talk about it are usually the ones who seem to be able to deal with it the best." He could tell by the look on Chris's face that he didn't believe him.

"Tell you what; sometimes the best person to talk to about stuff like this isn't your parents. Here's my card. If you ever need to talk—or just hang out—give me a call." He handed Chris his card, and Chris noticed that the man's name was Detective Ben Carlson.

"Thanks, I'll keep it in mind." Chris stuck the card in his pants pocket just as his father and the other two officers came around the corner.

"I see you've met Detective Carlson," one of the officers said, pointing to the man next to Chris. "It was a good thing he was headed home when he was."

"What do you mean?" Chris asked.

"Oh, he's just blabbering on," Ben said, waving his hand at the officer.

"Well, I'd like to personally thank you for everything you did for Chris," Larry said, shaking hands with Ben.

"Am I missing something?" Chris was getting frustrated with all the adults talking around him like he was a two year old.

"Detective Carlson was the one who saw the attack and called for backup," Larry told his son. "He tried to apprehend the boys but decided to stay with you instead. He sat with you until the paramedics arrived. If he hadn't come along when he did . . ." Larry ended the sentence before he said too much.

"Well, you definitely look much better than the last time I saw you," Ben smiled as he gave Chris a soft pat on the back. "I was also able to identify the three boys, so they'll be going away for a very long time."

"Well, I guess I owe you one for saving my life," Chris said. "Thank you."

"Don't worry about it. Just remember, my card is in your pocket," Ben said with a smile. He got up and stuck his hand out to Chris. "Friends?"

Chris shrugged his shoulders. "Sure, why not?" he said, shaking Ben's hand.

Chris was in a lot of pain after the trip to the police station, so he downed two Lortab instead of one like the prescription said. He went to bed, hoping to get the images of his attackers out of his head.

Larry was preparing lunch when Jody came up from her room. She was still wearing her pajamas. Her hair was ratted and her face was pale. He took one look at her and thought, *it serves you right.*

"You look like you've been run over by a freight train," he laughed. "Are you sick?" he yelled in her ear, trying to make a point.

"Don't yell, I have a terrible headache," she moaned, rubbing her hand across her forehead. "Do you have anything I can take for a sick stomach?" She sat down on a bar stool at the kitchen counter and laid her head down.

"I think what *you* need is something to eat," he said sarcastically.

He pulled out a bowl of tuna salad from the refrigerator and placed it in front of her, knowing how much she despised tuna. She took one look at the bowl, placed her hand over her mouth, and headed straight for the bathroom. Larry smiled in retaliation, hoping that he'd made his point.

After a few minutes she came back and sat down. "Okay, I get it. That was my lesson on drinking. Are you happy that you made me throw up?" she asked sarcastically.

"I'm not happy about any of this, so why don't you start off by telling me why you wanted to drink last night?" He was still trying this new, no yelling approach, but he was finding it very difficult to stay in control.

"Do we have to talk about this right now? I'm not feeling very good."

"Well, I could make you an egg salad sandwich instead."

"Okay, okay, I'll talk. Just no more food, please!" She gagged and covered her mouth again. "My friends and I were with some other fiends that we usually don't associate with. Well, they decided to stop at this party before we went to the dance. I didn't know they'd be drinking—honest. I wanted to say no—I really did, but they started calling me Molly Mormon, because I wouldn't drink, so I thought I would just hold the beer in my hand and pretend to take a drink. Nobody would ever need to know. But it came in a glass, not in a can, and they were playing quarters. Do you know what quarters is, dad?"

"I must have missed that game in high school."

"You sit at a table with a bunch of other kids. Everyone has a glass of beer in front of them. The idea is to bounce a quarter on the table and into the glass. If you miss, you drink. Well, I'm not very good at it."

She put her head down on the counter and let out a groan. "I don't ever want to see another beer for as long as I live."

"I really hope you mean that. However, you broke the rules, so there needs to be a consequence for your actions. What do you think your punishment should be?" He already had something in mind but thought he would ask all the same.

"You're asking me?" she questioned, cocking her head to one side in puzzlement. "Is this a trick?"

"Yes, I'm asking you, and no, it's not a trick. You know you broke the rules. Now, you come up with a punishment to fit the crime."

She looked at her dad as if he had lost his mind. But at the same time, she knew there was no drinking allowed, and she had broken the rule. If it were reversed, would she let him off so easily?

"Okay, how about no television for one week?" she asked, tilting her head to one side.

Larry cocked an eyebrow to let her know that it wasn't enough.

"And no going out with friends for . . . two weeks?" She added, asking a question rather than making a statement.

"Is that all?" he replied.

"No television and no friends—wouldn't you consider that punishment enough?" She was starting to get worried.

Larry momentarily considered her suggestions, and then he finally said, "Since this is your first offense, I think it will do." His arms were folded like a judge who had just passed a sentence. "What about talking to the bishop?"

"No! I'm embarrassed enough without talking to him. Besides,

I'm never drinking again—I promise! I just let my friends talk me into something really stupid, and I knew it was wrong. It won't happen again—trust me," Jody said with resolve.

"Then I'll put all my trust in you. I know you won't let me down."

A serious but sad look came across her face, and she hung her head. "Mom's probably really disappointed in me, huh?"

The question took Larry off guard. Jody had never wanted to talk about Barbara before, and fearing that it might push his daughter further away, he had been hesitant to bring it up. He walked around the counter and sat down on the stool next to her. "She's never been disappointed in you," he said, smiling. "She knows you're still young and you're going to make mistakes. The secret in life is to learn from your mistakes and not repeat them." He suddenly realized that he could benefit from his own advice. "Do you remember when you were ten and your mom wouldn't buy you a candy bar at the store, so without her knowing it, you put it in your pocket?"

Jody laughed. "When she found out she laid a huge guilt trip on me. She took me back to the store so I could return it."

"But she didn't force you to return it, did she?"

"No, I decided that all on my own. She just made me realize I'd done something wrong and needed to correct it. She also used the opportunity to teach about repentance."

"I remember how proud she was of you for making the right decision."

Jody understood where her father was going with this, but the memories of her mother were still too painfully fresh in her mind. She wasn't ready to take a walk down memory lane—not just yet. "Well, thanks for the pep talk," she said, abruptly leaving the room without looking back.

Larry watched as her blissful disposition changed to hurtful despair. At that moment he realized just how much Barbara's death was affecting everyone. He'd been dwelling on how bad things were for him, without regard to anyone else. Once again, he was only thinking of himself when he should have been thinking of his children and the hurt they were feeling inside.

He stood up from the stool and slammed both fists into the counter, disappointed in himself for acting so selfishly. He knew it was time to grow up and start acting like the adult. No more wallowing in self-pity!

His children were hurting just as badly as he was, and he needed to find a way to reach them.

As he prepared dinner that night, his mind went back to the scripture he'd read in the hospital. If he was to have hope, he needed to have faith.

Katie asked why he wasn't going to church and why he wouldn't say the prayer. He'd made one excuse after another, trying to avoid the real reason—a reason that up until now had made sense. But nothing was making sense anymore. He knew where he needed to be spiritually, but he had no clue how to get there.

Katie and Jody were the only ones actually going to church nowadays. Larry thought about going back to church several times, but when it came right down to it, he just couldn't bring himself to go. His hurt and anger ran deep, and his pride even deeper. At this rate, he wasn't sure if he'd ever get his family back on track again.

# Chapter 8

On a gray Tuesday morning, the dark clouds finally burst into a downpour. Larry grabbed his briefcase from the passenger seat of the truck and held it over his head to shelter himself from the rain. He should have listened to the weatherman when he said there was a thirty percent chance of rain, but Larry was hoping for some sunshine since it was the first day of May.

There was a time when he really loved the rain, but now it was a nuisance. He remembered when he and Barbara were first married and moved into an older home with a huge porch and an old porch swing. When it would rain, they would snuggle under a blanket on the porch swing and watch the rain come down. He thought it was terribly romantic to listen to the raindrops splash down and to smell the refreshing sent. When they moved, Barb pleaded with him to take the swing, but he wouldn't hear of hanging that old rundown swing on his new, three-story home. He recalled the disappointed look in her eyes, and he now wished that he had brought the old porch swing with them.

Larry hurried through the parking lot. He tried to avoid the puddles but managed to hit most of them. By the time he made it to the building, his shoes were soaked, his hair was dripping from the rain, and his spirits were as damp as his suit. He irritably brushed off the water and stormed into office, determined to eliminate the agonizing thoughts of the past.

As Larry turned on his computer and started going through his files, his thoughts returned to his son. It'd been a month since the attack, and Chris was still complaining about the pain. He kept insisting that he needed more medication. He got angrier by the day, insinuating that the doctor just wanted him to suffer. Most of the time he kept to himself and would mope around the house like he was mad at the whole world. At other times he would burst into an angry rage and start yelling for no reason. Chris's first few weeks back to school were tough for him. Although the patch on his eye was gone, it was hard to write with his arm in a cast. He would come home from school frustrated and angry.

Larry tried again to focus on the task at hand, but his gaze kept wandering away from his work and over to the family portrait he had sitting on his desk. He thought about the rain again and the old porch swing. Every memory he had included Barbara—memories that kept flooding his mind like an endless river. He was deep in thought when Mike, a fellow coworker, stopped by. Mike pulled up an office chair and sat down.

Larry met Mike the first day he started work at J.J. Jensen's. Mike had been there a little over three years and took Larry under his wing. They became best friends. He was two years older than Larry, and Mike's wife, Vicky, was the same age as Barbara. All four of them hit it off right away. Before Larry started putting in all the long hours at work, they would go out together almost every weekend. Mike had been trying to get him to go out to dinner with them for the last two weeks, but it didn't feel right without Barb there.

Mike plopped down in the chair and crossed his legs. "How ya doing buddy?" he asked cheerfully. "And don't give me the same bull you gave me over the phone Friday night. I want the truth."

"You don't need to hear about my problems," Larry said, dodging the question. "You've got your own family to worry about."

"I've been your best friend for over twelve years now. Are you really going to sit there and deny me the pleasure of trying to help you in your time of need? That's what friends are for," he said jovially.

Larry sighed heavily. He had been close to tears all morning. But men don't just burst into tears in front of other men, not even if he is your best friend. Larry swallowed the lump that had settled in his throat and tried to push aside his emotions.

"I miss her Mike, more than I ever thought I would. Some days it hurts so much that I don't even want to get out of bed. And I still do crazy things, like when Katie learned her first song on the piano. I thought to myself, 'I can't wait to tell Barb,' only to realize that she's not here to tell.

There's this empty feeling inside me that I just can't shake. And then there's the regrets and the what-ifs that eat at me. The kids miss her so much. They seem lost without her. Chris is lashing out at everyone, and I don't know how to help him. Jody gets close to opening up to me, and then she just shuts down. I don't know how much longer I can hold this family together." Larry looked at the floor so Mike couldn't see the tears that were welling up in his eyes.

"Be patient Larry, with your kids and with yourself. Let time be the healer and things will come together—you'll see."

"I don't know. Everyday I think it's going to get a little easier—a little better, but it hasn't."

"Hey, do you remember what I told you after the funeral?" Mike asked with a little excitement in his voice.

Larry shook his head. The day of Barbara's funeral was just a blur to him. He remembered going back to the church for a luncheon. Everyone was hugging him and asking him how he was doing, which made him feel even worse. He just wanted to go home and lock himself in his bedroom. Katie sat on Maggie's lap the whole time, not wanting anyone else to hold her. Jody kept busy helping serve the lunch, while Chris sat in the corner and refused to speak to anyone. It was like a long, drawn out, horrible nightmare from which he could not wake. He wasn't even sure he'd talked to Mike that day.

"Well I'll remind you," Mike said, noticing Larry's blank stare. "I have a cabin up Logan Canyon that we use during the summer. It's about a four-hour drive from here, but it's well worth it. It has two bedrooms downstairs and a loft, but no television or phone. It's just you, the kids, and Mother Nature."

Mike could sense that Larry wasn't interested, so he continued, "It's beautiful up there, Larry. There's a small lake just ten minutes away where you can swim and fish. There's also a small stream that runs right behind the cabin. I think it may be just what the doctor ordered," he smiled convincingly.

"Well, Chris still hasn't healed up, and school's not out for another three weeks. Then with the merger, I just don't know if I could take the time off to go."

"Excuses, excuses! You know very well you can get the time off work. I'll cover for you. Chris will be back on his feet about the same time school gets out, so take off and don't come back for at least a week."

Mike was determined to get them there.

"I'll see how things are in a few weeks. That's the best I can do," Larry said, trying to get Mike off his back.

"It'll be there when you're ready. Just let me know."

Mike jumped up and gave Larry a slap on the back. Larry continued trying to work but was interrupted with a phone call.

"Larry Porter," he announced into the receiver.

"Dad, this is Chris. I'm in a lot of pain and need you to excuse me from school." It wasn't a question; it was a statement. Chris would leave school with or without his father's approval.

"Chris, I excused you twice last week and three times the week before that. You really need to stay. Take some more Tylenol and let's see how you feel in a few hours." Larry was trying to understand, but he was afraid Chris was using his pain as an excuse to get out of his schoolwork.

"I knew you wouldn't understand! You never do! I told you before, the Tylenol isn't working! I need something stronger!" he argued angrily.

"The doctor said you would have to go off of the Lortab. They already gave you more than they thought you should have. The first few weeks off the medicine will be the hardest, but you'll adjust."

"Why can't they put me on some other pain killer? There's got to be more than just that one!"

"They all have the same effect, Chris. The doctor doesn't want you to become dependent on them. It can lead to more problems."

"Whatever! Are you going to excuse me or not?"

"Like I said, take the Tylenol and wait a few hours to see how you . . ."

"I knew you wouldn't care!" Chris interrupted. "I hate you for this!" He slammed down the receiver.

Larry hung up the phone. In despair and feeling terrible, he wondered if he'd done the right thing. He knew Chris needed to get back to a normal life, but he worried that his son would never be the same. Deeply troubled by Chris's reaction, Larry picked up the phone and called the school counselor for help.

"Mark Petersen," the voice on the other end of the line said.

"Hello, this is Larry Porter, Christopher Porter's dad."

"Yes, how are you, Mr. Porter?"

"Not so good, I'm afraid. I'm calling about Christopher. I've seen some changes in him lately that are disconcerting. I was wondering if you've talked to him since he came back to school."

"I've likewise been concerned about him and have tried numerous times to talk with him, but he has an excuse every time. I just saw him in the hallway this morning and asked him if he would drop by my office. He blew up and told me to leave him alone. In fact, I think his exact words were, "I'd rather be beaten up again than to have to sit in your office one more minute."

"It sounds like you're not making any more progress with him than I am. Do you have any advice?" Larry was hoping that since Mr. Petersen was a professional he would have some answers.

"Well, let's give him some more time and continue to watch his behavior closely. If you see any signs of depression, please call me right away."

"I will, thank you." Larry hung up the phone. He was discouraged about the way things were going, and now he was concerned that Chris might be depressed.

Chris skipped out the back door of the school and headed for home. He didn't need anyone's approval to leave. He'd leave if he wanted too. The walk home from school was a little more than a mile, so by the time he reached the house his ribs were throbbing horribly. He had the tremors again and felt cold and sweaty. How dare they tell him he couldn't have any more pain pills! He was still in pain!

He went straight to the upstairs bathroom and looked through the medicine cabinet, trying to find something that might help. He'd already taken all of the cough medicine, and now all that was left was cold medicine and aspirin. He felt a sense of desperation that he wasn't familiar with. It ate at him, tearing him apart from the inside. He knew he needed those pills.

*There's got to be something stronger in this house*, he thought frantically. Then he remembered his father's bathroom.

He searched through the medicine cabinet and looked through all the prescription bottles. There were some with leftover antibiotics in them, and then there were two with 'for pain' written on the label. One was Lortab and the other was Percocet. They were both in his mother's name, and he realized his father had forgotten to throw them out.

Feeling somewhat ashamed but mostly relieved, he stuffed the two bottles into his pocket. He then came across another bottle of medicine, way back in the top corner. It was in a clear bottle and had Morphine written on the label. Chris recalled how the Morphine had made him feel when he was in the hospital. He was spacey and lightheaded all the time. It was much too strong, so he decided to leave it there.

He rummaged through the drawers and found two unused syringes. He recalled walking in on his father giving his mother a shot. He was told it was pain medication that the doctor prescribed for her. The pain had progressed until the regular pain pills weren't enough and the injections were the only way to control it.

Feeling like an intruder in his own home, Chris put everything back the way he found it. He quietly opened the door, stepped out into the hallway, and then carefully closed his father's door behind him. That's when he heard Katie's voice.

"What were you doing in dad's room?" she asked innocently.

Chris panicked. He was not excepting anyone to be around this time of day, but now that he'd been discovered, he needed to think of something quick. "I'm buying him a present for father's day, and I wanted to know what cologne he wears so I can buy him the kind he likes. But it's a big secret, so you can't tell him I was in there, okay?" he explained, smiling convincingly.

Her face lit up like she'd just found out the biggest secret in history. "Oh, I won't tell. I can keep a secret." She zipped her thumb and finger across her lips and pretended to throw the key over her shoulder.

"What are you doing home so early?" he questioned suspiciously. "It's only one o'clock."

"I have a dentist appointment. I thought dad would already be here waiting for me," she answered. "What are you doing home from school?"

"Well, we're at lunch right now, so I thought I'd race home and find his cologne." Chris panicked again as he realized that his father was probably on his way home, and he knew he'd better make a hasty exit. "I've got to get back to school now, so promise me you won't tell dad," he added.

"I pinky promise," she said as she held out her pinky. Chris shook pinkies with her, although it bothered him to lie to his little sister. He then slipped out the side door just as his father pulled into the driveway and honked the horn. He waited in the bushes until the coast was clear, and then went back into the house to hide the pills.

He went to the kitchen and took two of the Lortab before hiding them in the bottom of his sock drawer. It was amazing the comfort he felt just knowing that he had those pills again. After an hour the pain faded, the shaking stopped, and he felt calm and in control once more.

When Larry and Katie arrived home later that day, Chris was in a much better mood. The kitchen was clean, the dishes were done, and Chris was making hamburgers for dinner.

"What's all this?" Larry asked with surprise. He certainly wasn't expecting to come home to dinner, especially after the way Chris had acted on the phone earlier.

"I just thought I would help out around here. Is that a problem?" Chris asked sarcastically.

"No problem. I'm just surprised, that's all. You said on the phone earlier that you were still in a lot of pain."

"Yeah, well, the Tylenol worked better than I thought."

After dinner was finished, Larry asked the girls to clean up the kitchen while he talked to Chris alone. Larry leaned his elbows on the table and folded his hands. He carefully watched Chris from across the table. "I talked to the counselor at your school today. He was hoping you would go in and talk with him."

"About what?" Chris was feeling a little spacey and was having a hard time focusing. His body felt numb and tingly, almost like he was floating.

"About the attack—or whatever else you might want to talk about. He just wants to help." Larry tried to be convincing but could sense Chris's resistance.

"Whatever," Chris mumbled, slurring his words and rolling his eyes. He slumped down further in his chair and looked in the opposite direction so his father couldn't read his face. He really just wanted to go to bed. The world around him was becoming distant, and he couldn't make much sense of what his father was saying.

"Are you feeling all right? You don't look so good," Larry asked suspiciously. He could see the glossy stare in Chris's eyes and noticed how distant he'd become.

"I'm really tired. I think I'll just go to bed early tonight." Chris grabbed the back of the chair as he stood, studying himself from the dizziness.

Larry watched in silent anguish as his pale-faced, incoherent son, staggered out of the room. Feeling another headache coming on, he rested back in his chair and rubbed his forehead. He could see Chris changing right before his eyes but was powerless to stop it.

Feeling a little more sluggish than usual, Chris went to his room and climbed into bed. As much as he liked the calming feeling the pills gave him, he hated feeling so tired all the time. At least when he was sleeping he wasn't thinking about the attack, unless one of those terrifying nightmares about the boys came into his mind. Nonetheless, he felt in control over his thoughts.

He stared off into the darkness and wondered what he would do when he was finally out of pills. Would he be able to get more? The thought of not having the pain pills was almost as frightening as the attack itself. However, there was one nagging question lurking in the back of his mind. How far would he be willing to go to get more?

# Chapter 9

Mother's Day was especially hard for everyone. Jody, Chris, and Katie loved to get up early and make Barbara a special Mother's Day breakfast in bed, which included chocolate chip pancakes. The aroma would fill the house as Barbara patiently waited in bed for her surprise breakfast. They would pick a fresh bouquet of flowers straight from her flower garden and wake her up with a smile. Barbara loved to watch their faces light up with pleasure as she raved about the food.

After breakfast, she was presented with a string of gifts. Katie would be first with something she'd created at school—a rose made from colored paper or a heart-shaped letter of love. Jody would be next with a scented candle or a new fragrance of body lotion from the mall. Chris would usually get her a statue that praised her as a mother and reminded her of how special she was to him.

Of course, she would have loved anything—or nothing at all—from them. She always felt that the greatest gift they could give her was their time, which was a concept that Larry had never understood. He would bring her flowers and gifts, but what she longed for was companionship. Barbara once told him that the time he spent with her meant more than any present he could ever give her.

Larry had always tried to make Mother's Day special for Barb. He would spend the entire day with the family, doing whatever Barbara desired. But Monday soon came and it was back to the same old routine. He never looked at it as taking time away from his wife and kids. He saw things from a different perspective at the time. He was providing them with the luxuries of life.

Larry worried all week about this day and how the kids would respond. He wanted to make this day special, even without their mother there. He thought about it and finally came up with an idea. He gathered all the kids together in the living room to hear what he had planned.

"I've thought about this day all week and I know that no matter what we do today, we're still going to miss your mother. But I'm hoping that we can remember her without missing her too much. So, I've decided that today we are going to do all the things your mother loved to do—starting with chocolate chip pancakes," he raved enthusiastically.

"Hurray!" Katie shouted and jumped up out of her chair. "Can we all help make pancakes just like if mommy was here?" she asked with excitement.

"You bet. Chris, Jody, would you help us?"

"But those pancakes were especially for mom on Mother's Day. It would seem weird to make them now that she's gone," Jody replied hesitantly.

"I think your Mother would be happy to look down and see all of you kids making her favorite breakfast on her special day. Wouldn't you agree?"

"You're probably right. Count me in," Jody smiled. She took Katie by the hand and headed off to the kitchen.

"What about you, Chris? Are you up to making some delicious chocolate chip pancakes?" Larry rubbed his hands together to show the excitement he was feeling. Chris sat on the couch with his arms folded and a scowl on his face.

"I've got a headache. I think I'll just go to my room until the pancakes are done," he grunted, unenthused.

"You've been acting strange all week. Are you sure it's just a headache?"

"I'm fine! I just want to go back to bed, so get off my case!" Chris barked harshly as he walked briskly out of the room.

Larry wiped the disappointed look off his face and joined the girls in the kitchen. As they made the pancakes, they laughed about the unforgettable memories and catastrophes. Like the time Chris dumped the syrup in the middle of the floor, making a horrible sticky mess. And the time Larry burnt the sausage, sending an unappetizing smoke-filled odor up the stairs, which set off every smoke detector in the house. Larry and the kids were devastated, but Barbara never laughed so hard in her life. She said it was one Mother's Day she would never forget, and they never did.

"Chris, breakfast is ready," Larry said, gently shaking Chris awake.

"I'm not hungry," Chris mumbled from beneath the covers. He'd taken two pain pills and now all he wanted to do was sleep.

Larry shook his head and wondered if this was a sign of depression. He worried that things were getting worse instead of better. Chris seemed to be in a downward spiral, with little indication that he would get better. Everything about him had changed—his attitude, his language, his friends, and his temper.

After breakfast they got ready for church. Barbara never missed a Sunday, especially on Mother's Day. Larry tried to find a way out of going, but he couldn't resist Katie's sad pleading eyes, so he gave up and decided to go. He was straightening his tie when Katie came into his bedroom. Her bright smile was gone and her eyes were full of concern. She looked like she was carrying the world on her tiny shoulders.

"Katie, what's the matter?" Larry asked as she slowly walked into the room. With her head hanging low, she plopped down on the bed.

"The Primary is singing Mother's Day songs today, but mommy's not here. What should I do?" she asked, genuinely distraught over her circumstances.

"Oh, Katie, mommy will be there in spirit. She wouldn't miss your songs for anything," Larry said, kneeling down beside her.

"Really?" she exclaimed with a gigantic grin.

"Really." He gave her a kiss on the forehead and sent her off to finish getting ready.

Larry tried to wake Chris, but once again Chris refused to go to church. Larry left him home with instructions to be ready to go by the time they got back, because he would be expected to spend the rest of the day with his family.

As Larry slowly approached the Fairview Fourth Ward church building, he felt more like an intruder than a ward member. After Barbara died, the members of the ward stopped by all the time. But as the days slipped into weeks and the weeks into months, he would only receive a call from time to time, asking how they were doing. The Bishop had called several times, but thanks to caller ID, Larry was able to dodge him.

Now he was there, climbing the stairs to the one place he thought he'd never come to again.

The guilt and shame weighed heavily on his shoulders as he opened the front doors of the church. The last time he walked through those doors was for Barbara's funeral. As he entered the building he felt the devastation of losing Barbara all over again, which quickly turned his guilt into anger and his heart into stone.

Bishop Geary was standing just inside and welcomed him with a friendly handshake. He asked Larry to come by his office and meet with him on Tuesday night.

*My first time back to church in three months and I'm already being called into the bishop's office,* Larry thought bitterly. He made up some horrible excuse that he was very busy and wouldn't have time. The bishop, however, being an inspired man, would not take no for an answer.

"You can come by when you get off work. I don't mind waiting," he said with a smile as he gave Larry a pat on the back.

Even though the bishop was a very understanding and patient man, Larry couldn't help but feel embarrassed. After all, he was holding the Lord responsible for everything that had happened. He was sure it was because of those feelings that Heavenly Father had withdrawn his spirit somewhat.

"I'll have to see about that," Larry said, not willing to commit to anything.

The congregation sang the opening song and Larry slumped further down into his back row seat. He felt like a rough, dirty pebble amongst the smooth, shiny diamonds.

The Primary presented the program, which included singing songs and reading stories about their mothers. Katie stood at the pulpit and told everyone why her mother was special. "She made me cookies, put bandages on my hurt knee, and she always, always, said, "I love you," before she kissed me good night. My dad told me she would be here today, watching me from heaven."

Larry looked around the chapel at all of Barbara's friends who were wiping their eyes as they listened to Katie praise her mother. Katie stood tall with confidence and had no doubt that her mother was there. So, with that in mind, she sang out the words of the Primary song, "Mother, I Love you."

Katie sang with pure love from her heart and total conviction that her mother was watching her from heaven. A tiny teardrop hung in the corner of Katie's eye, but it never did fall, and her warm, precious smile never faded.

Larry was dumbfounded by Katie's remarkable strength. His little girl was truly an inspiration to the whole family.

The meeting closed with the congregation singing hymn number eighty-five, "How Firm a Foundation." The words rang out through the chapel as if they had come straight from heaven and were intended just for Larry. They seemed to cut deeply through all of his animosity.

> Fear not, I am with thee; oh, be not dismayed,
> For I am thy God and will still give thee aid.
> I'll strengthen thee, help thee, and cause thee to stand,
> Upheld by my righteous, omnipotent hand.

He'd heard that same song at least a hundred times, but never before did the words make such an impact on him. His eyes filled with tears as he felt the spirit testify to him that God had not forsaken him in his time of need. It was such a powerful feeling, so strong that it left him speechless. Instantly, all of his anger and resentment were washed away, leaving him with a complete sense of hope and understanding. His heart softened as he sat and listened to the entire song, and he felt the true love of Christ surround him. Heavenly Father had not forsaken him. He had forsaken Heavenly Father, and he knew exactly what he needed to do.

After the closing prayer, Larry asked Jody to take Katie and wait for him in the truck. He nervously stood outside the bishop's office and watched for him to come down the hall. His palms were sweating and his heart was racing, but he had no doubt that he was doing the right thing.

"Brother Porter, what can I do for you?" Bishop Geary asked, surprised.

"I wanted to let you know that I will be here on Tuesday night around seven, if that's still okay."

"Of course! I look forward to visiting with you." Larry knew that if things were going to change, it would need to start with the Bishop.

When they arrived home from church, they quickly changed their clothes, picked some tulips from the flower garden, and headed for the park. Barbara loved to go to the park and feed the ducks. They found a perfect spot by the small pond and fed the ducks old crusts of bread.

Chris slumped down on the park bench and refused to take any part in what he called the "stupid duck-feeding ceremony." He wouldn't have come if his father hadn't threatened to take away his game cube if he didn't join them. His head was aching and his body hurt, but he was trying to make the pain pills last, so he hadn't taken any before he left the house. He had taken two Lortab twice a day just to get through school. Now he was down to just the Percocet, which was much stronger.

"Come on, Chris," Katie begged, pulling on his sleeve. "Push me on the swing, please? You used to like to swing with me."

"I don't want to, Katie," he snapped irritably and turned to face the other direction.

"Please, Chris, please?" Katie pleaded again, still pulling on his sweater.

"Leave me alone, Katie! I don't want to swing!" With one hard shove Chris violently pushed Katie to the ground, which sent tears flowing down her cheeks.

Larry heard Katie crying and rushed to her aid. He picked her up off the ground and dusted the dirt off her clothes. "What happened?" he demanded, eyeing Chris for answers. Chris sat up, and with cold, unfeeling eyes he glared at his father.

"I told her to leave me alone! I don't want to swing with her!" he shouted. He looked over at Katie who was still whimpering. "You are such a little crybaby!" he hollered, making her cry even harder.

"Christopher Porter, what has gotten into you?" Larry asked in disbelief. He couldn't believe what he was hearing. Chris had always cherished his little sister. He would never do anything to hurt her.

"Why do you always think it's me? Maybe she should leave people alone when they say to!" he yelled as he stormed off to the parking lot.

Jody heard the commotion from across the park and rushed over. "What's wrong with Chris?"

"I don't know. He got mad at Katie and pushed her down. I swear I don't know what's gotten into him lately. One minute he's making dinner and all smiles and the next he's acting crazy."

"Maybe he's still thinking about the attack," she said sympathetically, trying to find an explanation for her brother's unusual actions.

"I'm sorry daddy! I should've left him alone!" Katie sniffed as she wiped the tears away. "Do we have to go home now?"

"Oh, we're not going home. Chris will have to try a lot harder than that to ruin our Mother's Day tribute," Larry said, smiling. "Jody, you and Katie set up our picnic and I'll go talk to Chris."

Chris had decided to walk home. He'd had enough family fun time. He felt miserable and just wanted everyone to leave him alone. He was thinking about the six-pack of beer under his bed that his friend Brandon had given him. He found that if he drank a beer and took a pill, it intensified the craved effect.

Chris only made it two miles before he started feeling weak and out of breath. He was shaking and having cold sweats again. He'd come to realize that when this happened, only the pills could stop it. He sat down on the curb to rest, outraged that his father had made him come. He was angry with Katie for crying over the stupidest things. He was even mad at his mother for dying and leaving him alone in this idiotic world.

When Larry went to check on Chris he found the truck empty. His pulse sped up and he could feel a fiery rage starting to burn inside him. *This day was supposed to be about Barbara, not about Chris*, he thought furiously.

He drove up and down the streets until he found Chris walking though the video store parking lot. His hands were in his pockets and his head was hanging down. Larry pulled up next to him and rolled down the window.

"What do you think you're doing?" he asked Chris, who didn't stop walking.

"I'm going home. I told you I didn't wanna come in the first place, but you wouldn't listen to me!"

"Get in the truck, Chris, so we can talk."

"No, I don't want to spend the whole day thinking about my dead mother!" He blurted out disrespectfully. He continued to walk without looking at his father.

Larry couldn't take any more. He stopped the truck and got out. "Stop right there! I've had just about enough of your attitude!" he yelled harshly. Chris stopped walking and turned to face his father.

"Don't you have any respect for your mother's memory?" Larry shouted.

Chris shook even harder, and his anger escalated. With his eyes glaring like an enraged, wild animal, he shouted, "You don't know crap about making memories! You're a lousy father and you were a lousy husband!" Then he quickly turned to walk away, because he realized that his anger was out of control.

"What's the matter with you?" Larry said, reaching out to take Chris by the arm.

That was all it took to unleash Chris's hateful rage. He grabbed his father by the collar of his polo shirt and backed him into the door of the truck. Larry was stunned and breathless.

Chris lifted his right hand, which was still in the cast, and drew it back, ready to release his intense anger on his father. His posture was threatening and his face unfeeling as he fiercely glared into Larry's eyes.

"Don't you ever touch me again!" he threatened through clenched teeth.

Larry stood motionless as he looked into the cold eyes of a complete stranger. Chris rammed his fist into the side of the truck, just missing Larry's head and leaving a small dent in the door. He slowly released his grip and calmly walked away.

Larry watched him leave. He released the breath he'd been holding and stepped away from the truck. He watched as Chris turned the corner and walked out of sight. Astounded at what had just happened, he looked around the empty parking lot. He took a few deep breaths, and with a trembling hand, he wiped the sweat from his face. It was like a bad dream. He'd never seen such rage in anyone's eyes.

*This is either a sign of depression, or he's using drugs,* Larry thought. He was deeply troubled by his son's behavior. Whatever it was, he couldn't let the girls know what had happened. This was a side of their brother they didn't need to see. Larry took a few more refreshing breaths to stop his shaking, and then he headed back to the park.

"Sorry I'm late getting back," he said casually as he sat down at the picnic table next to Katie.

"Where's Chris?" Jody asked.

"He wasn't feeling well, so I took him home," he answered, trying not to sound as rattled as he felt. "But that doesn't mean the day is over for us."

"Where are we going next?" Katie said, gleaming with excitement.

"I thought we would take the flowers to the cemetery," Larry answered.

The cemetery was a short ten-minute drive outside of town. As they approached the graveside, they noticed that the ground was still unsettled, which made it seem as if it were just yesterday when Barbara passed away.

Jody brushed some pine needles from the headstone and Katie

carefully placed the tulips on top. They were all silent as they remembered Barbara. The headstone read,

### Barbara Marie Porter
### Born November 1, 1968
### Died February 26, 2007

Next to Barbara's name was the inscription, "Larry Doug Porter, born February 7, 1966," with no death date.

Between their names there were two hearts that were intertwined. In the middle it read, "Together for eternity, married September 28, 1988."

On the back of the headstone were their children's names: Jody Marie Porter, Christopher Larry Porter, and Katie Ann Porter.

Larry and Barbara had picked out the casket and the headstone together. It was something Larry wasn't ready for, but Barbara had kept insisting. He recalled the night when they were lying in bed together and she turned to him sadly. "I am going to die, Larry. Putting off the funeral arrangements is not going to prolong the inevitable, so please let me help you."

It wasn't easy for either one of them, and there were a lot of times when Larry didn't want anything to do with making decisions. He wanted to bury his head in the sand and pretend that everything was all right. It took several weeks to get everything in order, and all the while Larry kept waiting for his miracle.

After they left the cemetery the girls begged their father to take them to see their grandpa and grandma. They would be leaving on their mission in a week and would be gone for a year. Larry reluctantly agreed. He was still concerned about Chris.

Larry kept to himself during the visit. He was anticipating the confrontation that would occur with Chris when he arrived home. Maggie tried to pry out of him what was on his mind, but he just smiled and kept it hidden.

It was late when they finally arrived home from Maggie's. The house was dark and quiet. The girls went to their rooms and Larry checked on Chris. He listened at the door, but there was no sound coming from inside the room, so he turned the doorknob and cracked the door open a bit. He peeked in the room and could see Chris in bed sleeping. He thought about barging in and asking him what was wrong with him earlier, but he quietly shut the door instead and went upstairs. He was too tired to fight with Chris. A part of him just wanted to forget that it ever happened.

Larry stopped in to check on Katie before going to bed. She was already saying her prayers, so he waited quietly by the door. She blessed everyone she could think of, and then she came to Chris.

"Please bless Chris that he can be happy again and know I'm really sorry for today."

Larry closed his eyes and leaned against the wall. He was overcome with sadness. He realized Chris's behavior was affecting everyone, especially Katie. He knew he had to do something to change Chris's destructive behavior before it was too late.

When Katie was finished, she jumped into bed. Larry tucked her in and kissed her good night. "Chris loves you very much," he whispered.

"I know. I just wish he wasn't so sad all the time," she said, sighing. "Do you think mommy was happy we remembered her today?" Katie asked, her small round face smiling up at him.

"I know she is," Larry said, smiling back. He rubbed her soft brown curls. "I'm sure she is smiling down from heaven right now."

"I love you, daddy," she whispered, holding out her arms. He leaned over and put his arms around her and gave her a kiss on the forehead.

"I love you too," he said softly in her ear.

Larry went to his room. He knew he needed help. This was more than he could handle. He awkwardly knelt down beside his bed and hoped that Heavenly Father was listening. The words did not come easy for him. It had been a long time since he knelt in personal prayer.

He felt a little guilty about asking the Lord for help after the way he'd been feeling. Nonetheless, he asked Heavenly Father to give him guidance and to watch over Chris. He wished he had the faith that everything would be all right, but instead, he felt scared, lost, and confused. He was supposed to be the one leading his children down the right path, but he wasn't sure which path *he* was on.

# Chapter 10

"Dad wake up! Wake up!" Jody was frantically shaking Larry. He opened his eyes and sat up.

"What is it?"

"It's Chris. I think he's having a nightmare. Come quick," she said breathlessly, pulling Larry off his bed and toward Chris's room.

Jody was almost at a dead run with Larry right behind her. As they approached Chris's room they could hear him yelling in his sleep.

"I don't want to die!" Chris wailed over and over again. Larry sat down on his bed and shook him roughly.

"Chris, wake up!" Larry yelled. Chris was thrashing around so much that it was hard for Larry to hold on to him. "Chris, wake up!" Larry shouted again.

Chris opened his eyes and looked at his father. His gaze was filled with profound fear, and sweat was running down his frightened, pale face.

"Are you all right?" Larry asked him frantically.

"What are you doing in my room? Get out of here!" Chris blurted out, his fear shifting to fury and humiliation.

"You were having another nightmare. Do you remember what it was about?" Larry wanted desperately to get him talking. Chris started to shake uncontrollably, but he wasn't sure if it was from the dream or from the lack of pain medication.

"I'm fine! Just get out and leave me alone!" he demanded irritably. Jody immediately left the room, but Larry wasn't so intimidated.

"Chris, I'm worried about you. I want to help!"

"Nothing's wrong with me! I just want everyone to leave me alone!"

"Talk to me, Christopher. Tell me how I can help you!"

"You can help me by leaving me alone!" Chris almost screamed.

Larry walked out of the room and pulled the door closed behind him. Distressed and confused, he returned to his bedroom. He sat on the edge of the bed and looked at Barbara's picture. It had been a week since the incident with Chris on Mother's Day. Larry had tried to talk to him several times about it, but Chris was always in a hurry to leave, or he would tell Larry that they'd talk later. He had even been getting up early and leaving the house before Larry got out of bed.

Larry was almost at the end of his rope. He'd tried his best to be patient because of the attack and Barbara's death, and he knew Chris was dealing with a lot. But Chris had become mean and violent with everyone. One minute he would be calm and happy, and the next he was yelling profanity at everyone. Larry realized that the time was coming when he would have to confront him. If Chris was going to live under his roof, then his attitude would have to change. There would be no more outbursts like the one on Mother's Day.

As soon as Chris thought the coast was clear, he went to his dresser and took two Percocet and climbed back into bed. Why couldn't he just forget about the attack and move on? The only time he really felt at peace was when he was on pain pills, and he knew that would stop after this bottle was gone. He would have to do without them, and he was dreading it.

He closed his eyes and tried to go back to sleep, but he could see Jeff's brother's face staring at him with such hatred. He could hear their laughter and their taunting as he lay there on the ground, unable to move. He could still feel the stinging blows of their shoes as they drove them deep into his rib cage.

He opened his eyes and looked into the darkness of his bedroom. "Stop it, I don't want to think about this anymore!" he shouted, pounding both fists into the mattress.

He got out of bed and walked around his dimly lit room. He wanted to sleep so badly, but he couldn't seem to get those three terrifying faces out of his head. He walked over to his dresser and opened the top drawer. The bottle of pain pills seemed to be mocking him.

It had only been thirty minutes since the last one, and he knew he shouldn't take another, but he just couldn't sleep. He picked up the bottle and held it in his hand. He knew he was relying too much on them; nevertheless, he couldn't help but surrender to their brutal demands. He opened the cap and shook out one small white pill into the palm of his hand. *How odd*, he thought miserably. *How can something so small hold so much power over me?*

He swallowed it down, went back to bed, and waited anxiously for the effects he craved. He stared endlessly into the darkness until he felt his body become numb and tingly. He groggily wondered just who was in control: him or the drug, and then he shut his eyes and let the feeling overtake him. It wasn't long before he was unconscious.

Larry was back down in Chris's room leaning over him, trying to wake him up. It was not a nightmare this time that had brought Larry downstairs. Chris hadn't responded to any of his calls for breakfast. Larry was now shaking him and yelling out his name.

Chris finally opened his eyes halfway. He had a terrible headache and was having a horrible time trying to focus on the face in front of him. "Christopher, look at me. Are you all right?" Larry asked, concerned.

"Yeah, why?" Chris asked sleepily as he propped himself up on one elbow.

"It's seven o'clock in the morning. You wouldn't answer me when I called you for breakfast, so I came to see if you were all right."

Chris grunted and groaned. "I don't think I can make it to school today. I'm really sick." He pulled the comforter back over his head. He couldn't keep his eyes open and his head felt like it'd been run over by a garbage truck.

"Okay then, stay home. If it gets worse call me. I'll be at the office today." Larry was worried, especially after last night.

Jody and Katie had already left for school, so he picked up his briefcase and headed for the back door. The sky was covered in black clouds that were threatening rain, and after last time, he decided to play it safe.

He rummaged through the hall closet until he came across a black umbrella hiding in the back corner. He noticed an awful odor coming from the closet, and he couldn't quite decide if it was mold or smoke. Trying to locate the source, he took each jacket and coat that was hanging in the closet and smelled them. Then he grabbed Chris's blue and grey jacket. It was definitely the source of the smell, because it reeked of cigarette smoke.

Larry checked the pockets and pulled out a pack of cigarettes.

*That's just great*, he thought irritably. "Where is this going to end?" He took the cigarettes and headed back down the stairs.

"Christopher, wake up. I need to talk to you right now," Larry said coarsely as he shook him awake.

"Leave me alone—I'm sick," Chris grunted.

"Would you mind telling me why I found cigarettes in the pocket of your jacket?"

The statement caught Chris off guard, and he instantly flipped over to look at his dad.

"You went through my stuff?" he snapped.

"No, I was trying to figure out what the bad smell was in the closet, and it happened to be your jacket reeking from cigarette smoke." He held out the pack for him to see. "I found these in your pocket."

Chris gave him a blank stare. He tried to come up with another lie but found it difficult with the state of mind he was in.

"Well, my friend Brandon smokes and didn't want his mom to find out, so I told him I would hold them for him."

"You're telling me these aren't yours and that you don't smoke?" Larry hissed, unwilling to believe his son.

"Yes, now give them to me," Chris said, holding out his hand. He just expected his father to hand them over.

"I'll tell you what. You tell Brandon to come and talk to me about getting these back," Larry said, smirking. "If these are the kind of kids you're running around with, then it better stop."

"You can't tell me who I can be friends with!" Chris snorted angrily.

"You wanna bet? I know where this attitude is coming from! You're not to see those kids anymore!"

"You can't stop me from seeing my friends!" Chris bellowed as his father slammed the bedroom door. He didn't have time to argue with Chris about this; he had an important meeting to go to.

With butterflies in his stomach, Larry slowly walked down the hallway of the church. He didn't know why he was so nervous. It was just the Bishop, and he'd known him for years.

He felt bad about having to cancel their first scheduled meeting due to an emergency at work, but knowing he needed to get it over with, he had rescheduled it for 8 a.m. that morning. The door was already open when he reached the office. He wiped his clammy hands on his pant legs just before sticking his head in the door. The bishop was dressed in a suit and tie and was sitting behind his desk. A picture of the first presidency hung on the wall behind him, and a picture of Christ hung next to it.

"Come in Brother Porter and have a seat," Bishop Geary said with a smile. Larry shook the bishop's hand and sat down in one of the brown leather chairs next to his desk.

"I'm sorry to have to meet at such an odd time of day, but my schedule's been kind of crazy since the merger," Larry began. "I . . . um . . . wanted to talk to you about the reason I haven't been at church," he stammered anxiously. He took a deep breath and exhaled slowly.

"After Barbara passed away I became angry with the Lord and blamed him for everything," he continued, rubbing his trembling hands together. "In the beginning of her illness, I was convinced that if I did everything I was supposed to do, then he would heal her." He looked up to meet the bishop's caring eyes. "In the mission field, I saw prayers answered everyday. My companion and I would bless the sick and they would get better. We prayed for those who were struggling, and they found their way. They were healed and inspired because of their faith. But when it came to my wife, I couldn't save her. She had more faith than anyone I've ever known. So why didn't Heavenly Father give me the power to heal her?"

Larry felt the teardrops beginning to fill his eyes, and he quickly looked away from the bishop's gaze. He was feeling the hurt and anger creep up inside him again, but he was determined not to let it overcome him.

"I wish I had all the answers, Larry," the bishop said, sitting back in his chair. "You know I don't, but I *can* tell you this: Heavenly Father loves us, and he has a plan for us. Even if we don't understand why things happen, we must have the faith to know that he is aware of us and that everything happens for a reason."

He took out his scriptures from the top drawer of his desk, searched the pages until he found the passage he was looking for, and then read it to Larry. It was Doctrine and Covenants 121:7–8.

My son, peace be unto thy soul; thine adversity and thine afflictions shall be but a small moment; and then, if thou endure it well, God shall exalt thee on high; thou shalt triumph over all thy foes.

Larry could feel the bishop's love and concern, and he knew that he was truly called of God.

"But how do I get my faith back?" Larry asked. "After Barbara died, I didn't believe in anything anymore—not in the priesthood or in prayer. I turned all my anger toward the Lord."

"Let me ask you a question, Larry. Do you know without a doubt that the sun will come up in the morning?"

"That's a crazy question. Of course I do," Larry answered, a little confused.

"How do you know?"

"The sun has come up everyday of my life, so I know it will come up tomorrow as well."

"What if a storm was to blow in tonight, covering the sky with black clouds? Would you still know the sun is there, even if you can't see it?"

"Of course, it's just behind the clouds," Larry answered, beginning to see what the bishop meant.

"Faith can be much the same way. Just because your faith isn't shining through right now doesn't mean that it's not there. I want you to write down all the times your faith has helped you through difficult times in your life. Then you need to pray night and day, even if that's where your faith is wavering. Kneel down with real intent and pour out your soul to your Father in Heaven."

The bishop then testified to Larry that prayers are indeed answered, but not always in the way that we think they should be.

"Your faith is there, Larry," he continued. "If it wasn't, you wouldn't be sitting here right now."

Larry left the bishop's office feeling like a huge weight had been lifted off his shoulders. He knew he could now kneel in prayer without feeling guilt and shame. His faith was still there. It was just hiding behind the clouds.

# Chapter 11

*L*arry looked at the wood clock hanging on his office wall. It had only been eight minutes since the last time he checked, and ten minutes from the time before that. He sat impatiently at his desk and waited for the time to reach 5 p.m., another twelve and a half minutes away. He hadn't always felt this way about leaving work. In fact, there was a time when he wouldn't have left until the last chart was filed, the last paragraph read, and the last light turned off. He could now actually admit that he had been a workaholic. Since being at home with the kids, he now realized how much he'd missed it. It gave him a sense of obligation in knowing that he was needed at home.

At 4:54 p.m., he looked at the clock again. That was close enough. He closed the file he was working on and gathered his things. He'd almost made a clean escape when his boss, Charles Gibson the third, came through the door.

"Do you have a minute, Larry?" he asked, entering the room and closing the door behind him. With Charles being the boss, Larry felt inclined to say yes. Charles was second in command to the owner, Jacob Jeremy Jensen, so when Charles talked, his employees listened.

He came into Larry's office and dropped down into the chair next to Larry's desk. He was a large man in his late fifties and had graying hair. His horrible taste in clothing was offset by his expensive Rolex watch and the gold chain that hung around his neck. He wore black corduroy pants and a sky-blue silk shirt that was a flashback to the seventies.

"How are things at home, Larry?" he asked casually.

"Oh, we're managing all right, I guess," Larry answered. It was unusual for upper management to come in and shoot the breeze, so he was more than a little skeptical.

"Well, let me get right to the point of my visit," Charles stated, suddenly turning from caring employer to business as usual. "Now that the merger has gone through, we feel it would be in the best interest of the company to have you back to work full time in the office. Now, we understand that this may put a strain on your home life, so we're prepared to compensate your salary and promote you to office manager. How does that sound?"

Larry sat back in his chair and folded his arms. He was not about to be intimidated by Charles's power of authority.

"You know, I had originally thought that working from home would be stressful and inferior," Larry remarked. "But instead, it's been an eye-opener and a blessing. With Barbara gone, there would be no way I could ever go back to the hours I was working, and I don't think I'd want to." Larry watched Charles for his reaction. Charles wasn't the kind of man that was used to hearing the word no.

Charles looked at Larry in disbelief. "Are you telling me that you would pass up the opportunity of a lifetime to spend more time with your kids?"

With Charles having only one child—a son, whom he'd sent off to boarding school at the age of eight—Larry should have expected this kind of reaction from him. Still, it made Larry angry.

"Look, if you want to demote me, reduce my pay, or whatever else, that's fine with me. But I'm not working more hours," Larry stated firmly. He rose from his chair and walked to the door, insinuating that the conversation was over. He had never rejected a promotion, but he felt a rush of confidence in knowing that he was doing the right thing.

Charles rose and followed him to the door. "Office manager is not a position to be taken lightly. A title like that has to be earned, and I think you're the man for the job."

Larry opened the door and hesitated. "I have an important title—I'm a father," he announced proudly. "At the end of the day when all the work has been completed, the only people that really matter are the ones you go home to. I'm no longer willing to further my career at the cost of my family. I've missed too much of their lives already. Now, if you'll excuse me, I have a father-daughter dinner to attend."

Charles looked defeated. "I can respect your decision. I don't like it, but I respect it. I also think you are an excellent accountant and a valued employee, so how about a trade off? Two business trips a year, and you can continue working three days from home. What do you say?" He smiled as he held out his hand to seal the deal.

"Sounds like a good trade to me," Larry replied. He shook Charles's hand and was satisfied that he'd gotten the better end of the deal. He had previously been traveling six to eight times a year for business.

Anxious to finally get on his way, Larry rushed out of the office. He knew there would be an excited, bright-eyed eight-year-old waiting at the door for him. However, he was delayed again by road construction and had to detour off his usual path.

As he made his way down the two-lane back road, his surroundings soon became oddly familiar. When he rounded the second corner of 310 Maple Street, his heart skipped a beat. There on the right side of the road—right out of Barbara's scrapbook—stood the old house he'd once called home.

Feeling a little lightheaded, Larry pulled to the side of the road and turned off the engine. Unable to move or turn away, he sat in the truck and stared at the house. He was astounded that the old, two-story home still existed. As might be expected, the years had worn on the old house, but it still looked very much the same.

Built in the late 1920s, the house was home to a doctor, his wife, and four boys. After the doctor and his wife both passed away, the boys sold it to a contractor who had restored it in 1975. Then in 1990, Barbara was searching the paper for houses in the area and came across the ad. She instantly fell in love with it. It had everything she'd always wanted—a white picket fence, fruit trees, and a garden spot, and it was only ten minutes away from her mother. Larry was thrilled to be able to provide her with her dream home. He didn't realize it at the time, but that old house would soon become a thorn in his side.

When the money started rolling in, he felt that the house was beneath him. He wanted immaculate and expensive, and he wanted everyone to know that he was prosperous. It was the treasures of the world he was seeking and not the eternal wealth that comes from having a loving family at your side. The one concept he could never figure out was that a house doesn't make a home—a family does.

Larry got out of the truck and walked to the front of the house. He noticed that no one seemed to be home. Standing in the front yard was like taking a walk through time—a cluster of memories he'd once tried to forget.

He looked out over the yard and saw the crabapple tree they'd planted just after they moved in. It was now ten feet tall, with long, sturdy branches. He smiled as he remembered Barbara saying that it symbolized their growing family. Her flower garden was now completely covered with grass, but her beautiful rose bushes were in full bloom. Every piece of the house held special memories—memories that still haunted him.

He chuckled softly as he thought about the time Barbara forced him to dance with her in the rain. With their clothes soaked and their hair dripping wet, they laughed hysterically as he twirled her around and around in the rain.

That was what he loved most about her. Barbara was spontaneous and outgoing. She could make people smile and would brighten up a room just by entering it. She had a deep, genuine love for people and always found the good in everyone. Why she ever married him, he'd never understand, but he knew he was lucky to have her. Then slowly things changed—he changed.

He made his way to the porch steps and paused. He climbed the first step and then the second—each one awakening a memory inside him. He finally reached the top and heard the old familiar creak from the loose board he'd never fixed. He looked to his right and was overwhelmed with emotion when he saw the old porch swing still hanging exactly where they'd left it. It was an unforgettable image that he held most dear to his heart, but it also burned like fire.

He approached the swing and grasped one of the chains that held it securely in place. He felt each bumpy link as he ran his hand down the sturdy metal. He cringed, angry at himself for not taking the swing with them. It was a simple request, but one he'd rejected for his own selfish reasons.

He slowly sat down and started to swing. Even though it was not raining, he thought he could hear the rain falling softly from a darkened sky. He imagined Barbara sitting beside him, a sweet smile on her beautiful face and her silky brown hair blowing in the breeze. He could almost feel the warmth of her skin as her hand affectionately touched his. She laid her head on his shoulder and whispered, "I love you." He kissed the top of her head and smelled the refreshing scent of lilac . . .

Suddenly, the front door opened, and a small, elderly woman stepped out onto the porch.

"Can I help you?" she asked abruptly. She was startled to see a man sitting in her porch swing.

Embarrassed, Larry jumped out of the swing. "I . . . I used to live in this house . . . I was . . . reminiscing . . ." he tried to explain. He quickly came to his senses. "I'm sorry to have bothered you. I'll be going now."

"You don't need to rush off. You're welcome to come inside and look around—"

"Thank you, but I really must be going."

He was horrified to be confronted with all the regrets that the house held for him, and he quickly made his way down the steps. The emptiness inside him was overwhelming, which made it difficult for him to hold back the tears.

He escaped to the security of his truck and wearily leaned his head against the seat. He took one last look at the past and slowly pulled away from the curb.

As he drove home that night, a new kind of self-found freedom emerged from within him. He knew he could never go back in time and correct all of his mistakes. He would always savor the memories, but he was finally ready to put the past behind him and move forward, steadfast and strong, making positive changes that would ensure a better relationship with his children.

# Chapter 12

hris had spent eight long weeks with his arm in the cast, and it was finally time for him to have it removed. Summer vacation had officially started, which was a relief. He wouldn't have to put up with that stupid counselor chasing him down the hall to ask him how he was doing. However, he was still having the nightmares and taking the pain pills to cope with the horrible images that had been burned into his mind.

The doctor removed the cast, leaving a skinny and pale form of what Chris's arm used to be. Larry drove him to the doctor's office in hopes that they could talk, but Chris kept silent and avoided his father's gaze. Now on the ride home, Larry was determined to get his son talking.

"So I was thinking, maybe you would like to pick out another skateboard now that your arm is back to normal," Larry said cheerfully, hoping to break through the barrier that Chris had secured between them.

"I don't feel like skateboarding anymore," Chris replied calmly, keeping his eyes out the side window. The police had found his skateboard broken in half at the skate park. Chris was sure it was what they used to hit him in the head, so he really didn't care if he ever rode one again.

"You're very talented, and you shouldn't quit because of what happened."

"How would you know? You've never watched me skateboard before!" Chris snapped back sarcastically.

"You're right, I haven't. So why don't you show me now? Let's go buy a new board." Larry tried to sound upbeat and positive, but he could sense Chris's reservation.

With complete hostility, Chris jerked his head around and glared at his father. "Are you deaf? I said I don't want too!" He was not going to be pushed into doing something he didn't want to do, especially by his father.

"Look Chris, it's okay if you're still afraid. Just don't let your fear stop you from living a full life. You have to get right back up and keep on going," Larry encouraged, but he sounded a little like a drill sergeant on the first day of boot camp.

Chris was clenching his teeth tightly together and holding back the rage inside him. "I never said I was afraid!" he growled. "Just because I don't want to skateboard right now doesn't mean I'm afraid!" His fists tightened as the aggression swelled within him.

"All right, then. When you're ready to buy a new skateboard, just let me know." Larry could sense the tension between them and immediately backed off.

He pulled the truck into the driveway and Chris jumped out, violently slamming the truck door behind him. Feeling utterly helpless, Larry sat in the truck and leaned his head on the steering wheel. He wondered if there was any way at all to reach his son.

Jody had made dinner and was just putting it on the table when Chris came storming through the kitchen. "Hi," she said cheerfully, "Do you want some dinner?" Chris's anger was for his father, but Jody happened to be the one in the line of fire.

"Why would I want to eat your slop?" Chris blurted out disrespectfully. He could feel his heart beating faster and faster and his hands were trembling.

"Fine then! Starve!" Jody yelled back.

"What's going on?" Larry asked as he came through the back door.

"Ask him," Jody replied, pointing a finger at Chris.

"I'm going to my room!" Chris hissed loudly, knocking over a kitchen chair on his way out.

"What's the matter with him lately?" Jody questioned. Larry just shook his head. He really wished he could answer that.

Infuriated at the whole world, Chris went to his room and slammed the door. They were the ones with the problem—not him. Feeling much like a time bomb ready to explode, he paced back and forth. He stopped in front of the dresser, placed both hands on it, and scowled at himself in the mirror.

"I'm tired of everybody always on my case," he roared as he stared at his image in the glass. He was convinced that they all hated him. He slammed his fist into the mirror, which sent a crack down the center of it.

He opened the drawer, removed the pill bottle, and took out three pills. Then he slammed the drawer shut, which shook the entire dresser. He walked over and sat on the bed and took a couple of deep breaths. *I wish I were the one who died*, he thought miserably.

Larry heard the commotion from upstairs and went to investigate. He knocked on the door but didn't wait for an answer. He walked in and saw the broken mirror and Chris sitting on the bed. "Are you all right?" he asked.

"Did you hear me invite you in? This is still my room, isn't it?" Chris snarled.

"I was worried when I heard all the noise," Larry answered. He pulled over the chair from the desk and sat down face to face with Christopher. He wanted some answers.

"Your temper has gone through the roof lately. You're moody and emotional. What has gotten into you?" Chris rolled his eyes but didn't answer. "Are you doing drugs?" Larry asked bluntly.

Chris jumped up from the bed. He was outraged at his father's accusation. "What! How can you even ask such a stupid question? Just because I got ticked off, you're accusing me of doing drugs?" he shouted. His knees were trembling as he stood to confront his father.

"I wasn't accusing you! I was asking you a question!" Larry stood up as well. "That would explain your behavior the last few months."

Feeling backed into a corner, Chris's body tightened as he clenched his fists in anger. "I don't need you to stand there and tell me I'm doing drugs! Get out of my room!" Chris roared furiously. He flung open his bedroom door and pointed his finger in the direction he wanted his father to go.

"Christopher Porter, this has gone far enough! You're grounded until I get some answers!"

"You can't ground me, because I'm leaving!" Chris yelled. He grabbed his jacket from the bed and started for the door. Larry stepped in front of him and put his arm across the doorway to block his exit.

"You're not leaving this house!"

"Get out of my way, or I'll break your arm!" Chris raged.

Jody came downstairs to see what was going on. Katie also heard the yelling from up in her room and was now coming down the stairs. "What's the matter, Daddy?" she asked, her little voice full of concern.

Larry didn't take his eyes off Chris, who was still waiting for his chance to escape. "Jody, take Katie and go to your room—right now!" Larry hollered. He wasn't sure what Chris might do, or what he was capable of.

"Are you mad at Chris for going into your room?" Katie asked her father, tears welling up in her soft, brown eyes. "He was only looking for your cologne to . . ."

"Shut up, Katie!" Chris yelled at his sister.

Jody could hear the anger in Chris's voice, and it sent a chill down her spine. She took Katie by the hand. "Come on. Let's leave them alone," she said and pulled Katie into her room.

"What were you doing in my bedroom?" Larry demanded.

"I wasn't in your room. She's lying!"

"Somehow I doubt that."

"Of course you do, because she's your little angel, and I'm just the drug-addicted son. Now get out of my way!" Chris tried to go under his father's arm, but Larry wrestled him to the ground.

"You're not leaving this house!" Larry repeated firmly.

They momentarily scuffled on the floor, with Chris throwing punches at every chance he got and Larry struggling to block them. Larry felt Chris's strength, which was fueled by his anger, and Larry knew he was quickly losing the battle.

Chris finally broke free and got to his feet. He headed for the door, but Larry caught him by the ankle. Chris tripped and fell into the dresser, which caused the dresser to fall over on top of him. Worried that he might be hurt, Larry jumped up and pulled the dresser off Chris. Chris saw it as an opportunity to escape and bolted from the room.

Larry ran up the stairs and out the back door after him, but Chris was already halfway down the street. Larry knew he'd never be able to keep up with him. He let out a heavy sigh and hoped that Chris would come back once he had cooled off. He quietly closed the back door and headed downstairs to clean up the mess.

He'd put all the dresser drawers back in and was replacing the clothes when he realized what was wrong with Chris. There on the floor, beneath the socks, were the two pill bottles. He picked them up and held them in his hand. He was disappointed but not at all surprised. "Well, that answers a lot of questions," he said, sighing.

He went upstairs, sat on the edge of his bed, and rested his head in his hands. It was now obvious that Chris had a drug problem. The Lortab bottle was empty, and only three pills of the Percocet were left. He wasn't sure how many pills were in the bottles to begin with. Each time Barbara's pain had worsened, the doctor had put her on a stronger prescription, which meant there were leftover pills. As Larry thought about it, he remembered the bottle of morphine. He was supposed to return it to the doctor's office after Barb passed away, but he soon became distracted and forgot about it. He went to the bathroom and searched through the cabinets, only to discover that the morphine was gone.

Chris kept running until he was out of breath. He checked behind him to see if his father was following him. When he saw that he wasn't, he bent over with his hands on his knees and tried to catch his breath. He'd never run so fast in his life. His father would never understand how much he needed those pills, and Chris wasn't about to stand there and listen to a lecture on drug abuse.

He stuck his hand in his pants pocket and pulled out six dollars and thirteen cents. It wasn't even enough to get out of town. He stuck his hand in his other pocket and pulled out the bottle of morphine and a syringe. After his father left for work that morning, Chris had gone back to his room to get the morphine. He wanted to have it just in case he needed it.

He walked until he reached town. He noticed on the bank's neon sign that it was 10:38 p.m. The streets were empty, and even the fast-food restaurant was closed. The knots in his stomach tightened as the anxiety of being alone welled up inside him.

A few blocks to the east was the skate park. The thought of it gave him goose bumps. His father was right—he was afraid. He hadn't gone anywhere alone after the attack. His nightmares had increasingly worsened, and without the pills, they were unbearable. He always dreamed that his attackers were watching him from a distance, waiting for the right moment to finish what they had started. Were they watching him now?

As he walked down the sidewalk he heard footsteps behind him. He thought it might be his father and glanced over his left shoulder to take a look. It was a large man, probably in his late fifties, with a scruffy beard and mustache. He made Chris extremely uncomfortable, so Chris walked faster in hopes of losing him. Memories of the attack came rushing back, and he fearfully wondered what this stranger could possibly want with him. Maybe it was someone in Jeff's family coming to finish him off.

Chris walked a little faster, but the stranger kept pace with him. Faster and faster he hurried, trying to escape a confrontation.

"Hey kid, wait a minute," the stranger finally called out to him.

Chris turned the corner and ducked into the doorway of the jewelry store. Panting heavily, he picked up a large rock. He would not be a victim again. When the stranger came around the corner, Chris swung the rock at him. The man caught Chris's arm just in time to avoid taking a blow to the head.

"Hold on a minute, kid. I just want to know where the bus stop is," he said irritably.

"Oh, I'm sorry!" Chris apologized. He dropped the rock when he realized that the man wasn't trying to harm him. "It's just two blocks over and one down."

Chris could still feel the adrenalin in his veins long after the stranger left. He could see now that he was not over the attack. Fear was consuming him. It restricted him from doing the things he loved. The pills made him feel light-headed and spacey. They clouded his thinking and judgment. He decided it would be better to go back home and face his father than to face his fear of being alone.

As he started back down the street, Chris heard a car pull up behind him. It was a police car. He instantly remembered that he had the morphine in his pocket and wondered if his father had called the cops on him. He nervously stuck his sweaty hand into the pocket of his pants and tightly clutched the bottle. He could feel his face heat up and was sure his guilty conscience would betray him.

The officer got out of his car, and Chris knew him right away. It was Officer Carlson.

"Hey, Chris! What are you doing out here so late by yourself?" he asked, smiling.

"Me and my dad had a fight, so I was just walking off steam."

"Are you headed back home?"

"Yeah, I thought I would." He worried he might be slurring his words, so he tried to stay focused on what he was saying.

"Can I give you a lift?"

Chris was panic-stricken. What if he knew about the drugs and was taking him to jail instead of home? "I can walk," he instantly responded.

"Come on, after what happened, I just can't leave you out here in the dark by yourself."

Chris realized there would be no getting rid of him. As nervous as he was, he reluctantly consented. He hesitantly walked around to the passenger side of the police car, all the while feeling the morphine bottle bulging in his pocket.

They talked about the attack and how Chris was handling things. Chris smiled warmly and said all the right things as he nervously counted the blocks to his home.

"Hey, Chris," Officer Carlson said as he pulled up to the house. "There's no shame in asking for help—for anything."

"Yeah, I know," Chris muttered. He thanked the officer for the ride home and ran to the house. He was relieved to finally be out of the car.

All was dark and quiet as he entered the house through the back door. He wondered if his father had even been worried about him. He thought for sure he would have come after him, which left Chris thinking that he really didn't care about him.

He didn't bother to turn on any lights. He guessed his father was sound asleep by then. He found his room back in order and the drawers back in place. He opened his top drawer and searched through his socks and underwear for the pill bottles. He slammed the drawer shut after realizing that his father had found them. He needed a secure place to hide the morphine—somewhere no one would find it. He looked around the room and found the perfect spot.

Larry was waiting in the corner of the dark kitchen. It was 11:45 p.m. when he heard the back door open. He didn't say a word; he just followed Chris down to his room. The door was open just enough for Larry to watch Chris hide the bottle of morphine in his guitar case and place the case in the back of his closet. Feeling overwhelmed and more discouraged than ever, Larry quietly went back upstairs. Smoking was unacceptable, but Larry could deal with it. Drugs, however, were intolerable.

He dropped to his knees beside his bed and with tears streaming down his face he prayed for strength and guidance. In a moment of great anxiety, he realized that he was still searching for the faith that he so desperately needed.

# Chapter 13

The next morning when Larry awoke, he knew what he needed to do. He felt inspired to take the kids to Mike's cabin. He needed to get everyone away for a while, and after last night, he knew Chris was in trouble and needed his help. Jody and Katie sat down at the table for breakfast with lots of concerned questions about Chris. Larry avoided the inquiries with talk about the cabin in the mountains.

"We could spend a week like mountain men, fishing and sitting around a campfire. Mike said there was a lake nearby that we could swim in. So, what do you think?" he asked with enthusiasm.

Katie was all smiles. "That sounds great! When can we leave?" she squealed, her eyes beaming with excitement.

"As soon as Jody agrees, then we'll start packing." He looked over at Jody, waiting for her approval, but not quite able to read her expression.

"Is there a phone or a television?" Jody asked hesitantly, not looking up from her plate.

"Nope! That's the beauty of it. It's just us and Mother Nature. No phones and no television to distract us. What better way to get reacquainted with each other?" He waited a few seconds to see how Jody was going to react. Every time he'd mentioned family in the past, she was quick to remind him how many times he'd blown it, especially when it came to camping.

They had planned a camping trip last year to Strawberry Reservoir. The trailer was packed and they were ready to go. Then the office called. One of Larry's coworkers had become sick and couldn't fly to New York

City for a conference. Larry didn't even hesitate to say yes. Barbara ended up taking the kids herself, while Larry took the next flight out. It was another one of those unfavorable memories he wished he could block out. However, it served as a constant reminder of the life he would never go back to.

"Look, Jody, like I said before, I know I've messed up in the past. But if you'll just give me another chance, I promise things will be different this time," Larry said gently.

After a few more seconds she looked up from her plate and cocked her head to one side. "Does this mean you'll actually take time off work to go?" she said, smiling, which gave him the approval he was waiting for.

"Can you believe it? I tell you I'm a new man!" Larry stated with enthusiasm as he placed his hand firmly on his chest.

"Hurray! We're going to be mountain men!" Katie shouted for joy as she lifted both arms high in the air. She suddenly got a serious look on her face and became quiet. "Is it okay if I'm a girl mountain man?" she questioned sincerely.

"Of course! Girls make the best mountain men!" Larry said, smiling. He was trying hard not to laugh at her innocence.

After breakfast Larry gave the girls money and sent them to town to pick up some things for the trip. He wanted to talk to Chris and was unsure how he would react. But first he needed to talk to someone who had been through drug addiction and overcome it. He picked up the phone and called his brother.

Alan was twenty-two when he started using marijuana. He was in his first year of college and all his friends were trying it. He used only a little at first, such as on weekends and at parties, but he was eventually doing drugs every day. He soon became addicted to cocaine.

Larry suspected all along that there was a problem because of the way Alan acted toward the family. He became more and more distant from all of them. When Larry would try to talk to him about it, he would tell him it was none of his business. You could never tell when he was going to blow up. Larry thought back over the last several weeks and realized that for some time Chris had been showing a lot of the same signs.

Alan ended up in jail on drug charges. He was totally broke and called Larry to wire some money to bail him out. Larry refused to help him. He wanted Alan to realize that what he was doing was not only deadly but also illegal. After that, Alan wouldn't talk to him or Barbara and wouldn't return any of their phone calls. Larry even flew there to try to talk to him, but he slammed the door in his face.

Before long, Alan's car was repossessed, he was thrown out of his apartment, and he lost his girlfriend. He finally admitted that he had a problem and checked himself into a rehab center. He went through the twelve-step program and eventually made amends with his family. He'd been clean for over ten years, so Larry thought for sure he would be able to give him some much-needed advice. Larry explained everything that had been going on with Chris and asked what he should do to help him.

"Luckily, you've caught onto it early," Allen said, still in disbelief over Chris's circumstances. "It'll be easier to get him off the drugs. If he's acting like you say he is, then he's probably having withdrawals, so he's aware he needs the pills and is dependent on them. But you need to get the morphine away from him."

"Should I call a doctor or a counselor?"

"It would be better if you could convince him to go into drug counseling on his own. I found out that if it's not your own decision to go, then it usually doesn't work. You need to make him realize that he has an addiction."

As they talked, Larry began to realize the horrendous obstacle he was up against.

Larry paced back and forth in front of Chris's bedroom door trying to muster up the nerve to go in. Finally, taking a deep breath, he flung the door open. "Chris, wake up. I need to talk to you."

"What do you want?"

"We're all going on a family camping trip, so get up and get packed," Larry blurted out excitedly.

"I don't want to go! Just leave me home!" Chris rolled over and faced the wall.

"Okay, but if you don't go, you'll have to stay with Aunt Jenny."

He knew Chris hated Aunt Jenny's house. Jenny was Barbara's younger sister who lived in Salt Lake City, Utah. Her ten-year-old son, Trevor, worshipped Chris and would never stop talking. He followed Chris everywhere.

"What?" Chris grunted. He threw off his blankets. "You know I can't stand Trevor! I'll just stay here."

"Oh, you can't stay here. I'm having the house sprayed for termites and everybody has to be out for forty-eight hours." Larry was lying through his teeth and was hoping that Chris would buy it.

"We don't have termites," Chris argued. He looked at his dad as if he were crazy.

"Yes, we do, so I'll go call Aunt Jenny and tell her to expect you in a couple of hours." Larry turned to go, anticipating Chris's reaction.

"Fine, I'll go. Just don't call Aunt Jenny, please!" Chris thought for sure this would be a week of drug counseling, but anything was better than spending time with Trevor.

"Great! You jump in the shower and I'll find a suitcase for you."

Larry waited at the top of the stairs until he heard the water turn on. Chris never took long showers, so Larry knew he didn't have much time. He opened the closet door and found junk everywhere. He frantically searched the back of Chris's closet for the guitar case. His heart was pounding loudly and his adrenaline was pumping fiercely. He never imagined he would be invading the privacy of one of his children in search of drugs.

He found the guitar case in the back corner of the closet. He pulled it out, opened it, and took out the guitar. The case was completely empty. He slid his hand across the lid and down along the bottom. He came across a lump in the bottom of the case and took a closer look. There was small rip in the lining. He stuck two fingers into the rip and pulled out the bottle of morphine and the syringe.

Even though he'd seen Chris hide the morphine, it wasn't real until now. As Larry held the bottle in his hand, he realized that his son was in way over his head.

He quickly replaced the guitar and slid the case back into the closet so that it was exactly where he found it. He headed for the door and ran right into Chris.

"What are you doing in my room?" Chris blurted out angrily. "Were you going through my stuff?"

Larry realized there would be no easy way out of this, so he held up the bottle. "With good reason apparently," he said gravely. "Do you want to explain this?" he added calmly.

Chris looked at the bottle in disbelief. He thought he had hid it where no one would ever find it. He hesitated, knowing that he'd been busted.

"What do you want me to say? I'm a druggy and I stole my dead mother's drugs? Fine then! I'm a druggy! Now get out of my room!" Chris yelled pointing at the door.

"Are you addicted to the pain medication, Chris?"

"No!" Chris shouted. "I'm still in pain from the attack. I needed more medicine, and the stupid doctor wouldn't give me any, so I took them from your medicine cabinet. No one was going to use them anyway. I can quit anytime I want too."

"Fine, then prove it. I've got the rest of the pain pills, so I'll throw them and this bottle out. Do you have any more?"

"You're holding the last of it."

For once Chris was telling the truth. He was sure he wasn't addicted to the pills. Nevertheless, he felt a little uneasy watching his father take away the last of the painkillers.

Larry flushed the pills down the toilet. He got out the hammer and smashed the bottle of morphine in the sink. As he turned on the water and watched the medicine diminish down the drain, he couldn't help but wonder if this was truly the end. Part of him wanted to believe that Chris was telling the truth, but his mind was telling him otherwise.

As Chris packed his suitcase, he could feel the tension build and his anxiety escalate. He knew he didn't have access to any more pain medication. It would be tough—there was no question about that. He realized that he was taking the pills for all the wrong reasons, but he was no drug addict, and he was determined to prove it to his father.

# Chapter 14

*I*t was a tedious four-hour drive to the cabin. Larry and Katie sang songs and played *I Spy*. Jody and Chris brought their MP3 players so they wouldn't have to join in the annoying singing. They stopped in Logan just before entering the canyon and bought some food and drinks to take with them.

After thirty minutes of traveling up a winding mountain way, they turned off onto a small dirt road lined with enormous pine trees. They rolled down their windows to smell the fresh pine scent and the brisk mountain air. The road suddenly made a sharp turn, which exposed a beautiful two-story log cabin. It had a forest green roof, green shutters, and a large porch. The porch had two green wooden rocking chairs and a small table. Larry thought it looked like something you would see in a travel guide.

The girls took the loft with the queen-size bed. Chris took the smaller room on the main floor with the twin bed, and Larry took the larger one with the king-size bed.

The cabin had log furniture throughout, including an exquisite log table in the dining room. Larry couldn't help but think how much Barbara would have loved the cabin with all its beautiful furniture and the backwoods country feel.

On the back of the cabin was a deck with a scenic view of the mountains and a small, rocky stream. To the right was a fire pit surrounded by logs to sit on. The whole place had its own personal charm. Larry could already feel a difference just by being there.

After unpacking the truck, Larry stood on the deck and took a deep breath of refreshing mountain air. He felt his lungs expand, and his worries began to fade. It was like medicine for his soul. He was sure this week would be the turning point for everyone.

Katie came and stood beside him, her innocent little face looking up. "What do mountain men eat?" she asked. "I'm starving."

"Well, I thought we would start a fire in that there fire pit and cook us up some good old hot dogs," he said, trying to sound like an old cowboy.

Katie laughed at her father. "You don't sound anything like the cowboys on TV."

They roasted hot dogs over the open fire and laughed about some of their family trips. Katie was too young to remember most of them, which made Larry feel even worse. He decided that starting tonight, he would make more memories. The only problem was they wouldn't have Barbara in them.

Before he started working the long hours, they traveled to places like Yellowstone, Disneyland, and the Grand Canyon. Each summer they would plan one big vacation and spend a week or more together as a family. Then, like everything else, Larry slowly let it slip away. He traded the priceless memories for more money. It had been a least three years since they'd been on a family vacation.

The sky soon turned dark, and the stars and moon glowed brightly. Larry and his family gazed up into the starlit sky and were hypnotized by its beauty.

"It's absolutely breathtaking," Jody exclaimed as she watched the stars shimmering in the night sky.

"There are so many of them," Katie observed, with her mouth gaping open. "How come we don't have this many stars where we live, daddy?"

"You just can't see them like you can when you're way up here in the mountains," Larry said, smiling happily. He was enjoying watching the night sky and was indeed pleased that his children were likewise impressed.

Chris suddenly felt small and insignificant as he stared up at all the twinkling stars in the sky. He wondered why God would create such a wonderful world and then let terrible things happen.

For the second time in 10 minutes, Chris looked over at the clock sitting on the nightstand. It was 2:46 a.m. He rolled over, wearily thinking that it was no use trying to sleep in the condition he was in. His head was throbbing, the shakes were back, and he'd broken out in a cold sweat. He'd been without any pain pills for well over twenty-four hours, but he was determined to make it though this. His father was wrong about him, but he knew he would never take Chris's word for it.

He wiped his cold, moist, face with his trembling hands and turned on the lamp next to his bed. He opened his suitcase. Thank goodness he'd gotten his hands on some cigarettes before coming to the mountains. He thought it might take the edge off the shakiness. He got out of bed, pulled on his jeans, and went outside to have a smoke.

He sat down in one of the wooden rocking chairs and looked around. The moon was still shining brightly in the night sky and lit up everything in its path. It was so quiet and peaceful. The only noise he heard was the sound of the creek running. There was a slight breeze that made the tops of the aspen trees sway back and forth.

Hoping for some relief from his agonizing symptoms, Chris lit up a cigarette and inhaled deeply. He'd called Brandon right after his dad left the house that morning. They sat and talked about life and how his dad found his pain pills and took them away. Brandon was surprisingly sympathetic and wrote down the name and phone number of a person who could get him some more pills if he needed them. Levi Curtis was his name, and he lived in Logan. Chris was determined to go without them, but stuck the piece of paper in his pocket anyway.

He finished his cigarette, and, being careful not to wake anyone, he quietly slipped back into the cabin. He went to the medicine cabinet to see what Mike had stashed in there. He found allergy medicine, cold medicine, and aspirin, but nothing of importance. Hoping it would help him sleep, Chris removed the allergy medication and took four.

He returned to his bedroom and went back to bed. He stared into the darkness and thought about those same three boys who were still haunting his thoughts. He wondered if a day would ever come when he didn't think about the attack.

Larry was up bright and early to cook breakfast. The bacon and eggs sent an appetizing aroma up to the loft, which woke Katie and Jody.

Larry went to wake up Chris, hoping for the same enthusiasm he saw last night. He bent over and roughly shook the blankets. "Rise and shine sleepy head. It's a beautiful day outside," he bubbled excitedly.

"I want to sleep—leave me alone!" Chris grunted irritably. He was so tired he couldn't even pull his head off the pillow. His entire body felt drained of energy.

"Didn't you sleep well?" Larry asked as he tried to uncover Chris's head and look at his face.

"No, I didn't sleep well," Chris said, holding tight to the covers and hiding from his father's interrogation.

"Okay, but we're going to the lake to go swimming and have a picnic. I'd really like you to come with us."

"I'll come up later for lunch."

Chris really didn't care if he ever got out of bed again. He felt totally wasted and nauseated.

Larry closed the door, disappointed he couldn't convince him to come, and worried that he was having withdrawals from the pain pills.

After breakfast, Larry, Jody, and Katie packed a picnic basket and headed for the lake. It was a short ten-minute walk from the cabin and was just as Mike described it. The lake was surrounded by pine trees and aspens. There were huge patches of purple and yellow wild flowers growing around the edge of the water, making it picture perfect. The water was calm, crystal clear, and sparkling, but it also looked cold, so they decided to go exploring until it warmed up a bit.

They followed a trail up the side of the mountain and looked out over the lake. The view was exquisite. Katie saw a squirrel and tried to follow him, but she found he was much too fast for her. They gathered different types of tree leaves and unique rocks as they explored the mountainside.

Back at the cabin, Chris looked over at the clock that hadn't seemed to move much. It was only 10:24 a.m. He sat up on the side of the bed and ran his fingers through his hair. His head was throbbing again and he was trembling. He checked the cabin and found it empty, so he went outside for a smoke. He took in long, deep breaths trying to stop the uncontrollable shaking. All it managed to do was make him sick and light-headed.

He went back to bed to try and sleep it off, but the shakes continued to get worse, until his entire body felt like it was going to explode. The cold sweats had started up again and he had an awful jittery feeling. It was just too much for him to bear. "I can't do this," he cried out as he threw the covers off and climbed out of bed.

He searched his father's room until he found his cell phone. He went out to the front porch, removed the paper from his pocket, and dialed the number, only to find that there was no cell phone service. Willing to do whatever was necessary, he went back into the cabin and frantically searched for the keys to his father's truck. He was just about to give up when he saw them hanging from a nail by the front door.

Since he'd only driven once before, with Jody as his teacher, he was a little skeptical as he climbed behind the wheel of his father's expensive truck. Pushing aside the guilt that was stirring inside him, he took a deep breath and started the engine. He carefully backed up and started down the tiny dirt road. He pulled out onto the paved highway, picked up speed, and headed for the town they had stopped in on the way to the cabin.

The water in the lake was still cool but felt very refreshing as Larry, Jody, and Katie jumped in. They splashed and played in it until they felt like icicles and finally had to climb out to get warm. Jody found a nice grassy area and spread out the blanket for their picnic. They feasted on sandwiches, chips, and cookies while soaking up the majestic atmosphere around them. The mountains seemed to have a peaceful serenity that caused their burdens to simply melt away.

When they were finished, they lay in the soft, green grass, looked up at the pure blue sky, and tried to find animal shapes in the white fluffy clouds. Katie's short attention span soon got the best of her, so she headed off to pick wild flowers.

Jody turned to her father and propped herself up on one elbow. She was feeling a connection to him that she hadn't felt in a long time. "Thanks for bringing us," she said. "I think it's just beautiful here."

"I'm glad to hear that," Larry said, smiling with pleasure. He sat up and looked her in the eyes. "I need to ask you something since we're here alone." He paused briefly, contemplating her response before he could even ask the question. "I need to ask you for your forgiveness."

"My forgiveness? For what?"

"You were right. I wasn't around enough to help your mother, or to notice when she started getting sick. Believe me, I wish I could turn back the clock and start over. Knowing I chose my job over my family all these years just kills me inside." He was tearing up as he struggled to say the words that needed to be said. "But I now realize how short life can be, and I don't want to take it for granted anymore."

"What do you mean?" Jody sat up, touched by her father's openness.

"I love you more than anything in this world, and I want to live each day as if it were my last. I want to spend all the time I can with you, Chris, and Katie. I want to be there for you when you graduate from college and when you find that special someone and go to the temple to be married. I want to be there to hold my first grandchild."

Jody had only seen her father cry one other time, and that was when they closed her mother's casket. As she watched him, with tears now flooding his eyes, she could feel his sincere love for her. She felt a new kind of security, one she hadn't felt since her mother's death.

She scooted over, wrapped her arms around his neck, and gave him a reassuring hug. "I love you too," she whispered, her eyes filling with tears. "I know we all make mistakes. I've made lots too. I'm sorry for giving you such a hard time. I just really miss mom," she said, sobbing.

"I know honey, I miss her too. But we have each other, and together we can get through this. So what do you say, can we make a fresh start?" he asked, wiping her tears away.

Jody smiled tenderly. "I'd like that."

Katie ran toward them with an armful of purple and yellow flowers. "Why are you crying?" she asked sweetly.

With trembling hands, Chris made the phone call as soon as he reached the bottom of the canyon. When he heard Levi on the other end, he knew he had phone service.

Chris explained his situation and where he was. It was critical that he got something immediately. Levi told him that he could get anything he wanted, but it would cost him for the short notice. Money wasn't an issue for Chris; he'd found his dad's wallet while looking for the cell phone, and he took seventy dollars from it.

Chris told Levi what he was wearing and gave him the make and model of his father's truck. Levi instructed him to wait in the grocery store parking lot and they would find him.

"How long is it going to take?" Chris snapped, agitated and worried that his father would be coming back from the lake at any moment. It was apparent to Chris that Levi could care less about his urgency. He waited around for fifteen minutes before a red sports car pulled up beside him.

"Are you Chris?" the man with extra-large biceps and a tattoo asked.

"Yes, I am." Chris nervously scanned the parking lot for anyone who might be watching.

"It's fifty dollars—cash," the man firmly stated.

Chris handed him the money and was given a small, brown paper sack. The men immediately left the parking lot. Chris looked inside and found a small plastic baggie with ten white pills. He hadn't even bothered to ask what they were, and at that point, he really didn't care. He just wanted instant relief from the torturous shaking. He downed one pill, started the truck, and took off for the cabin.

Fearing his family might already be back from the lake, he sped up the road. He wondered what excuse he could possibly come up with. He wasn't even thinking about his speed until he saw the flashing blue lights behind him.

"No! No! No!" he shouted, fiercely slamming both fists into the steering wheel. Deciding it would be useless to try to run, he slowly pulled to the edge of the pavement and stopped the truck. While the officer was getting out of his car, Chris stuffed the paper sack as far under the seat as he could.

"May I see your license and registration, please?" the officer politely asked.

"Well, sir, I . . . left my wallet with my license in it at home. But I have the registration right here." He took the registration from the glove box and handed it to the officer. "It's my dad's truck. I'm just borrowing it."

"You know, son, you're never supposed to drive without your license on you," he lectured. "You look rather young to be driving. When is your birthday?"

"My birthday is . . . um . . . April 14, 1991. I just turned sixteen," he answered nervously. He was indeed tall for his age, but he still had a childlike face, which gave him a fifty-fifty shot at the officer believing him.

The officer gave Chris a questioning look. "Wait here while I run the plate."

"I'm dead. I'm so dead," Chris groaned, lightly thumping his forehead on the steering wheel. He thought about speeding off and trying to outrun him, but he realized that would be stupid, considering the officer had the registration. Feeling like a mouse that had just sprung a trap, he sat helplessly awaiting the outcome.

The officer rushed back and handed the registration to Chris. "This is your lucky day, son. There's been an accident a few miles back, and I'm the only officer in the area. Make sure you slow down, and remember your license next time." He gave Chris a friendly smile and tipped his hat.

Chris thanked him and eagerly pulled back onto the road. He silently rejoiced that he wasn't going to jail. As soon as the officer was out of sight, Chris sped up again. He was positive that they'd be back by now.

He parked the truck exactly where he'd found it, reached under the seat, and took out the bag. He rolled it up tightly and stuffed it in the back pocket of his blue jeans. Then he quietly walked up to the house and peeked in the front window. Maybe he'd gotten away with it after all.

"Well, look who finally got out of bed, and before three o'clock," Larry said, laughing. He, Jody, and Katie had just come around from the back of the cabin. Chris quickly stuffed the cell phone and keys into his pocket and tried to act normal.

"Yeah . . . so you're just getting back from the lake?"

"Yes, and it was a blast. You really missed out," Katie announced happily.

"Maybe we can talk you into it another time," Larry commented, noting the panicked look on Chris's face.

As they changed out of their swimming suits, Chris quickly put his father's cell phone and keys back where he found them. Then he went outside and pried up a loose board on the deck. He placed the baggie and pills in the deck and carefully replaced the board.

With a sense of relief, he went back to his room. The pill was already beginning to work, and he savored the effects it had on him. He'd actually gotten away with it—stealing the truck and taking the cell phone. It had all worked out to his advantage. But as Chris lay there and watched the ceiling swirling above him, there was one thought that kept pestering him. As much as he tried to ignore it, he knew exactly what all this meant.

# Chapter 15

$\mathcal{L}$arry got up extra early the next morning and sat in one of the green rockers on the porch. He loved to watch the morning sun, especially after what the bishop had told him. Now, every time he saw a sunrise, he thought about faith and how even in the darkest times it was still there waiting to shine. He never realized how beautiful a sunrise could be until now. The colors of orange and yellow appear long before the sun shows its face. You wait, in anticipation, until the sun finally peeks over the tallest mountain. Once it begins, it only takes a few minutes before the sun is totally exposed.

Illuminating everything in its path, the sun shone out brightly over the entire mountain valley. *What a wonderful thing that God created for us*, Larry thought. *The Lord gave us something beautiful that we could look forward to each day.*

Feeling inclined to give thanks for the beautiful earth and everything in it, Larry knelt in front of the rocking chair and began to pray. He thanked Heavenly Father for giving him this time with his children and being able to overcome some of their differences. He asked for forgiveness for being so angry, and asked Heavenly Father to give him the strength he needed to conquer life's trials.

He felt at peace as he prayed and was comforted by the Spirit. Finally, after all the anger, resentment, and blame, he felt at ease when talking with the Lord. He knew without a doubt that the Lord was listening and loved him deeply.

When Larry finished, he sat down again and listened to the birds chirping. He felt a slight breeze as it blew through the tops of the trees. Out of the corner of his eye he saw a movement in the doorway and looked up to see Jody standing there. She was wrapped in a blanket and was still in her pajamas.

"I didn't mean to interrupt you," she said.

"I was just listening to Mother Nature. Come sit with me," he said, smiling contentedly. "Why are you up so early?"

"I couldn't sleep. I've had something on my mind all night, and I wanted to talk to you about it."

So many emotions had run through Jody since she arrived at the cabin; things she longed to tell her father but could never find the words. Now was the right time. She could no longer hold them in.

Larry could see the anxiety in her eyes and tried to comfort her fears. "It's all right, Jody. You can tell me anything."

Jody sat down in the chair next to him and rested one knee against the armrest. "When I was Katie's age, I was so proud that you were my dad. You gave me piggyback rides and played basketball with me. You even came to my tea parties. I would climb on your knee and you'd read me a story, give me Eskimo kisses good night, and call me your little wildflower."

Larry chuckled at the memory. He'd forgotten about that.

"I felt like I was a princess in a castle when I was with you. But then one day something changed, and you weren't around much anymore. When I tried to talk to you, you told me to go away, you were too busy. I wasn't sure what I did, but I knew you didn't want me anymore. So I stayed away and told myself it was okay because I didn't really need a dad anyway."

Jody wept as she remembered the devastating rejection she'd felt. She had built her tiny world around her father, only to have him crush it with his absence.

"Oh, Jody, I'm so sorry I made you feel that way. I did want you! I was just too stupid to realize how much." His eyes filled with tears, and he sighed regretfully.

"I've kept this bottled up inside for so long, too scared to tell you what I was feeling, and holding you responsible for every little thing that's gone wrong," she said, sobbing. "But yesterday at the lake, when you were crying, I realized that you really do love me, and I really do need a dad."

Larry knelt down by her chair and held her tightly in his arms. "You're still my wildflower—just not so little anymore. I love you Jody. I always have and I always will. I just wish it hadn't taken me so long to figure out where my priorities are. Can you forgive me for making you feel that way?" he said, looking into her red, swollen eyes.

"Well, that's why we have second chances in life. When we blow it the first time, we can get right back up and try again," she said, smiling. "I know mom would want us to try again."

"You're absolutely right, and this trip has been a blessing from heaven. It's brought us together again." He gave her a kiss on the cheek and wiped away her tears.

Larry put his arm around her as they walked back into the cabin. He could see that the back door was open and curiously walked out onto the back porch. In doing so, he caught a glimpse of Chris smoking a cigarette down by the stream. Jody also saw what was going on and decided it would be best to stay upstairs until breakfast.

Clueless that his father had been watching him, Chris finished his smoke and walked back to the cabin.

"Did I misunderstand you?" Larry asked him irritably. "I thought you said you didn't smoke."

"Would you rather I pop pain pills?" Chris blurted out sarcastically.

"This isn't a negotiation, Chris," his father said firmly. "Hand them over." Larry held out his hand. He was enraged that Chris had ruined his whole expectation of their trip. He'd actually thought he was getting through to him.

"You're in luck; that was my last one," Chris said, walking past Larry, bumping shoulders with him to let him know that he was not in control. He wasn't about to tell him about the pack he'd hidden under the dresser.

"Why don't I believe that?" Larry sighed, shaking his head. He dropped the argument because Katie had come downstairs and wanted to help make breakfast.

He shook off the hurt and disappointment and put a smile on his face for Katie's sake. After a delightful breakfast of pancakes and sausage, Larry announced that they would be going on a little excursion that would include Christopher.

As they started on their way, Larry noticed a difference in the gas gauge. It seemed rather odd, but he quickly forgot about it. The last thing he wanted was to ruin their time together.

They drove over the mountain to Garden City, a small town near beautiful Bear Lake. Katie was astounded at the size of the lake and wanted to go swimming right away.

Katie splashed in the water and made sand castles, while Chris found a comfortable spot to sleep. Larry and Jody sat on the beach and talked. He wanted to know everything about her; what she wanted to do with her life, what her favorite subject was in school—everything she was willing to tell him. She even opened up to him about her mother.

After a few hours at the beach, Larry gave each of his children twenty dollars to spend at the souvenir shops in town. When he opened his wallet, he was flabbergasted at the amount of money that was missing. Although he kept quiet, he watched Chris closely and wondered if by some chance he might have taken it.

Jody bought some fresh raspberry jam and post cards to send to Grandma Maggie and Grandpa Bob.

Katie couldn't decide what to buy, but finally bought a small, brown fishing hat and a tackle box. She also bought some live worms, which she wouldn't touch. She convinced her father to buy a fishing pole so they could be real mountain men. Larry couldn't resist her pleading brown eyes and the glow of excitement on her face.

Chris bought a twelve pack of Mountain Dew and a pack of gum, and then put the rest of the money in his pocket.

On the way out of town they stopped at a small diner—Bubba's Barbeque. Larry sat the kids down in a corner booth and told them to order while he slipped outside to call Mike. He wanted to let him know how much they were enjoying the cabin. Since Mike was the last person he'd called before leaving, he hit the redial button.

"Hello," A male voice on the other end said. It didn't sound a thing like Mike. Larry held out the phone and looked at the number. It wasn't Mike's.

"I think I may have dialed the wrong number. Who am I speaking too?" Larry asked out of curiosity.

"This is Levi. Who are you?" Levi said rudely.

Larry instantly hung up the phone and checked to see when the call was made. It all started to make sense—the missing gas, the money from his wallet—and now the phone call.

Larry was silent through dinner. He was angry but struggled to conceal it from his children.

When they arrived back at the cabin, Larry told Jody he needed to talk with Chris alone. After seeing Chris smoking that morning, she was more than willing to oblige. She took Katie on a walk to find bugs.

Chris was lying on the bed listening to his MP3 player when his father entered the room. Larry unzipped Chris's suitcase and with one hand dumped everything out onto the floor.

"What do you think you're doing?" Chris yelled as he jumped off the bed.

"Where are your drugs, Chris?" he demanded furiously. "I know they're here somewhere!"

"I don't have drugs! Stop going through my stuff!" Chris wailed loudly. Larry grabbed Chris by the arm and forcefully set him down on the bed.

"I've lost all patience with you, Christopher! Enough of the lies! When is this going to end? Now you're calling drug dealers to get your pills?"

"What? I don't have a drug dealer! I'm not doing drugs! Just because I smoke doesn't mean—"

"Just shut up! I'm not talking about smoking! I'm talking about the fact that I have less gas, less money, and the number for somebody named Levi on my cell phone!" Larry was in Chris's face and was releasing the fury that had built up inside him for some time.

Chris's mouth gaped open. He was stunned that his father had figured it out. He hadn't even thought about erasing the phone number.

"Just leave me alone!" he bellowed in frustration. He slipped from his father's grasp and headed for the front door. He pulled on the knob just as his father came up behind him and slammed the door shut. "You're not running away this time!"

"What do you want from me?" Chris whined, strung out and close to tears.

"I want some honest answers. Who is Levi? Did you buy drugs from him?"

Chris racked his brain to come up with an answer that his father would accept.

"My friend Brandon gave me his number so I could get some cigarettes. I drove your truck into town and paid for the smokes with the money I took from your wallet." He tried to act calm and in control. If he was going to be in trouble, he would rather it be for smoking and stealing the truck, not for buying drugs from a drug dealer named Levi.

Larry ran his hand through his hair. "So you're telling me all this is about smoking?" Larry asked, unconvinced.

"Yes, and if you don't believe me, I'll prove it to you."

With Larry close behind, Chris got up and went to his room. He got on his knees, reached under the dresser, and pulled out an unopened pack of cigarettes. "That's what I bought from Levi," Chris said, handing them to his father.

"So you're addicted to cigarettes?" Larry asked, still skeptical. Chris looked his father in the eye and shook his head. He was pleased with himself that he'd come up with such a good alibi.

"This must have been one expensive pack of cigarettes," Larry said, scowling. He knew Chris was lying, but without knowing where the drugs were, he couldn't prove it. "You'll be grounded for a month when we get home." Larry took the cigarettes and ordered Chris to clean up the room.

Later that night, Larry opened his Book of Mormon to search for inspiration. He felt helpless when it came to Christopher. It seemed as though they were in a boat in the middle of the ocean and Chris had fallen overboard. Larry was reaching for him, trying to get him to take his hand so he could pull him aboard, but Chris wouldn't reach out and take it. The more Larry tried to reach him, the deeper Chris sank.

Larry wondered if this is how our Father in Heaven feels when we fall from the straight and narrow path into murky waters. If we're drowning in the sea of life, do we reach out and take his hand so he can pull us back up?

Larry knew he'd come close to drowning. His pride and stubbornness had almost sunk him. He would jump into the deepest waters to save Chris, but there was one question that seemed to torment him—did Chris even want to be saved? Can you help someone who doesn't want to be helped? Larry desperately flipped through the pages of the Book of Mormon for answers.

He was reading in Ether when he came across a verse that was of interest to him. It was Ether 12:6.

And now I, Moroni, would speak somewhat concerning these things; I would show unto the world that faith is things which are hoped for and not seen; wherefore, dispute not because ye see not, for ye receive no witness until after the trial of your faith.

Still thinking about the verse, Larry turned off the lamp and knelt in prayer. He knew his faith would stand up to the trials placed before him, and he decided to leave it in Heavenly Father's hands. He knew that if anyone loved Chris as much as he did, it would be our Father in Heaven.

# Chapter 16

"Daddy, wake up!" Katie shouted joyfully as she jumped on top of Larry. "We're going fishing today, remember?" Her voice rang with excitement as she hopped up and down on the bed.

Larry rubbed his hazy eyes and wondered why he'd bought that stupid fishing pole. "All right, Katie. I'm awake. Just give me a few minutes," he yawned sleepily.

Katie went to the kitchen to get a bowl of cereal while Larry slowly pried his weak, old body out of bed. The strain he felt from the problems he was having with Chris was starting to wear on him. He wasn't sleeping because of worry, and self-doubt was starting to creep up inside him. Unanswered questions hung in the back of his mind, which added to his stress and frustration. He wondered if he was the best person to help Chris. If not, then who *could* help him?

Jody didn't think fishing sounded all that fun, so she found a good book to read. Larry woke up Chris and insisted that he come with them. He reminded him that he hadn't done much of anything with the family the whole trip, and since he was already in trouble, it would be in his best interest to do as he was told. Chris wasn't in any mood to argue, so he reluctantly agreed.

"Hurry up, Chris! Let's go!" Larry yelled impatiently.

Dressed in their fishing gear, he and Katie had been waiting on the front porch for the last ten minutes. Chris felt burned-out and agitated, so he decided to get a little help. With Jody in the loft reading a book and his dad and Katie out front, he quickly located his stash and took one pill from the baggie.

"All right, I'm ready," he said, sticking his hands in his pockets and casually walking out of the cabin.

By the time they reached the lake, Chris could already feel the effects of the pill. He found a nice grassy area and plopped down in it.

"You don't want to fish?" Larry asked, disappointed.

"I'm still tired. I think I'll just lie here for a while."

Larry didn't push it. Instead he found a nice shady spot by the lake where he and Katie could fish. He showed her how to bait the hook, and to his surprise, she even wanted to add the worm. He demonstrated the proper way to cast the line out into the lake. After ten minutes, when they hadn't caught a thing, Katie went off to play while Larry stayed with the pole.

Larry sat on the ground and peacefully watched as tiny waves splashed against the rocks. He closed his eyes, inhaled deeply, and felt the warm breeze against his face. He knew Barbara would have loved it here. He wished she were here with him. She loved to fish, camp, or just spend time with her family.

He pictured her sitting near him. She had a pole in one hand, a smile on her face, and was wearing a fishing hat that was much too big for her. He remembered how she used to tease him, saying, "Last one to catch a fish has to make dinner," even though he would always be the one who would end up cleaning and cooking the fish. It was the one thing about fishing she couldn't stand. Oh how he wished she were beside him and not just in his mind!

Finally, a small tug on the line sent Larry to his feet. "Katie, come quickly! We caught a fish!"

Katie rushed to him and put her hands on the pole with his. They tugged and pulled and reeled until they finally brought in a small rainbow trout. Katie's little face lit up with excitement, and she clapped her hands and jumped for joy.

"We caught a fish, Chris," she hollered. Chris waved his hand and kept right on sleeping. Larry wanted to teach Katie how to clean and fillet the trout, just the way his father had shown him. He took out his knife and sliced it open, releasing a musty fish odor into the air. Katie took one look and plugged her nose.

"Oh, that's disgusting!" she grunted and ran off to play.

Larry just smiled and continued cleaning the fish. He was almost finished when he felt the cold, sharp blade of the knife penetrate the palm of his hand.

He quickly grabbed his jacket from the ground and wrapped it tightly around the wound to stop the bleeding. Feeling the throbbing pain run through his fingers, he decided to head back to the cabin for the first aid kit.

"Chris, wake up," Larry said, tapping his shoulder. Chris sat straight up when he heard the urgency in his father's voice. He was having trouble comprehending what his father was trying to tell him. "I've cut my hand and need to go back to the cabin. Can you wake up and watch Katie for me?"

"Can't we all go back to the cabin with you?" he whined, thinking about his warm, comfortable log bed. "Katie, come on! Let's go!" Chris shouted.

"I don't want to go!" she stubbornly replied. She folded her arms and stomped her foot in disapproval. She'd been occupied with building a castle out of rocks and didn't want to be interrupted.

"Chris, I need to go. Just keep an eye on her. Can you do that much for me?"

"Fine, I'll watch her." His head was spinning and his body felt numb and tingly. Irritated that he was left to babysit, he waited until his father was out of sight, and then he flopped out on the grass again.

Larry rushed back to the cabin and found a first aid kit. The cut wasn't as deep as he had originally thought. Jody heard him come in and helped clean and bandage the wound. She then offered to go back with him.

They were almost to the lake when they heard Chris's earth-shattering scream for help. Larry and Jody ran up the mountainside. Larry's heart was beating harder and harder with every step in anticipation of what he'd find at the lake.

As they reached the top of the hill, they could see Chris. He was kneeling down and sopping wet. They saw Katie lying on the ground beside him. Larry's heart momentarily stopped beating when he realized what had happened. He turned to Jody, who let out a scream in terror. Larry grabbed her by the shoulders.

"Jody, take the truck and the cell phone. Drive down the mountain until you get service. Call for an ambulance. Hurry, Jody! Hurry!" he cried in desperation.

An alarming sensation of horror came over him as he finally reached the lake. Chris was kneeling over his sister, crying hysterically, and shaking her wet and lifeless body. He was pleading with her to wake up. Larry shoved Chris out of the way and dropped to his knees next to Katie.

He put his ear to her cold, pale face and placed two fingers against her neck. There were no signs of life. A gut-wrenching panic flowed through him, and for an instant he was lost in hopelessness. He'd learned CPR years ago but wasn't sure if he still remembered how to do it. He closed his eyes for just a moment and asked Heavenly Father to give him the strength and wisdom he needed to save his daughter's life.

Suddenly, as if a fog was lifted from his mind, he knew exactly what to do. He opened his eyes and started chest compressions. After fifteen compressions, he plugged Katie's nose and gave her two shallow breaths, watching to make sure her chest rose with each one. Then he repeated the compressions, followed by another two breaths.

Larry put two fingers on her neck to check for a pulse. "Come on, sweetie," he pleaded breathlessly. There was nothing. Despair severed his hopes, leaving him slightly disoriented as to what to do. "Keep going," the voice inside him said sternly. He started the compressions again, followed by two more breaths. Sobbing uncontrollably and repeating how sorry he was, Chris frantically paced back and forth behind his father.

After the fourth set of compressions, Larry again checked for a pulse. He eagerly waited for a sign. He felt a faint thumping. His heart jumped with excitement as he gave her two more breaths. Katie started coughing and choking up water. He set her up and administered a couple of hard blows to her back.

"Katie, can you hear me?" he asked as he leaned her back on his lap.

She opened her eyes, blinked from the bright sunlight, and gave him a dazed look. "My chest hurts," she whispered softly.

Larry smiled and gave her a hug. Those big brown eyes never looked so beautiful! Tears of joy streamed down his face, and he looked up to heaven. "Thank you! Thank you for saving my little girl!" he sobbed.

Chris dropped to the ground beside them. His body was trembling from shock. "I'm sorry! I'm so sorry!"

Larry wasn't about to wait for the details. Without saying a word, he picked Katie up in his arms and headed for the cabin. Chris saw the disappointment in his father's eyes and felt his cold disapproval. Trying to outrun the guilt and shame, Chris recklessly dashed off into the trees.

Larry couldn't help but be angry with him. He was supposed to be watching over his sister. But Larry was even angrier with himself. He knew better than to leave Chris in charge.

By the time they reached the cabin, Katie's small body was trembling, and her once bright face was now grayish in color. Her breathing was shallow, and she was still coughing up water. Larry took off her wet clothes and wrapped her in a warm blanket. He gently laid her on the couch and caressed her damp hair. "Everything is going to be all right now," he gently assured her.

Larry listened for Chris, but the cabin was quiet. He irritably wondered if he was off sulking somewhere. It was just like Chris to be thinking only of himself. Praying that the paramedics would get there soon, Larry stayed by Katie's side. After about ten minutes, Jody returned in the truck, followed by a police car.

The police officer was driving up the canyon when Jody caught his attention and got him to pull over. The officer entered the house and approached Larry and Katie.

"I'm Officer Abbott. The paramedics are on the way," he said kindly.

Jody was shaking all over and was still crying. Larry was sitting on the floor next to the couch. He motioned for Jody to come to him. Jody slowly walked over and looked down at Katie's pale face. The sight of her frail condition made Jody cry even harder.

"Is she going to be all right?" Jody asked. Larry nodded and smiled. He was still concerned about her breathing, but she was awake and alert.

The officer took out a pad of paper and a pen. "Can someone tell me what happened today?" he asked, looking at Larry and Jody.

"There's only one person who can answer that. Jody, will you please go find your brother so we can get to the bottom of this?"

After a few minutes, Jody came back into the room. Chris was nowhere to be found.

*That's typical,* Larry thought angrily. When the going gets tough, Chris always manages to leave. He wasn't worried. He knew Chris was hiding out until things calmed down.

The ambulance and first responders finally arrived. They brought in a huge blue bag that contained all of their equipment. They started Katie on oxygen and then proceeded to check her vital signs.

It had been almost an hour since Chris disappeared, and Larry was now getting worried. He asked Jody to stay with Katie while he searched for him.

Larry walked outside and called Chris's name but got no answer. He walked around the back of the cabin and noticed a board pulled up from the deck. He had an uneasy feeling and frantically began calling Chris's name. He finally spotted him slumped under a tree next to the stream and rushed to his side.

"Chris, are you all right?" he asked anxiously. Chris's eyes were open, but he was in a daze. Larry knelt down beside him and hoped that his intuition was wrong. He placed one hand on Chris's shoulder.

"Chris, did you take something?" He spoke loudly, trying to bring him out of his stupor. Chris turned his head toward his father. His eyes were glossy, and he slightly nodded his head.

"Oh, Chris!" Larry gasped frantically. He quickly lifted him into his arms and ran for the cabin.

"Somebody help me!" Larry cried as he carried Chris through the back door. Two of the paramedics and the police officer came running to his aid. They took Chris from his arms and gently laid him on the kitchen floor. "He's taken some kind of drug—probably pain pills—but I don't know what or how many!" Larry explained loudly as he nervously paced back and forth. He feared for his son's life.

The paramedics checked Chris's eyes and they were dilated.

"Christopher, can you tell us how many pills you took?" a young, skinny paramedic asked. He was trying to keep Chris awake. Chris turned his head away and closed his eyes. He wanted to surrender to the darkness that beckoned him.

"Chris, stay with me!" the paramedic shouted loudly. He tapped the side of Chris's face and brought him back around. "Chris, just nod your head. Was it pain pills?" Chris barely nodded. "Was it more than five pills?" Chris nodded again, his eyes still closed.

"Christopher Larry Porter, how many pills did you take?" Larry demanded furiously as he stood over his son. "Tell them Chris, right now!"

"Sir, please, just step back and let us do our job," the older paramedic instructed. He pushed Larry back a few feet to give them room. "I'll call dispatch for another ambulance," he said to the other paramedic.

He turned to Larry, who was still anxiously pacing the floor. "We need to get him to the hospital right away and have his stomach pumped.

Katie is in stable condition and can wait for the other ambulance."

"Is he going to be all right?" Larry asked breathlessly.

"We're doing everything we can."

Larry could hardly believe what was happening. He exhaled loudly and ran his hands through his hair. "Get a hold of yourself," he whispered. He knew it was not the time to fall apart. Chris and Katie needed his strength.

As the paramedics picked Chris up off the floor, Larry could see how limp and lifeless his body was. He could hear Katie crying for him, her daddy. He felt torn between the two of them, both of them needing his utmost attention. They had started Katie on an IV and her little eyes were squinted and full of concern.

Larry went to Katie's side and picked up her cold hand. "Daddy, I'm scared. Please don't leave me!" she begged as she tightened her grip. Larry looked into her small, frightened face and knew that as much as he wanted to be with Chris, Katie needed him more.

"Chris is going to the hospital too, so I'll just go see him off," he said, gently rubbing the top of her head. "I'll be right back." Jody stayed with her while Larry went outside to the ambulance.

"Could I see him for a minute before you leave?" he asked the driver. The driver nodded, and Larry climbed in the back. They'd wrapped him in a blanket and started an IV. His eyes were trying hard to close, but the paramedic was keeping him awake by speaking to him loudly and slapping his skin.

Larry sat down beside him and took his hand. "Chris, I'll be right behind you in an ambulance with Katie. I love you," he said tearfully. "May I give him a quick blessing?" he asked the paramedic. The paramedic nodded, and Larry placed his hands on Chris's head. He had no consecrated oil, but he had faith that the Lord would hear his prayer.

He blessed Christopher by the power of the priesthood and by his faith in the Lord that he would make it through this trial all right. Larry was also inspired to bless him with the strength of Helaman that he would overcome his addiction. He closed the prayer, and with much hesitation, he let go of Chris's hand. He climbed out of the ambulance and let the paramedics take over.

Larry's fear subsided as he watched the ambulance drive away, and he was left with a calm and peaceful feeling. He knew that Heavenly Father would watch over and protect Chris.

The other ambulance arrived shortly after the first one left. Larry asked Jody to follow in the truck so he could ride with Katie. As he climbed into the back of the ambulance, he quickly pointed out to Katie all of the really cool stuff. He was trying to get her mind off the ordeal, but she was not her usual curious self and was not the least bit interested.

He sat next to Katie, holding her hand, but his thoughts were with Chris. It wasn't his condition he was concerned about—it was his addiction. He was deep in thought when Katie tugged on his shirt to get his attention.

"It wasn't Chris's fault," she whispered. "I was playing on the rocks where you told me not to, and I slipped."

"We don't need to talk about it right now," Larry replied gently. "I don't want you to worry about a thing."

He knew now why Chris wasn't paying attention to Katie and why he had been so moody. Larry had to face the fact that his son was addicted to pain pills and needed more help than he alone could give.

# Chapter 17

When they reached the hospital, the driver instructed Larry to go on inside and check Chris in. As he entered the automatic doors of the emergency area, he was directed to a small room to fill out paper work. This was all too familiar to him—the insurance information, birth dates, medical histories, and signatures. After it was all complete and the hospital knew exactly who was going to pay the bill, he was directed to the nurse's station down the hall.

The doctor gave him the details of Chris's condition. They had to pump his stomach and give him a charcoal substance to absorb any of the medication that was still in his system.

"Your son is one lucky kid," the doctor told Larry as he escorted him into the room where Chris was. "If you'd found him any later, he might not have been so lucky."

Chris was lying very still with his eyes closed. His hands and feet were tied to the gurney and he had black charcoal around his mouth. The doctor explained that Chris had put up such a fight that it was necessary to restrain him for his own safety. He closed the door and left Larry alone with his son.

Larry sat down next to Chris and picked up his hand. "I love you, Christopher," he whispered softly. Chris opened his eyes and looked at his father.

"Hey, there. You gave us quite a scare. Are you feeling okay?"

Chris got a funny look on his face. He was miserably lost somewhere between being grateful and angry.

"You should have let me die," he exclaimed, his voice full of resentment. He tried to turn away but the restraints held him in place, which irritated him even more.

"How can you say something like that?" Larry said, stunned. He felt as if someone had just given him a blow to the head and he was having trouble hearing. "You can't possibly mean that, Christopher."

"Yes, I do!" Chris answered furiously, his face turning red with anger. "Just leave me alone! Get away from me!" He started thrashing around, trying to break free from the restraints, and turned red in the face from screaming, "Get out! Get out!"

A large African-American woman, who was wearing purple scrubs with smiley faces on the shirt, came into the room. "You need to go now, sir," she said firmly. She held the door open for him to leave.

"I'm his father! I have a right to know what's going on!" Larry insisted, refusing to leave his son. Chris was still thrashing around and had begun to swear.

"Sir, please leave. I will come get you when he calms down." Larry shook his head in disgust and reluctantly left the room. He stood in the hallway, watching through the window as Chris stubbornly fought to escape the straps that restrained him. Larry stayed quiet, but he was filled with anger. He needed to know what was going on with his son.

Just then Jody came down the hall. She was trying to find Larry. "Katie wants you," she said, concerned. She nonchalantly glanced through the window. "What's going on in there?" she asked innocently and immediately recognized her brother. "Is that Chris?" she gasped. She reached for the doorknob, but Larry caught her arm, preventing her from going in.

"I think we'd better talk," he said, sighing heavily.

Larry stopped to check on Katie, who was sitting up, eating an orange Popsicle, and watching cartoons. She was still on oxygen but looked much better. Then he and Jody went to the cafeteria to talk. He wanted Jody to know everything that had been going on with Chris. She deserved to know the truth.

It was after seven in the evening and the kitchen was closed. They sat down at one of the tables in the dining area and settled for a sandwich and a soda from the vending machine. Larry explained to Jody what had happened on Mother's Day and how Chris had taken the medicine from his cabinet. Finally, he told her about Levi and the drugs Chris bought from him while they were at the cabin—the same drugs that nearly cost him his life.

Jody kept her eyes on her food and picked at her sandwich. When her father was finished talking, she looked up at him with tear-filled eyes.

"I knew there was something wrong, but I didn't think it was drugs," she said sadly. "I thought he just really missed mom and was taking it out on all of us." She paused and then added, "How can we help him?"

"Well, I'm going to talk to the doctor about admitting him into a drug rehab program."

"Is that really necessary? I mean, why can't we just help him at home?"

"I've tried to talk to him about it, but he just blows up. He assured me he could stop using, so I gave him the benefit of the doubt. Obviously he can't quit by his own volition, and I don't know how to help him." Larry sighed regretfully as he sipped his root beer.

"Do you think Chris will go to a drug rehab?" Jody questioned, her eyes full of doubt. She thoroughly disagreed with what he was proposing.

"Well, whether he will or not, I'm going to admit him. He's under eighteen, so he won't have a lot to say about it." It sounded cold and ruthless when he said it out loud.

"You're going to force him to go? He'll never forgive you if you do." Defiantly challenging his decision, she slammed her Sprite can onto the table and looked directly into his eyes.

"That's a chance I'll have to take in order to get him the help he needs," Larry answered firmly. He couldn't believe he was defending his decision. He thought Jody would back him up.

"It's just pain pills—not cocaine or something worse. Can't we be the ones to help him?" She pleaded. "School's out, so I can watch him during the days when you're at work. I can even help keep an eye on him in the evening." She was worried that her brother might go off the deep end if he was confined to a rehab.

"Jody, I've tried everything. Look, I'll check into all my options before making a final decision. That's the best I can do." With Jody's skepticism, Larry was now wondering if he was making the right choice.

Jody shook her head to let her father know that she did not agree. She thought he was making a huge mistake. She knew Chris would never willingly go to rehab.

Back upstairs, things had calmed down. The doctor had given Chris a light sedative to relax him. Because of the attempted suicide, the doctor admitted Chris into the psychiatric ward of the hospital. Larry and the doctor stood in the hallway and discussed Chris's options, including a drug rehab program. They were waiting on the hospital psychiatrist, who was coming in that night to talk to Chris. Larry still hadn't made up his mind, but he consented to let the psychiatrist talk to Chris anyway.

Katie was resting peacefully. They had moved her to the pediatrics wing on the third floor. Her room had red and green balloons on the walls and there was a playroom just down the hall.

Larry kissed her softly on the forehead and pulled her covers up around her. She had Peggy snuggled tightly under her right arm. He knew Barbara was still watching over their little girl, even if it was just in spirit.

As Larry watched his daughter sleep, he realized how close he had come to losing two of his children that day. Without the Lord watching over them, this day may not have turned out as well as it did. He said a prayer in his mind to thank Heavenly Father again and to make a solemn promise that from this day on, he would never again let his faith waver.

He quietly closed the door and found Jody talking to the nurse at the desk. Jody had learned that a motel was just down the street a few blocks from the hospital. Larry was hesitant to leave, but it was late, and they were both exhausted. The nurse assured him that she would call if there were any problems. The psychiatrist had not yet come to talk to Chris, but the nurse encouraged Larry and Jody to get some rest. Larry finally agreed and gave her his cell phone number.

They checked into the motel and settled into a room with two double beds. They had no clothes with them because everything was still back at the cabin.

Exhausted, they climbed into their beds. Larry turned out the light and stared into the darkness. He couldn't stop worrying about his son.

"Dad, are you awake?" Jody asked from the next bed.

"Yes."

"Do you think they're okay?"

"Probably."

"I just don't understand why Chris would want to take his own life," she said sadly.

Larry could tell from the tone of his daughter's voice that she was just as worried as he was. He wanted desperately to comfort her, but at that moment he couldn't, because he was scared to death. The life-altering decision he was facing was eating him up inside. What if he made the wrong choice? There would be no going back once he agreed to admit Chris into rehab. Was he strong enough to incarcerate one of his children? He had to keep reminding himself that it would be for Chris's own good. He desperately wished that Barbara could be at his side to guide him in the right direction.

"That's why I think he needs help. Things with him are getting worse instead of better," Larry said, trying to make her see his point of view.

"I understand that. I just wish it didn't mean locking him up," Jody said with a sigh. "I wish he would talk to me about stuff. He used to tell me everything, but now he just shuts me out. I really miss our conversations. He was teaching me how to play the guitar before mom died."

"I don't think I've ever heard him play. Is he good?"

"Wow, is he ever. How could you not hear him playing his electric guitar?" she asked in surprise. "He plays it downstairs in his bedroom all the time, and when he plays, his music fills the entire house."

"I thought that was his stereo! You mean to tell me that he was playing that music?" Now it was Larry's turn to be surprised.

"His stereo broke a long time ago!" Jody said, laughing. "Mom always said he should start his own band."

Larry hadn't realized how talented his son was and wished he'd taken more of an interest in his children's accomplishments.

"I've really missed out on a lot, haven't I?" he asked remorsefully.

"Well, it's not too late to start now. We've put aside our differences and made a fresh start. I know Chris will come around and do the same," she said, yawning.

"You'd better get some sleep," he said softly. "Good night, Jody."

"Good night, dad. I love you."

"I love you too," he said with a smile.

# Chapter 18

Larry awoke to the sound of rain tapping on the windowpane. He looked at Jody sleeping peacefully in the next bed. He checked his cell phone for missed calls and messages and was relieved to find none. It was 7:30 a.m., and he was anxious to get back to the hospital.

He got out of bed, walked over to the window, and pulled open one side of the heavy blue curtains. The sky was covered in dark clouds, and the rain was coming down in torrents. Judging by the size of the puddles in the parking lot, it looked as though it had been raining most of the night. He cracked open the window just enough to let in the brisk, clean smell of the morning rain. It once again brought back memories of Barbara and the past. He tried to push the thoughts out of his head. He needed to think about the present, not the past.

However, the past was where he wanted to be right now. When the kids were younger, his only worry was a skinned knee or a temper tantrum over a piece of candy. Barbara would always be the first to give in, letting them get away with just about anything. Now, he, on the other hand, grew up in a very strict home with a lot of rules. Barbara would laugh at him and say, "Rules were meant to be broken." She was always so patient with the kids, and in a way, he was envious of that. He knew he had a temper that at times was hard to control. It only got worse when he started working longer hours. Now that he thought back on it, Barbara had a lot of patience with him as well. Back then he couldn't wait for the kids to grow up. Now he wished they were five again and a piece of candy would make everything better.

He quietly closed the window and went back to his bed. Jody was still sleeping, so he knelt down beside the bed to pray. He tried hard not to complain to the Lord, but his heart was heavy with burdens. He was still struggling with the decision of putting Chris in a program and asked the Lord to guide him in the right direction.

"Dad, are you all right?" Jody asked with concern when she saw him on the floor.

"Yeah, I was just saying my morning prayers," he said, smiling.

"I'm glad to hear that. I was getting a little worried about you," she said, grinning.

"I was too," he chuckled and sat down on the bed next to her. "You don't need to worry anymore. I was lost there for a while, but I've found my way back again."

He would never know how much those words comforted her. She had noticed how distant he'd become from the church, and it terrified her. The one thing she had always held onto was the thought of seeing her mother again and being an eternal family. With Chris acting the way he was and her father falling away from the church, she was worried she'd lost her family forever. He leaned over and kissed her on the forehead. "Everything will work out, you'll see."

As they entered the hospital, Larry's cell phone rang. There would be a meeting at 9 a.m. to discuss Chris. Since they had some time to spare, Larry and Jody stopped by the cafeteria to grab a bite to eat and then headed upstairs to meet with the doctor.

The doctor was a heavyset man with thick-framed brown glasses, and a bald spot on the top of his head. He was holding a clipboard and introduced himself as Dr. O'Brian, the pediatrician in charge. He had already been in to check on Katie and was happy to report she would make a full recovery. Larry's quick response with CPR had saved her life. They could now focus their attention on Chris. Jody went to stay with Katie while Dr. O'Brian escorted Larry down the hall to a small conference room.

Dr. O'Brian introduced the two other people sitting around the large oval table. There was Dr. Nash, the hospital's psychologist, and Leslie Holtz, the director at Sunrise Youth Center, a drug rehab. Larry could feel his heart thump as he was introduced to Leslie. He hadn't made up his mind about a rehab program, so this came as quite a shock.

"I told the doctor last night that I haven't made up my mind about anything yet," he said firmly.

"We aren't here to tell you what to do," Dr. O'Brian pointed out. "Dr. Nash spoke to Chris last night and called Leslie to come in just to give you an idea of what kind of help is available. It will still be your choice whether or not you place him in a rehab program. However, I think it would be beneficial for you to at least listen to what they have to say." He acted like he had all the answers and that drove Larry nuts. Larry sat down, folded his arms, and nodded his approval. His body language insinuated that he would not be influenced to doing something he didn't want to do.

"Okay, I'll go first," Dr. Nash said, opening a red folder on the table in front of him. "As Dr. O'Brian said, I was able to talk to Christopher last night and I'm deeply concerned about his drug abuse and his mental stability. When we first started talking, he gave me the usual response. He told me where to go and how to get there. But after sitting with him for a while, I could see that there are a lot of emotions running through him, and the biggest one is anger. That anger was the key that led to the drug use you reported last night."

"Don't tell me what I already know," Larry said irritably.

"All right, then, Christopher needs help immediately. With all the anger and depression building up inside of him, I think he will try this again," Dr. Nash said, directing the responsibility onto Larry.

Larry unfolded his arms and leaned forward to place them on the table. He looked directly into Dr. Nash's eyes. "So you're telling me that if I don't put my son in this rehab program, he'll attempt suicide again?" Larry was already frustrated with the way things were going, and he didn't like feeling pressured.

"I'm saying that it's a very good possibility. The pills he's addicted to are downers and only intensify his anger and depression, so I think we should start by trying to help him overcome his drug addiction." He turned to Leslie, who was sitting in the chair next to him. "Leslie, why don't you tell him about your program?"

Leslie was sitting straight across the table from Larry, and he noticed what a nice-looking woman she was with her blond hair and blues eyes. He thought she was young, maybe in her mid-twenties. She was aggressive when she spoke, as if she knew what was best and was going to make sure everyone agreed with her.

"Our facility is one of the best in the state. We're located just outside Provo, so it will be close for you. After talking to the doctors, I would advise a sixty-day program for Chris. My recommendation is based partly off of how long he's been using and what kind of drugs they are." She removed a picture from her briefcase and slid it across the table to Larry. "The home sits on 10 acres with stables and horses. We're a smaller facility with only eight rooms and two kids per room. There are three counselors available, one psychiatrist, and a doctor who comes in daily."

"Is it a secure facility?" Larry asked, thinking Christopher would probably take off on a dead run the minute he got there.

"There's an eight-foot chain-link fence that covers the entire property, with a security guard at the gate. The kids earn points that move them up to different levels. Each level gives them special privileges, such as watching movies or riding horses." She handed Larry another piece of paper with prices. Money wasn't really a concern to him. He had the six thousand dollars in the bank that they were asking for the sixty-day program. He more or less was trying to find an excuse not to send Chris away for two months. "We have one opening right now, so we could take Christopher straight from here to the program. Sometimes it makes the transition a little easier." She was acting like it was a done deal.

Larry looked over the papers and was torn as to what to do. He felt like his back was against the wall, with all three of them waited for his response. He wanted to flee from their opposing stares, to think things through and make a rational decision. "Can I take an hour to think it over?"

"Certainly. My cell phone number is on the bottom of the paper," Leslie answered in a friendlier tone.

"Thank you. Now, if you'll excuse me, I'd like to go check on my children."

Walking down the long hallway back to the pediatrics unit, Larry couldn't help but admit that it sounded like a good program that might help Chris get off the drugs. It had its advantages. It was secure and close to home. Maybe this was the direction the Lord wanted him to go, but if it was, why was he having such a hard time doing it? The thought of watching strangers take his son away was wrenching his soul.

Katie was just finishing up her breakfast of scrambled eggs, bacon, and toast when Larry walked into her room. The soft, rosy color was back in her cheeks and she was grinning from ear to ear. "Daddy!" she shouted excitedly. "Look what the nurse gave me." She proudly held up a fabric doll wearing a hospital gown. "She said I was real brave to stay all by myself."

"I knew you would be all right without me," he said smiling, and he gave her a kiss. She was now off the oxygen and back to her usual energetic self.

"I want to go to the playroom daddy, please," she pleaded. His thoughts were still on Chris and he was anxious to get downstairs to the psychiatric wing. Jody could see the distress on his face and knew it was because of Chris.

"Dad needs to go take care of Chris right now," she said, giving him the okay to leave. "He can come later." She took Katie by the hand and led her down the hall. He watched them until they turned the corner into the playroom. He was thankful that he had such a wonderful daughter to take over for him.

The psychiatric unit was totally locked down, and Larry had to show his ID just to get in. The rooms were also locked from the outside to ensure the safety of the patients and the staff. The nurse unlocked the door to Chris's room and informed him that Chris had gone into a rage of anger when they denied him painkillers. If he didn't calm down, they were going to have to restrain him again.

Wondering what he would find inside, Larry hesitantly opened the door. Chris was lying in bed facing the wall. The evidence of his fiery rage was left untouched. His breakfast tray was upside down on the floor, and food was scattered everywhere. There were no covers left on his bed; they were scrunched up in the corner. The recliner was on its side, and the mini blinds had been ripped from the window.

Chris turned over, saw his father, and turned back to face the wall again. He thought for sure it would be the police standing there holding out the handcuffs. After all, he'd stolen his father's truck, bought illegal drugs, and let his little sister almost drown. That should buy him some time in the slammer.

Stepping over the scrambled eggs and toast, Larry carefully walked across the room. He sat the recliner in an upright position and took a seat. "I can't blame you for not wanting to eat. Hospital food is horrible," he said, laughing and trying to make light of the situation. "How are you feeling?"

"Fine," Chris muttered, annoyed. What he really wanted to say was that his head throbbed, his body ached, he felt sick to his stomach, and he was shaking all over. He would do anything right now for a pain pill. He was already making plans to call Brandon just as soon as he returned home.

"Chris, can you turn around and talk to me?"

"I don't have anything to say to you. Just leave me alone!" he grunted.

"Chris, you told me you could quit taking the drugs. You told me you didn't have any more drugs at the cabin, and you told me you only bought cigarettes from this guy Levi. Now, why don't you tell me something truthful for a change?" Larry could feel anger edging its way to the surface. "Chris, look at me!" he shouted.

Chris turned over. His eyes were filled with hateful rage. "I didn't feel like quitting, all right? It's my body! What do you care anyway?" he roared.

"I do care, Christopher. If I didn't care, do you think I would be sitting here right now?" Chris rolled his eyes as the tension escalated. "Why did you try to kill yourself?" Larry asked.

"Why don't you just leave me alone? Go be with Katie. She's the one who needs you! She almost drowned thanks to me!" Larry could hear sadness and despair breaking through his son's anger.

"That was an accident, Chris. That wasn't anyone's fault."

"That's a lie and you know it! You left her in my care and I blew it. Why don't you just say what you're really thinking? Say what you really mean?"

"What are you talking about, Christopher?"

"You wished I was the one in that lake yesterday, and then you could have let me drown! Don't deny it! I could see it in your eyes when you picked Katie up in your arms!"

"No, Chris. I was just scared. I didn't—"

"Just get out of my room!" Chris yelled. He pointed his trembling finger at the door.

Larry was dumbfounded. He didn't know how to respond to something so outlandish. "I love you Chris," he said gently.

"Go to ——!" Chris raged, his face red with fury.

Larry stood up, looked helplessly at his inconsolable son, and stepped out into the hallway. He softly closed the door behind him. He went to the nurse's station, picked up the phone, and dialed the seven digits of Leslie's cell phone number.

There were no more questions to ask, no more excuses to be made. It was apparent what he had to do.

# Chapter 19

$\mathcal{L}$arry impatiently paced back and forth, waiting for the people from the program to arrive. He had met with Leslie an hour earlier to go over the paperwork and the rules. Visiting hours were every Saturday for one hour, except the first week. Chris would start on level one, and with cooperation, he would move up a level each week and receive special privileges, such as horseback riding, going into town, and eventually going out for the day with family. If all went well, he was to return home on August 15, just before his sixteenth birthday.

She pulled out the final paper for Larry to sign, which gave Sunrise Youth facility temporary custody of Christopher. Larry grasped the pen in his trembling hand, paused, and stared down at the empty black line. Once he put his signature on the paper, Chris would be theirs for the next two months. He suddenly felt like he was relinquishing his parental rights and giving up on his son altogether. Recalling the events that had led up to this decision, he reminded himself that this was the best thing for Chris.

Leslie could see his hesitation. "This is only temporary," she reminded him. "We can help Chris if you'll let us." Her voice was soft and sympathetic. He looked into her caring, soft, blue eyes and knew if anyone could help Chris, it would be her. Larry put the pen to the paper and signed his name, which left a cold, empty feeling in the pit of his stomach.

Nervously awaiting the arrival of the others, he went in to check on Chris. Much to his surprise, Chris was already dressed and tying his shoe laces. "What are you doing?" Larry asked.

"Leaving. You've done it enough, you should recognize the signs," he exclaimed bitterly.

The harsh words stabbed deeply into Larry's already broken spirit. "You can't leave. The doctor isn't finished with you yet."

"You signed my release papers, and now we're leaving."

"Wait a minute. I need to talk to you first." Larry knew it was time to come clean, with or without Chris's approval.

"Look, if you want me to see the school counselor again, I will. I just want to go home now," Chris said sorrowfully.

"Chris, a counselor isn't going to be enough. I've admitted you into a drug rehab program."

Chris stared at his father in disbelief. "I'm not going to any rehab program! I'm going home, even if I have to find my own ride!" he growled loudly. He opened the door and smacked right into Dr. Nash, who was with Leslie and two other men from the facility. The two men were dressed in white polo shirts and khaki pants. "What's this?" Chris questioned loudly as he angrily glared at his father.

"These are the people I was referring to from the rehab program. They're here to take you to the center." Larry was trying his best to sound upbeat and positive, but on the inside, he was falling apart.

"You've already called them without talking to me first?" Chris was feeling a sense of fear creeping up inside him. "You can't make me go!" Leslie stepped forward to take control of the situation.

"It's not up to your dad anymore. I'm the one you need to blame for this," she firmly stated. Larry felt a huge relief from the burden she was taking off his shoulders. He silently stood back and let her domineering personality take over. "You will be coming with us to the facility. Your father can send your things later."

"Whatever!" Chris responded. He would go along with their plan, at least long enough to get out of the hospital.

They took the elevator to the first floor. Chris went along, walking beside his father calmly, quietly, and respectfully. That was until they reached the outside of the hospital. Suddenly, Chris bolted through the parking lot and was immediately followed by the two men.

The rain was down to a light drizzle but had left large puddles in the parking lot. Chris frantically ran through cars and trucks trying to lose his pursuers. One of the men came around a large truck and cut Chris off, blocking his escape. He grabbed Chris around the middle and picked him up off the ground. Chris was fighting as hard as he could. He kicked his legs and swung his arms in an attempt to free himself, but the large, muscular man overpowered him and threw him over his shoulder.

"Let go of me! Get your hands off me!" Chris hollered.

"Come on, little man. Let's not make this any harder than it has to be," the man said calmly. When Chris saw his father, he tried a different approach.

"Dad, please don't send me away! I promise I'll be good from now on," he pleaded as the two men forced him into the van.

"Chris, I'm doing this for your own good. They can help you." Larry could feel the tears welling up in his eyes as he struggled to do the right thing.

"Dad, I promise I won't take any more drugs. Please don't make me go!" Chris yelled from inside the van.

The two men sat Chris in the second seat of the eight-passenger van and strapped nylon restraints across him. Two restraints went over his chest so he couldn't move his arms. The other two were over his legs. A terrifying feeling of captivity came over him as they secured the last strap around his legs. He felt like a prisoner.

"Mr. Porter, it's best if we leave now before things get worse," Leslie said sympathetically. Larry nodded and stepped a little closer to the van to say good-bye. He could see that Chris was red in the face from his useless struggling.

"I will see you a week from this Saturday," Larry said, feeling a little like a judge who had just sentenced his son to sixty days in jail. "Everything will be okay."

Chris could see that all of his endeavors to escape had been useless, and it sent him into a rage of anger. "I hate you! I hate you!" He screamed at his father. "I will never forgive you! Never! You're dead to me now!" They closed the door of the van with him still screaming.

Larry turned away to hide his tears. Chris's words cut like a knife into his broken heart. "Doing the right thing isn't always easy," Leslie said, trying to comfort him.

Larry nodded his head and walked back into the hospital, all the while watching the van as it pulled out of the parking lot. He would see Chris in a week, but a week seemed like an eternity.

Chris could no longer hold back the tears, and they streamed down his face. Thoughts of jail and prison bars flashed through his head as his tough-guy act transformed into childlike weeping.

"This doesn't have to be tough, Christopher," Leslie said from the front seat of the van. "It's all up to you." When she got no response, she turned and buckled her seatbelt for the two-hour drive.

Chris stared out the window at the rain coming down and wished his mother were there. Thoughts of her flooded his mind. He wouldn't be on his way to purgatory if his mother had been there. No one understood him like she did. She had a way of turning everything around to make it better. His father hated him—that was evident now. But he didn't care. He didn't need him anyway. He didn't need anybody! He would do their stupid program and then get far away from his father.

He laid his head against the window of the van. The cold glass felt soothing against his aching forehead. He closed his eyes and pictured his mother, which comforted him. He let himself relax into a peaceful sleep, dreaming of better days when his mother was alive and well.

A huge bump knocked his head into the window pane, jarring him back into his grim reality. He looked out the window just as the van turned into the long driveway of an enormous white Victorian-style home set against the Wasatch Mountains. It was surrounded by tall, leafy, green trees and elegant flower beds. The sun was brightly shining, and there were several teenage kids outside playing ball on the basketball court. Others were just sitting around on the grass in the beautifully landscaped yard. It didn't look anything like Chris expected.

The van came to a halt, and Leslie turned around in her seat. "Well, here we are. Ready to get those restraints off?" she asked with a smile on her face. Chris was more than ready, but he wasn't about to give her the pleasure of hearing him say so. He shrugged his shoulders and looked out the window.

"All right, then. I'll just leave the door open, and when you're ready, just holler at one of the kids to come in the house and get me," she said with a cold, icy stare. She and the men got out of the van and walked toward the house, leaving Chris strapped to the back of the seat.

"You've got to be kidding!" he shouted as he watched her go into the house and close the door. *If she thinks I'm giving in that easy, she better think again*, he thought angrily.

The restraints were feeling snug around his arms and he tried to reposition himself in the seat. The shakes had started up again, which added to his already miserable situation. His stomach was sick, probably from not eating any breakfast, and he was extremely agitated. He wiggled this way and that, trying to find a comfortable spot. He thought for sure that any minute her guilt would finally get to her and she would come back to set him free.

"Lunch!" somebody called from the front porch, which sent all the kids from the yard and running for the house.

"That's just great! Now if I want to be free there's no one out here to hear me," he whined to the back of the driver's seat. He wasn't ready to call uncle just yet. He rested his head on the back of the seat and looked up at the ceiling. *Time passes slowly when you're strapped to the back seat of a van*, he thought anxiously. "That stupid witch isn't even going to come get me for lunch!" he hollered loudly.

"Who are you talking to?" said a pretty, redheaded girl standing in the doorway of the van. She looked like she was about his age, with green eyes and freckles. He thought she was terribly pretty and was now embarrassed of the fact that he was tied to a seat talking to himself.

"Nobody, I was . . . was just talking to myself," he stammered. "What do you want, anyway?" he said brusquely, trying to regain some dignity.

"Nothing, I just thought I would come see what you were doing in here. Now I guess I know," she said, smiling brightly. She had a slight southern accent that Chris thought was very appealing. "You might as well give in. Ms. Holtz won't, that's for certain. She's very stubborn and would rather cut off her right arm than give in to anyone. The sooner you realize that, the faster you'll get free."

"Oh yeah? Well I think she's a witch, and I'm not giving into her twisted game!" he stated with confidence.

"Suit yourself." She turned to go, her long red hair whipping around as she spun on one foot to leave. "Good luck getting out of there."

"Wait a minute!" Chris called after her. "You're not going to help me out of these restraints?"

"Why should I? I don't even know you," she replied bluntly.

"So what? You could still help a stranger in need," he replied, thinking guilt was his ticket out of there. "Could you just loosen the straps a little? They're really starting to hurt." He shot her a painful, pleading look.

"They do?" she asked with concern. "Well, maybe I could just loosen them a bit." She climbed in beside him and reached across to unloosen the strap. He could smell the flowery scent of her shampoo and feel the touch of her soft skin.

"What are you two doing?" Ms. Holtz abruptly asked. They both looked up to see her scowling at them.

"I was just loosening them a little," the redheaded girl quickly responded. "He said they hurt and—"

"All right! Run along to lunch and let me have a word with our new friend."

The redheaded girl glanced over at Chris, who gave her an "I'm sorry" look, and then she jumped out of the van.

"So, plan A didn't work out so well for you. Do you have a plan B, or are you ready to ask for assistance?"

Chris irritably looked the other direction. He felt much like a participant in the game of chicken and wondered who would swerve first to avoid the collision.

"Well then, I'll check on you later." She turned around to walk off and Chris could see he was not going to win this one. Besides, he had to use the bathroom something awful.

"Wait," he said softly, swallowing his pride. "I'm ready to get out of these restraints."

"I'm sorry, I didn't hear you," she said, placing her hand up to her ear. Chris was tempted to wet his pants rather than give in to this overbearing, overconfident witch.

"I said . . . I'm ready to get out of the restraints!" he shouted in an obnoxious voice.

"I don't respond to kids who speak to me in that tone of voice. I'll see you in an hour." She turned and started to walk away once more.

"Fine!" Chris yelled from the van. He struggled to move the words past his stubborn lips. "I'm sorry! Could you please help me out of these restraints?" he asked politely, restraining himself from what he really wanted to say.

"Why, yes, I will." She climbed in the van and released the binding straps. Chris softly rubbed his arms where he'd been bound.

"You might as well forget trying to run anywhere. The whole place is fenced in, with a security guard at the gate," she said, pointing down the driveway.

Chris wasn't thinking about running. Now that he was standing, he could feel his knees shaking terribly. It was all he could do to not fall over.

"Can I go to my room now?" he asked irritably. She could see that he was pale and trembling all over.

"I think you should see the doctor first. Follow me."

The house was even more immaculate inside. It had hardwood floors throughout and a beautiful fireplace in the living room. The dining room was off to the right with a long wood table and chairs. Above the table hung a crystal chandelier. The next room down the hall was the doctor's office. It had an exam table, a desk, and a sink. Ms. Holtz introduced Chris to Dr. Letzo. He was a tall, thin, Hispanic man with glasses. He shook hands with Chris and escorted him to the exam table, while Ms. Holtz waited outside the door.

"Welcome," he said, overly cheerful. His English was good, but you could still hear an accent. "It looks like you're having some withdrawals."

"Some what?" Chris asked, confused and agitated.

"Withdrawals," he said again. "It's what happens when you've been continually giving your body drugs and then just up and stop cold turkey." He snapped his fingers together to make his point. Chris thought he acted like a quack. "Your body's trying to tell you it needs more drugs. That's why you start shaking and feeling sick, but I can give you something to help your symptoms." He talked while taking Chris's blood pressure and temperature. Then he went to the cupboard, took out a bottle of pills, shook one out, and handed it to Chris. "This should help," he said.

"More drugs? Isn't that defeating the purpose?" Chris asked, snorting obnoxiously. He looked down at the small green pill in the palm of his hand.

"Well, you could tough it out on your own, but I should warn you, it only gets worse before it gets better." Chris decided if they were stupid enough to offer him more drugs, who was he to say no? He downed the pill with a glass of water and watched as the doctor put the pill bottle back in the cupboard. "Good, I'll see you tomorrow for a full examination," he said opening the door for him.

Ms. Holtz escorted him up the huge, hardwood spiral staircase to the second floor. Down the hallway there were three rooms on the right and two on the left. The last door on the right was his room. There were two twin beds, one on each side of the room, with matching blue and green checkered bedspreads. Each side of the room had a desk, a small closet, and a nightstand with a lamp and clock on it. It was very small compared to Chris's room at home.

"Where's the bathroom?" he asked, looking around the room.

"Back down the hall, third door on your left."

"We have to share a bathroom?" he asked disgustedly.

"Did you think you were checking into the Hilton?" she said sarcastically. She handed him a blue folder with a bunch of papers inside. "This is all the rules and regulations, as well as an agenda for the next week. You will receive a new agenda each Saturday morning. It will go over all the activities for the whole week. If you're caught breaking a rule, you will be reprimanded, so learn them, love them, and live them," she said as she closed the door behind her.

Chris sat down on the end of bed and stared at the back of the bedroom door. There was a large plastic sign hanging by two nails that read, "You can do it!" in big, bold, black letters. Chris fell back on the overly firm mattress and looked up at the ceiling.

"Great, my dad has sent me to boot camp," he grumbled softly.

# Chapter 20

hris could hear music blasting from across the room and placed his pillow over his head to drown out the noise. Soon his roommate, Keith, was standing over him, poking him in the back.

"Time to get up!" he said in a loud voice.

"Go away," Chris grunted sleepily.

"Suit yourself—I'm not your mother," Keith shot back and left for breakfast.

Chris was in no mood to get out of bed that morning. He had a horrible headache again and all he wanted to do was sleep. He'd finally dozed off again when he heard a loud banging sound coming from the doorway. This was going too far. Keith was a good guy, but this was too much. He pulled the pillow off his head and sat up.

"What's your problem, man?" he screamed, trying to get his eyes to focus on the glaring face in front of him. He rubbed his eyes and took another look. Staring down at him was the evil eye of Ms. Holtz, who had been banging a wooden spoon on the back of a black metal pot.

"I told you to read your agenda," she lectured sternly. "Breakfast is at eight, chores at nine, and group therapy is at ten." She looked down at the floor and saw the folder lying underneath his jeans and T-shirt. She walked over, picked it up, and threw it on his lap. "You have one hour to learn everything in that folder. There will be a quiz on it." She waltzed out of the room like the head prison guard, softly closing the door behind her.

"She's got to be the devil!" he groaned miserably. He collapsed back on his bed and rubbed his hands over his face. He did not want be here, and he wasn't about to adhere to any of her commands.

He looked over at Keith's already made bed. *What a suck-up*, he thought irritably. The alarm clock read 9:15 a.m. Chris briefly met his roommate last night. He had sandy-blond hair, green eyes, and was tall and skinny. Several of his teeth were missing, and he told Chris it was due to using crystal meth for the last year. He was from Boise, Idaho, and had been in the program for seventy-two days out of his ninety-day sentence. His father was running for state legislature in Boise and was embarrassed by his son's drug habit, so he sent him away, telling everybody he was at military school. As he talked about his father and his home life, Chris soon came to realize that Keith's father was worse than his own. His mother was killed in a car accident when he was three, and his step-mother wanted nothing to do with him.

Chris unwillingly pried himself from the soft, warm covers and went downstairs to find something to eat. He hadn't eaten much yesterday, and his stomach was now protesting loudly. He was wearing Keith's pajama pants and an old T-shirt until his father could send him some clothes. As he walked down the stairs, he could feel his knees start to shake. His breathing was rapid and he was feeling jittery and agitated. After visiting the kitchen he would need to go see Dr. Quack again for one of his little green pills. They didn't seem to work as well as the pain pills, but it was better than having nothing at all.

Watching for anyone who might see him, he quietly made his way to the kitchen. The large wooden table was cleared off, and luckily nobody was in sight. Looking out of the kitchen window, he could see the kids doing their chores. Two were mowing the grass, three were washing the van, and the others were doing odd jobs in the yard. Chris quickly took out the ham, mayo, and bread to make himself a sandwich. He slammed the refrigerator door just as the cute redheaded girl from the day before came through the doorway.

"Well, I see you finally got out of the restraints. Does that mean you finally came to your senses and relinquished to her demands?" she said, smiling sweetly.

Chris just smiled back, not willing to admit to anything. "I'm sorry I got you into trouble yesterday. I didn't mean to," he said sympathetically.

"You didn't. Ms. Holtz may be stubborn, but she's also very understanding."

"You could have fooled me," he said, laughing. He really wished he'd gotten dressed and combed his hair before coming to the kitchen, but she was the last person he expected to see. "By the way, I'm Chris," he said, anxiously waiting to learn her name.

"I'm Amanda, Nice to meet you," she said, holding out her hand to shake his. He took her hand in his and gave it a gentle shake. His hand felt cold and sweaty against her smooth, warm skin, and he quickly pulled it away with embarrassment. She gave him a warm smile. "It's okay, I was nervous too the first day I was here. You better not let Ms. Holtz see you eating that. We're not supposed to help ourselves to the kitchen without asking permission first."

"I'm not scared of that old witch," he scowled, putting on the tough act for Amanda.

"Did I hear someone call my name," Ms. Holtz chattered, coming into the kitchen.

"We were just talking . . . about . . . a movie . . . *The Wizard of Oz*," Amanda stammered fearfully.

"Obviously, we need to go over some of the rules, don't we?" she asked Chris. She folded her arms in disapproval. "You can go to group now, Amanda."

Ms. Holtz turned her sights to Chris, who was stuffing down his sandwich. He was not the least bit intimidated by her authority. "Why is it you're determined to put me in my place?" she asked respectfully. "Do I intimidate you?"

"No!" Chris blurted out through bites of sandwich. "Why is it you're so determined to make me bow down and kiss your feet?"

"So, that's what you think. And you don't answer to anyone, right?" She was eyeing him up and down as if she'd already figured him out.

Chris covered his insecurities with a tough outer shell. "Why should I? I'm my own person with my own brain. I can act for myself, and I can think for myself." He was not going to let her control the conversation. "I don't need anyone."

"Were you thinking and acting for yourself when you started using drugs?"

He should have known she'd turn this whole thing around into a counseling session. He felt her opposing stare, trying to read him like an open book. "That was not my fault! I got hurt in a fight and the doctor put me on prescription pain pills. If he'd controlled my pain better, I wouldn't be in this position," Chris argued.

"So it's not your fault you started using, it's the doctors?" She was backing him into a tight corner and he hated it.

"I didn't say that! Don't go twisting my words around to fit into your delusional world of drug therapy. You don't know anything about me, so why don't you go find someone else to torture, and leave me alone?" He angrily threw down the rest of his sandwich and headed for the door.

"Hold on, Mr. Dynamite with a short fuse. I'm not finished." She stepped in front of the door to block his exit. "The time is now 10 a.m., and that means its group therapy. Let's go."

"Like this? I need to get dressed first," Chris complained irritably.

"Maybe you should have thought about that before you came downstairs to raid the refrigerator. There's no time now—everybody's waiting for us," she said, taking him by the arm.

"Don't touch me! I'm perfectly capable of walking on my own!"

When they got to the therapy session, kids were sitting on two couches, two love seats, and anything else they could find. Chris looked around the room and noticed that there were no empty seats. There were five girls, including Amanda, and nine boys. They were all gawking at him in his pajama pants. He could feel the perspiration run down his back as he searched for an available seat. He was furious at Ms. Holtz for embarrassing him in front of all the other kids.

Chris finally found a spot on the floor in the back of the room and slumped down into it. He hated Ms. Holtz with every bone in his body and wondered how anyone could be so pretty and yet so ruthless.

"Christopher?" Ms. Holtz called from the front of the room when she noticed he wasn't by her side. He slouched down even lower in an attempt to hide from her piercing eyes. "This is your seat up here," she said, discovering him in the corner. She gestured to the seat right next to hers.

"I'm fine where I'm at," he said, hoping the floor would crack open and swallow him up.

"You don't understand," she said sternly. "You're the new kid on the block, so you get to sit in the hot seat."

He knew very well he was playing into her game, but he went ahead and asked anyway. "What's the hot seat?"

"Somebody didn't read his folder," she said with a slight ring in her voice. "Can anyone tell our new friend what the hot seat is?" Several hands went into the air, and Ms. Holtz called on a blond girl sitting on the couch.

"It's where the new kid sits and tells us about himself. It's also for anyone who would like to share an experience or talk about their feelings," she explained, glancing over at Chris.

"Thank you, Tina. Now, Christopher, would you please come take your seat so we can get to know you a little better?" Chris wanted nothing more than to reach over and rip her teeth out, but he calmly walked to the front of the room instead. He really wished now he hadn't eaten that sandwich. It was creeping up his throat, threatening to cause a scene.

"Are you happy now?" he quietly grumbled as he passed Ms. Holtz and took his seat. She could see he was having more withdrawal symptoms, but she was determined to get him through group therapy before sending him to the doctor.

Chris told them the usual stuff, like where he was from and what grade he was in at school. Then she asked the kids if they had any questions for Chris. He hated being put on the spot, especially when he wasn't feeling good.

One boy raised his hand and stood up. "What do you like to do for fun?" he asked.

"Ska . . . um, play my guitar," he said, timidly looking at the floor. He didn't want to bring up the whole skateboarding thing. Ms. Holtz would have a heyday with that one.

"Oh, do you like to skate as well?" she asked curiously.

*So much for leaving it in the past*, Chris thought, agitated. "Not anymore." His voice was full of sorrow as he kept his eyes on the floor. Leslie realized she'd hit a sore spot and backed off.

"Why are you wearing your pajama pants?" a young girl asked.

"Hey, those are my pajama pants!" Keith joked and made everyone laugh.

Chris was quick to shoot Keith a thank you look before Ms. Holtz moved on with the subject of the day, taking the attention off Chris.

The group discussed how to handle certain situations and how their choices determine their future. She had everyone break off in pairs and handed out slips of paper with a scenario on each. The pair was to discuss the situation and come up with an appropriate action. Chris was the odd man out and became Ms. Holtz partner. She turned her chair to face him and read the scenario.

"You've just completed your program here at the facility and are finally home. On your first day back to school, your old buddy comes up to you with a full bottle of pain pills. He put them in your hand before you could tell him no. There you stand holding the very thing that caused all your problems to begin with. But at the same time, you remember how good they made you feel and you really want to take one. What would be your action?" she asked, looking at Chris.

"What do you think I would do?" Chris snarled bitterly. "I would throw them away and never talk to that friend again." This was like one of those stupid games you play on the first day of school, and he hated it. He thought he'd said exactly what she wanted to hear, but he underestimated her.

"Well, that would be the typical response, now wouldn't it? But you'll never get off level one with that attitude. So why don't you try telling me what you would really do? How would you feel?" She was purposely edging him on, searching for his strengths and weaknesses.

"I don't know, scared I guess."

"Come on, Chris. You can do better than that. What would be going through your head at that very moment?" He could feel her witchery as she pried deep into his soul, trying to pull out all of his hidden secrets. It enraged him and started his blood boiling. He'd had it with her holier than thou attitude! Who did she think she was anyway?

"What do you want from me?" he yelled. He shot up out of his seat, knocking it over backward. All of the kids stopped talking and were staring at him. "Fine, I would take every last pill in that bottle and finish the job that I started at the lake!" She didn't seem intimidated by his outburst of anger. She sat calmly and let him vent. "Is that what you want to hear?" He turned around to see everybody staring at him, and that infuriated him even more. He let out a loud growl and kicked the chair across the room on his way out.

He ran up the stairway and back to his room, violently slamming the bedroom door. His heart pounded harder and harder as he paced back and forth in the tiny room. He was shaking uncontrollably, and the rage from being locked away was overpowering him. All he could think about was taking another pain pill. The thought entirely consumed him, altering his judgment. At that moment he realized he would do anything to get drugs. Lie, steal, or kill—it didn't matter to him. He wanted it more than anything he'd ever wanted in his life. But it wasn't just the want, it was the need. It was like they'd taken away his air and he was suffocating.

Suddenly, there was a knock at the door, but Chris hesitated to open it. His anger was out of control and he could easily attack anyone who crossed him. The door swung opened and there stood Dr. Letzo.

He led Christopher to his office and closed the door. "Chris, if I'm going to help you, you need to tell me a little about your drug dependency." He had a syringe in his hand ready to give Chris an injection.

"Hold on!" Chris shouted, and jumped off the exam table. "I don't need a shot! Just give me that green pill you gave me yesterday!"

"This will work much faster than the pill—trust me," the doctor said, tapping the syringe. Chris reluctantly sat back down and took the stinging injection.

Chris's mind wandered over the last three months. He'd taken so many different drugs—Lortab, Percocet, over-the-counter cold and cough medicines, even alcohol and tobacco. They might lock him up and throw away the key if they knew he'd taken some kind of drug every day for the last three months.

The doctor watched as Chris twisted and squirmed, looking the other direction to avoid the question. "Chris, I can't help you if you're not honest with me," he said sympathetically.

"Well, try!" Chris demanded harshly and jumped off the table again, his fists tightly clenched together. He stood tall, shoulders arched, ready to unleash the fiery rage from within.

"Christopher, try and calm down—"

"Don't tell me what to do!" Chris said loudly. "I'm sick and tired of everyone always telling me what to do!"

Doctor Letzo could see that he wouldn't be getting any answers from Chris at that time, so he called in the two security officers that were standing outside the door. They each took Chris under one arm and escorted him down the hall to the last room on the right, with Chris fighting them all the way. They opened the door, pushed him inside, and with a click of the lock, he was a prisoner once again.

The room was very small, with one window that didn't open and a cot with a pillow on it. The walls were bare and there was a small sink and toilet behind a room divider.

Chris paced back and forth like a caged wild animal. He twisted and tugged on the doorknob, but without success. He took his fist and punched the door repeatedly. He hated this place. He hated Ms. Holtz, he hated his father, and at that moment, he even hated his mother. There was a powerful punch for each one until his knuckles gaped open and blood was dripping on the floor. He took off the pillow case and wrapped it around his hand to stop the bleeding. He sat down on the cot, finally coming to terms with the intense rage he'd felt.

The room was quiet. The only sound was a faint hum coming from the light that hung from the ceiling. No one was coming to check on him. No one cared. He was utterly alone, confined by the four small walls around him. The room began to spin, which gave him a strange floating sensation. "What did that idiot doctor give me?" he grumbled under his breath as he lay back on the cot.

He looked up at the ceiling, which was spinning in circles. How did everything get to be so crazy? Why couldn't he go back in time and not punch that kid in the nose? Maybe he wouldn't be lying here right now. Or maybe he would have succeeded with killing himself and he would be with his mother. He hated this life and he wanted out! Nothing had gone right since the day he said good-bye to his mother.

That day remained agonizingly clear to him. He remembered seeing his mother lying on the hospital bed, her petite, frail body only a fragment of what it used to be. Her hair was soaked with sweat, and her face was deathly white. The sight of her burned harshly into his mind. He sat down in the chair next to the bed and was scared to touch her. She struggled to hold up her hand and motioned for him to take it. He reached out and took her limp, moist hand in his and broke down.

"Please don't die, please!" he pleaded tearfully as he laid his head softly on her shoulder, just the way he'd done when he was a small child and needed his mother's comfort. She just smiled and caressed his hair.

"I'll never really be gone," she whispered softly. "I'll always be here in spirit, watching over you. I love you, Christopher."

"I love you too," he sobbed, and softly kissed her forehead. He took one last look at her before he left the room, realizing that it would be the last time he saw his mother alive.

Feeling helpless and angry, he walked down the hallway of the hospital, ignoring his father's pleas to talk to him. He bolted out the front doors, jumped on his skateboard, and flew down the sidewalk, tears streaming down his face. He vowed from then on to shut the whole world out. That way he would never be hurt again.

Chris closed his eyes. The memories of that day were so vivid. He took a deep breath and exhaled slowly. No longer able to fight the effects of the drug, he fell into a deep slumber.

# Chapter 21

"Christopher? Christopher, wake up." Chris opened his eyes and focused in on Ms. Holtz standing over him, shaking him gently. "Now that you're calmer, why don't you come with me?"

"Where are we going?" he asked sleepily. He sat up and stretched his arms above his head. The bleeding had stopped, but his knuckles were bruised and swollen. He wiggled his fingers, which sent shooting pain through his whole hand. Ms. Holtz saw the bloody pillowcase lying on the bed and took a look at his hand.

"It looks like you may have broken it," she said, gently inspecting the damage. "Dr. Letzo will be coming back soon, and we'll have him take a look at it." She walked toward the door, motioning for Chris to follow her. "Come on."

He was still a little dizzy but otherwise felt much better. He followed her down the hall and through the living room. The house was quiet except for their footsteps on the hardwood floor. He looked through the front window and could see it was still light outside, but he wasn't sure what day it was. For all he knew, he could have been asleep for a week.

"What day is it?" he asked, still a little dazed from the medication.

"It's still Friday," she laughed, as they entered the dining room. There was a plate of food on the table with fried chicken, mashed potatoes, and corn. It looked wonderful, and he was starving. "Sit down, Chris, and have some dinner." She pulled out a chair and sat down across the table from him.

"What time is it?" Chris asked through bites of chicken. That shot had really knocked him out, and he was still trying to figure out how long he'd been asleep.

"It's about 6:30 in the evening. I wanted you to sleep a long time so you would be in a better frame of mind to talk." It was like he was talking to a totally different person than this morning. The tough drill sergeant act had vanished into a gentle, sympathetic friend.

Chris remembered that morning and was now embarrassed at the way he'd behaved. It was like he was watching himself from the outside. He knew he was out of control, but he was powerless to stop it.

"Chris, do you think you need help with your drug problem?" she asked bluntly, deciding to tackle him head on.

The question took Chris by surprise. No one had ever asked him what he thought, or how he felt about all of this. They'd just told him this was what he was going to do and slammed the door. Although he was wondering that very same thing, his ignorance got the best of him.

"I think I could quit on my own if I really wanted to. I don't need anyone's help," he answered positively, but then he wondered just who he was trying to kid. He had finally realized that morning just how important the drugs were to him.

"Do you mean you don't want to quit?" She wasn't particularly surprised by his response. She'd gotten this tough guy act plenty of times in the past. But she was a little disappointed that she hadn't gotten through to him yet.

"I haven't decided. But when I do, you'll be the first to know," he smirked sarcastically. He wasn't about to let her control the conversation by manipulating him into saying what she wanted to hear. Besides, acknowledging he had a problem and needed help would be like handing the remote control over to her, letting her push whatever buttons she desired.

"Well, I'll ask you again in a few days. But if you have no intention of quitting, then I'm not going to waste my time and your father's money."

"What do mean? I can just leave?" Chris was getting more confused as the conversation progressed.

"Not exactly. You'll be taken in front of the judge, and he will decide what to do with you." She looked him straight in the eye, wondering if he'd call her bluff.

"I don't believe you," he snorted irritably.

"Believe what you want. I'm only trying to help. But hey, if you don't need me, then there's no use sitting here any longer," she sighed, shaking her head.

She stood up and briskly walked away, leaving him questioning everything. Was she really telling the truth that he'd have to face the judge? Or was it another one of her conniving tricks? He felt like she was skillfully baiting the hook, waiting for him to bite.

By the time Chris finished his chicken, Dr. Letzo had arrived to examine his hand. Luckily it wasn't broken but was just badly bruised. He bandaged it up and gave Chris some aspirin for the pain. Chris argued that he would need something stronger, but the doctor would not accommodate him.

"Chris, I'd like you to try to get through tomorrow without the help of pills. The pills are only meant to be a crutch to help you through the first forty-eight hours. After that, it's up to you to fight the addiction," Dr. Letzo explained. "I know it will be tough, but I am confident that you can do it."

Chris shook his head in disgust and silently left the office. He knew it was no use to argue his point, because no one was listening. Lost in despair, he went back to his room. He felt alone and barricaded behind the brick wall he had built for himself.

"Hey, Chris," Keith exclaimed excitedly as he came through the bedroom door and plopped down on his bed. "You missed a killer movie!"

"Oh yeah, what'd you see?" Chris asked, covering up his emotions and putting back on the tough guy act.

"Transformers. It was awesome! Sorry you had to spend the day in the tank. That really sucks," he said sympathetically.

"The tank?" Chris laughed. "Is that what you call that prison cell I was in?"

"Yeah, I've done some time in there myself. But you'll soon find out that it's better to just play things their way. You tell them what they want to hear and soon you'll be out of this place."

"You sound like an expert."

"Well, let's just say this isn't the first rehab center I've been in," he boasted.

"How many have you been in?"

"This is my third, and it's been the most fun. They all have this high and mighty attitude that they can make your life better. Well, my life is better when I'm on the drugs. Then I don't have to deal with life, and it drives my old man crazy. What's better than that?"

Chris was taken back by Keith's attitude. When Chris first met him, he talked like he knew that the drugs were bad for him and that he was going to change his life. Now Chris could see that it was all an act.

"You mean you don't plan on staying clean when you leave here?"

"Are you kidding? I couldn't handle things without the meth. It's the one thing I can do that my dad has no control over. He could actually care less if I do drugs or not. It's his reputation he's worried about. The rehabs are just a way to get rid of me for a while. I'll be eighteen in six months, and my father's already told me I'm not his problem after that." There was a slight distress in his voice as he spoke, and Chris could hear the hurt child in him crying out. "Do you know the only time he's come to see me in the last seventy-two days was when Ms. Holtz personally called him to come for a visit?" He looked down at the floor, suddenly realizing he was letting his emotions show. "I don't really care. I think I hate him just as much as he hates me!"

Chris was silent. He didn't know what to say. How could a father care more about his reputation than his own son? "Aren't you worried that the meth might finally kill you some day?"

"Nah, I know how much I can take and when I should stop. Hey, maybe when you get out of here we can hook up. I've got some friends you might want to meet. They can set you up with anything you want."

"Yeah, maybe," Chris said, astonished at what Keith was implying.

Chris pulled the covers up and rolled over to face the wall, hoping to indicate to Keith that he was tired and wanted to go to sleep. He didn't want to talk about drugs or what the future might hold for him. The truth was that he was uncertain about a lot of things lately. He'd changed so much in the last three months that he hardly recognized himself. Taking drugs, the alcohol, the smoking, the uncontrollable outbursts of rage— that wasn't him at all. In fact, he wasn't sure who he was anymore.

Keith turned off his lamp, and before long Chris could hear a slight snore coming from across the room. Chris, however, tossed and turned before finally getting up and going downstairs for a glass of water.

It was after eleven and the house was completely quiet. Just to make sure he wouldn't wake anyone up, Chris went to the kitchen without turning on any lights. The full moon helped light the house just enough so that he could see where he was going. He stood at the kitchen sink and looked out the window at the beautiful garden in the back yard. The light of the moon made the entire garden glow. The flowers reminded him of his mother's flower garden. Her flower garden was the envy of the neighborhood. She would say, "Flowers are a lot like children. They both need a lot of love and attention so they can grow into something beautiful." He chuckled as he thought about how disappointed she must be in him right now.

He grabbed a piece of leftover chicken from the refrigerator and started back upstairs. He turned the corner and smacked into someone who let out a high-pitched squeal, making him drop his chicken on the floor.

"Amanda, is that you?" he asked, staring at her in the soft moonlight. She was wearing flannel pajamas and had fuzzy slippers on her feet.

"Yes, you scared me to death. What are you doing sneaking around down here?" she panted breathlessly.

"I was getting a drink of water and some leftover chicken." He bent over and picked the chicken up off the floor. "What are you doing?"

"I couldn't sleep, and I love the full moon, so I thought I would come into the living room to get a better view. I wasn't expecting to run into someone this late at night."

"The moon is pretty incredible tonight. Do you think we could sneak out to the porch to get a better look?" he said, smiling. He threw the chicken in the trash and walked toward the front door.

"I don't think that would be a good idea," she said hesitantly but followed him anyway.

Chris opened the door a crack and paused, looking around the room. "I don't hear any alarms going off," he teased as he stepped out onto the porch. "Come on, live a little." He reached back through the doorway and took her by the hand. She gave him a smile and reluctantly let him pull her out onto the porch.

The moon was completely full and beautiful. They both sat down on the porch step and looked up at the night sky. "It reminds me of being up in the mountains," Chris said, remembering sitting around the campfire with his family, gazing up at the stars and moon.

"I love the nighttime," Amanda sighed as she tilted her head back to look into the sky. "It's so peaceful and beautiful. It's like you're the only one on earth." Chris wasn't watching the sky, he was watching her. With her radiant red hair and her green eyes, she was even more beautiful by moonlight. She sensed his stare and turned to look right into his charming green eyes. They were face to face, both too nervous to move and too afraid to speak. Chris shot her a warm smile to break the awkwardness between them. When he saw the corners of her mouth start to turn up, he knew she felt the same.

"Do you live around here?" he asked, breaking eye contact. He could feel the sweat in the palms of his hands, and quickly ran them down his pajama pants to dry them.

"I'm from Arkansas. Do you know where that is?"

"That explains the accent," he laughed. "I live in Fairview. It's about an hour drive from here. What grade are you in?"

"I'm going into tenth grade this year. What grade are you in?"

"I'm going into tenth grade too. But I'm one of the oldest in my class. I'm going to be sixteen on August 31. Then I can get a job and a car and get out of my house," he said bluntly.

This took Amanda by surprise. "What's wrong with your house?" she asked gently.

"My dad for one. He hates me! The only reason he sent me here was to get me out of the way! He's never wanted me around, and as soon as I get out of here, I'm leaving!" Chris could sense Amanda's apprehension and shot her a smile. "Sorry, I didn't mean to lay all that on you. My dad just makes me so mad sometimes."

"What about your mom? Do you get along with her?"

"She . . . died, four months ago," he said softly, looking down at the ground.

"Oh, I'm so sorry! I didn't know." There was an awkward silence between them. Chris stared at the ground, kicking himself for even bringing it up. The last thing he wanted was to be a sympathy case. Chris took two deep breaths and looked up at Amanda who had been quietly watching him.

The wind had come up and was blowing her long, silky, red hair in her face. She shivered as she tried to keep her hair from blowing in her eyes. Chris hadn't noticed until then how cold it had become. A few clouds had gathered in the starry night sky and the treetops were dancing in the wind. Chris hated to end this night, but he could see the goose bumps rising on both of her arms.

"I guess we better get back inside before somebody figures out were missing and sends the guard dogs after us," he said, smiling. He stood up and offered his hand to help her up off the stair. She gladly took his hand

and stood up, coming face to face with him once more. He felt as if a team of butterflies were playing football inside his stomach. "Thanks for listening to me ramble on," he said, sill holding her hand.

"Any time," she said, smiling warmly. He let go of her hand and held the door open for her. "Good night, Christopher."

"Good night, Amanda."

Chris went back upstairs. He closed the door softly and went to bed with a smile on his face. He had never felt this way about a girl before. He always thought girls were too loud and giggly. But Amanda was different from all the other girls he'd known. She was down to earth, smart, and understanding. Maybe staying here for fifty eight more days wouldn't be such a bad thing after all.

# Chapter 22

Christopher, time to get up," someone said in a loud, obnoxious voice.

Chris pulled the covers up over his head. "Leave me alone!" he grunted coarsely. He wanted to stay in bed all day, regardless of the stupid agenda. He could care less about breakfast, and he wasn't about to do any chores with the throbbing headache he had. He knew if he got out of bed it would only get worse, and there would be no pills to help him through the day.

He drifted off to sleep once again, into a place without counselors, without rules, and without Ms. Holtz. Suddenly he felt his soft, warm blanket being yanked from his bed, leaving him in nothing but his pajama pants. He abruptly sat up, ready to do to battle, when he was cruelly greeted with a bucket of cold water over his head. It gushed down over him, drenching his entire body and soaking the bed.

He jumped up from the saturated bed sheets, ready to fight. "What do you think you're doing?" he bellowed furiously. Standing in front of him, with a satisfied grin, was none other than Ms. Holtz. Dumbfounded and breathless from the icy bath, he gave her a blank stare.

"Since you obviously don't care about the agenda, let me remind you again. Breakfast is at 8 a.m. sharp," she said, scowling.

Chris stood motionless as goose bumps rose on his cold, wet skin, water dripping from his extremities. "I know, but I . . ."

"No buts about it, Christopher!" she interrupted angrily. "We went over this yesterday. So, starting tomorrow morning you will be placed on a.m. kitchen duty for one week. You will report to the kitchen every morning at 6:30 a.m., where you will help prepare and serve the food."

"Serve the food? I'm not . . ."

"If you are even one minute late, your sentence will be carried out another day. Do I make myself clear?" She was pacing back and forth like a military sergeant.

"That's not fair!" Chris protested.

"Whoever said that life was fair?" Ms. Holtz replied teasingly. "Now get your bed stripped down and take a shower. I want to see you in my office in one hour."

"I hate this place!" Chris screamed as Ms. Holtz closed the door behind her.

With fire raging from within, Chris lost control, swinging at the bedside lamp and knocking it to the floor with a loud crash. He stripped the bed down, just like she had demanded, but threw all of the sheets out the window. Seeing the folder still lying on the floor where he'd left it, he picked it up, took out the pages, and fiercely ripped each one into tiny shreds before flinging it across the room. "This is what I think of your program, Ms. Holtz!" Chris shouted.

The door opened, and Chris threw down the folder, ready to defend his actions. Keith walked in, saw the paper strung across the room, and began to laugh hysterically. "Having a bad day, are we?" He folded his arms and cocked an eyebrow at Chris.

Chris pointed his finger at him, infuriated at the whole world. "Don't start with me, man," he bit back harshly.

Keith just smiled. Being in his shoes many times before, he knew exactly how Chris felt. He held up both hands in defense. "Hey, if you want to redecorate your side of the room, be my guest. But leave my side alone."

He turned and left as quickly as he'd come, leaving Chris alone, wet, and angry.

Chris drenched his frustrations in a hot shower, letting the water burn deep into his back. The refreshing water felt good against his sore, achy muscles and somewhat rejuvenated his spirits. He could feel his knees start to shake and his head start to spin. He desperately wanted a pill to take away his tormenting symptoms, but he recalled what the doctor had said and tried to push the cravings aside. He realized he was on his own now.

The water soon turned cold, forcing him from his peaceful sanctuary to face the judgmental world once again. He slowly got dressed, reluctant to visit the office of the one person he despised the most. He was absolutely positive the only purpose Ms. Holtz had in life was to make his miserable. She didn't understand anything, and she didn't understand what he was going through. He wondered why reading a couple of text books and taking a few tests made a person an expert on drug abuse. He could feel the tension tighten at the thought of her sitting in her chair all high and mighty, preaching about something she'd never had to experience firsthand. Nevertheless, if he didn't show up, he knew she would hunt him down, so it was best to just get it over with.

As he made his way to the kitchen, he could feel the anxiety building inside of him. It was like a ticking time bomb, with no indication of when or where it would blow. He entered the kitchen, surprised to see two boys about his age still doing the morning dishes.

Chris walked past them, and they started to giggle. Ignoring their odd behavior, Chris pulled out a muffin from the bread box and started to eat. The boys continued to chuckle and whisper amongst themselves until Chris could take it no longer. "What is your problem?" he snarled.

One of the boys looked over at him and pointed out the window. "Are those your bed sheets sitting on the front lawn?" he laughed.

"Yeah, so what?"

"Well, if I'd wet *my* bed, I sure wouldn't have thrown my sheets out the window for the whole world to see." The two boys innocently started laughing uncontrollably, which ignited the bomb inside of Chris.

He angrily threw his muffin onto the floor and tackled the boy to the ground, throwing punches into his stomach and face. The other boy jumped on Chris's back and pulled him off, pinning his arms behind him. He held Chris tightly, giving the advantage back to the other boy, who gave Chris a crushing blow to his nose, sending blood gushing to the floor.

Before they could get in another hit, a male counselor came through the door to break up the fight. The boy loosened his grip and Chris pulled free, pushing the counselor out of the way as he bolted from the kitchen and ran up the stairs.

He grabbed some tissue and held it tightly on his nose, pacing back and forth, enraged with anger. He had to find a way out of this place. There had to be some way past the fence, past the security guard, and past

Ms. Holtz's intimidating stare. He would risk anything to get out.

There was a knock at the door, and Ms. Holtz came into the room. "I want to see you in my office!" she demanded, pointing her finger at the door for him to leave. Chris rolled his eyes but did as she commanded.

He sat down in the chair next to her desk, avoiding her accusing eyes. "I've got one side of the story. Do you want to tell me yours?"

"What can I say? No matter what I tell you it won't be good enough, so just give me my punishment and I'll leave," Chris snapped impatiently.

"You are going to be put on restriction, but you need to stop playing hardball with me!" She sat on the edge of her chair, staring at Chris with worry and frustration, wondering how to break through his barriers.

Chris rolled his eyes again and looked the other direction as she continued her interrogation. "Christopher, how did it feel to lose total control? Can't you step back from yourself long enough to see what the drugs have done to you? The drugs are uncaring and unforgiving. They will consume you entirely, destroying every shred of the person you used to be."

Chris continued to stare off in the other direction, unwilling to surrender to his own crying child inside. "Christopher, will you try something for me?" Ms. Holtz asked.

"What?" Chris grunted.

"I want you to close your eyes for a minute."

"What for?"

"Please, just for once, do something I ask."

"Fine," Chris sighed and reluctantly closed his eyes.

"I want you to recall a time in your life when you were the happiest. It can be a specific day, month, or a whole year." She paused for a moment and waited for him to capture the memory. "Do you have it?"

"Yeah," Chris answered, thinking of a time when his mother was well, his father was home more, and their family was happy.

"I want you to concentrate really hard on that particular time. How did you feel about yourself, and how did you feel about your family?"

Chris continued to concentrate on the way things used to be. The love he felt from his family, the security, the peace, and the happiness. It was a time when everything was in harmony.

"Now, I want you to picture yourself in the present. How you feel about life, about your family, and about the drugs. Is there a difference in the way you feel now, versus the way you felt back then? If so, then what was the changing factor in your life? Yeah, life has dealt you a pretty bad hand, but instead of asking for help to deal with it, you turned to drugs, which made a bad situation even worse."

Chris popped open his eyes and glared deeply into hers. "What do you know about turning to drugs? You think just because you have a degree, you know everything?" Chris snorted angrily.

Ms. Holtz sat back in her chair and folded her arms. "On the contrary! It's not my degree that makes me an expert; it was my addiction to cocaine." She watched as his frustrated expression changed to curiosity.

"You were addicted to cocaine?"

"Yes, and it nearly killed me. I was sixteen and I thought I knew it all. I soon found myself doing things I would have never done. I lied, I stole from my family and friends, and I even sold myself. I didn't care about anyone or anything. All that mattered was the drugs."

"Did you go through rehab?" Chris asked, looking into her soft, caring blue eyes.

"Yes, I did. It was similar to this one. After I stopped blaming everyone else for my addiction and realized I needed help, my life changed. It felt liberating to take back my life again. I hadn't realized how much I was allowing the drugs to control me. Then, when I turned twenty-four, I got my master's degree in counseling and opened this place. I wanted to help kids get their lives back on track. So you see Chris, you're not alone in this battle. Everyone here has gone, or is going through exactly what you are now." She spoke with sureness and sincerity.

"Well, I wasn't taking the hard stuff. It was only pain pills, and they don't control me."

"Are you sure about that?"

"Positive!"

# Chapter 23

Chris ran fearfully down the deserted back alley, his legs feeling like cement blocks with each leap he took. His heavy arms were dangling at his sides as he struggled to take another step. His side began to ache, and he knew he could not make it much further. He saw a large, blue, tin dumpster toward the end of the alley and took refuge behind it, squatting down with one hand braced firmly against the dumpster for support. He panted breathlessly, trying hard to keep silent.

It was late and the alley's forbidden darkness seemed to come as a warning to all those who trespassed. Chris felt terror sink deep into his soul, sending an icy chill down his spine. No one was around. No one was there to hear his screams. A small street light about one hundred feet away dismally lit the murky, dark alley. It flickered off and on, making a terribly loud buzzing noise.

Chris sat quietly waiting, hoping he would not be discovered by the intimidating threat that was following him. He heard a crunch, and then a crack. His heart started beating harder and faster as he listened to the sound of footsteps coming closer. Sweat dripped from his forehead and he tightly closed his eyes, praying they would walk right by him. He held his breath, hearing his heartbeat echoing inside his head.

Suddenly, a large muscular arm reached behind his safe haven, and with a firm grip roughly caught him by the collar of his shirt. Chris went wild, punching, kicking, and screaming for help. But the strength of three overpowered him, violently knocking him to the ground and leaving him gasping for air. He stared down at the pavement, motionless, listening to them mock him, laughing at his inability to get up after the crushing blow to his stomach.

Chris stayed on his knees, helplessly accepting his defeat. But the three remorseless boys would not accept his surrender and pulled him to his feet to confront his attackers. Feeling the sharp pain as it ran through his abdomen, he locked his knees so he could stay standing. He raised his weary head and looked straight into the cold, hate-filled eyes of Jeff's brother.

Chris opened his eyes in a panic and looked into the darkness of his bedroom. Breathing heavily, he sat up on the edge of the bed. He ran his trembling hands over his sweat-soaked face, the images of the nightmare still taunting him. It was still all too real for him, the pain still fresh in his memory and his fear unwavering. The attack had left more than just a scar across his forehead. They'd stripped him of his self-confidence, his courage, and his dignity, leaving nothing but an empty shell. He could no longer go anywhere by himself without horrifying images of the attack creeping into his mind. So even if they were locked away, they had still won.

Unwilling to subject himself to the ridicule of the darkness any longer, Chris got out of bed and slid on his blue jeans. He glanced over at Keith, who was sleeping soundly, and decided to take a walk to clear his head. He could feel his knees beginning to shake as he made his way down the spiral staircase. He was angry and agitated. He wanted freedom from his thoughts and freedom from this miserable situation he'd so helplessly been forced into.

Chris plopped down in one of the chairs at the dining room table. He could feel the secluded darkness closing in on him. He yearned for the pain pills to help him escape from the world around him. Without them, he felt vulnerable and weak, surrendering to his worst fears and grim reality.

His cravings intensified, urging him to find something that would take away the jitters. He walked down the hall to the doctor's office and tried the doorknob. "Of course it's locked, you idiot," Chris whispered irritably. He went to the kitchen in search of something he could use to pick the lock. After rummaging through three drawers, he finally found a large paper clip and decided it would have to work.

Chris straightened the paper clip and made an angle close to the end of it. He inserted it into the keyhole and pressed up, hoping to release the mechanism inside. When it didn't budge, he tried again and again, his hands trembling and sweat running down the sides of his face. He reached up with one hand and wiped his forehead, determination egging him on. He had to get to those pills! There was no other way to eliminate the agonizing symptoms.

Suddenly there was a click, and the doorknob turned. He carefully and quietly opened the door and stepped inside, feeling a little like he was betraying a friend. He left the lights off and used the little bit of light coming from the outside to see his way over to the medicine cabinet. He reached up and tugged open the glass door, revealing an assortment of different drugs.

He checked through them until he came to the one bottle that contained the small green pills. He picked up the container and held it gently in his hand, remembering what Dr. Letzo had said. They were meant only to be a crutch for the first forty-eight hours. After that, it was up to him to fight the addiction.

As Chris stood there, looking down at inevitable relief, he was divided in two. As badly as he wanted those pills, he couldn't help but wonder if Ms. Holtz was right after all. The thought of putting the bottle back and walking away was like trying to put out a burning building. The craving blazed inside him, finally taking over his better judgment. He stuffed the bottle into his pocket and shamefully left the office.

Chris was up at 6:30 a.m. and helping to prepare breakfast. He woke easily due to the fact that he hadn't slept most of the night. Between the guilt from stealing the pills and the frightening images dancing around in his mind, there was not much room left for sleep.

When he returned to his bedroom the night before, he'd felt so ashamed that he couldn't bring himself to take a pill. He placed the bottle safely under his mattress and had lain in the dark for hours, wondering how he'd become the monster everyone said he was. He could feel the tremendous thumping of his heart and the constant hunger for relief as he aggressively fought back the demons that were lurking inside of him.

As Chris ate his breakfast, his thoughts returned to the container of pills and the alluring effect they seemed to have over him. He realized how easy it would be to just pop off the cap and take one, but he'd been restrained by his own personal struggle between right and wrong. Even though he'd taken his mother's pills and had bought drugs from Levi, something felt very different this time.

"Can I have everyone's attention please?" Ms. Holtz announced as she walked into the dining room, followed by Dr. Letzo. Her voice was firm and direct as she spoke. "Dr. Letzo is missing some pills from his office this morning. I would like to give that person the opportunity to come clean and return the bottle. I will give you one hour to come see me; otherwise we will start searching rooms. Until that time, all of you will remain confined to your bedrooms." She shot Chris a look of disappointment, and he wondered if she already knew.

Everyone slowly rose from the table and walked silently back to their rooms. Chris sat down on the edge of his bed, wishing he'd never taken the bottle of pills. He lay back on his bed and stared at the ceiling, wondering what fate had in store for him. Keith flipped through the pages of his magazine, sensing Chris wasn't in the mood for conversation.

Chris watched the clock beside the bed as each number changed, creeping closer to the one-hour mark. He closed his eyes, thinking about the past three months. Things had gotten out of control. He never meant to keep taking the pills; he just wanted sanctuary from his pain and from his thoughts. But it was now evident that he couldn't quit on his own. He had handed the control over a long time ago, permitting the drugs to lead him down a destructive path of anger and despair.

He looked over at the clock again as it changed. With only five minutes to spare, Chris climbed off the bed, knelt down on the floor, and retrieved the bottle from beneath his mattress. He sat on the floor with his knees up, holding the bottle in his hands and feeling utterly disgusted with himself.

"Oh man! You're the one who took the bottle of pills?" Keith exclaimed, seeing Chris holding the bottle.

"Yeah," Chris said, sighing.

"What are you going to do now?"

"I guess take it back and fess up," Chris said remorsefully as he stood up from the floor. He was feeling a little shaky, but knew it wasn't just from the withdrawals. He was mortified to face Ms. Holtz.

Keith jumped off his bed and stood by the window. "You know, we could take the bottle and chuck it out the window. No one could prove it was you who took it."

"No, I did it, and I should confess."

"Why? You don't owe this place anything." Keith stated in disbelief.

"I know, but it's the right thing to do," Chris said sorrowfully as he opened the bedroom door.

"All right, but don't blame me if you're on kitchen duty for next two months."

As Chris made his way downstairs, he could feel his knees trying to buckle underneath him. The house was quiet as he walked down the short hallway to Ms. Holtz's office. Her door was already open and she was sitting at her desk. Chris reached out his trembling hand and knocked on the door to announce his arrival.

Ms. Holtz looked up, not really surprised to see him standing there. "Come in Christopher," she said softly.

Chris walked over and sat down in one of the chairs next to the desk. He reached over and placed the bottle of pills in front of her. "They are all there. You can count them if you like," he said quietly, trying to avoid looking into her eyes. "Before you say anything, would you ask me your question again?" Chris kept his eyes on the floor, waiting for her to speak and anxiously wondering if it was too late for him.

Ms. Holtz took the bottle in her hand and leaned up in her chair. "Do you think you need help with your drug problem, Christopher?"

Chris could hear the empathy in her voice, which put his mind at ease. "I really wanted to believe I didn't have a drug problem, and I wanted everyone else to believe that I was in control of it. But last night I wasn't in control. In fact, I don't think I've had much control over my life since I started taking the drugs. All I could think about was getting to those pills, no matter what the consequences were. And then when I got back to my room, I couldn't take one. I was angry and disappointed in myself knowing I'd let the drug win. For the first time, I was really scared, wondering if I'd ever be able live a normal life without the drugs." Chris looked up into her understanding eyes and for once gave her an honest answer. "Yes, I do need help to quit taking drugs," he said, feeling a sense of redemption come over him.

They talked for over an hour about the past and about the future. Chris was finally able to open up and talk about the attack, his father, and even his mother and the devastating emptiness that he felt. He was able to talk about everything—except Katie. When she asked him how his drug abuse had affected Katie, he shut down and crawled back behind his barrier.

"I think that's enough for today," Ms. Holtz said, noticing his reaction. "I want to see you every day for counseling. Because you came to me with the pills, I'll limit your punishment to five days, and you'll continue to work in the kitchen for the next week."

Chris nodded his head in agreement, realizing it could have been much worse. He walked over to the door and turned around. "Thank you Ms. Holtz," he said sincerely.

"You should be proud of yourself, Christopher."

"Proud? I'm disgusted and ashamed, not proud," Chris grunted.

"You had the courage to stand up and take responsibility for your actions. You openly admitted that you need help and that you're willing to try and make the program work. That in itself is a huge accomplishment." She was grinning from ear to ear, like a proud coach that had just led her team to victory.

"I guess so," Chris said, still not totally convinced.

"Well, just remember, Rome wasn't built in a day. It even took the Lord six days to create the world. You've only been here four."

# Chapter 24

All the way upstairs Chris could smell the appetizing scent of bacon frying. It reminded him of Saturday mornings with his mother. When he was younger, she would put the bacon in the shape of a smiley face on top of his pancakes with the eggs as the eyes. She was always doing crazy things like that just to make him smile. Like the time she helped him build a skate ramp in the driveway. Even though he couldn't talk her into trying it out, she stayed and cheered him on as he tried new moves on his skateboard. He cherished those memories of her and was not about to let his father try and replace them.

Two weeks had gone by quickly. He was, for the most part, over the withdrawal symptoms—or so Dr. Quack said. He could never tell when the doctor was being serious and when he was joking around. He tried much too hard to fit in with the younger crowd, which was irritating to Chris. He seemed to know his stuff when it came to medicine, though, and Chris was feeling much better now.

Chris spent the last week setting goals, talking to counselors, and going to group therapy, although he hadn't sat in the sharing chair again since his arrival. He wasn't ready to share everything about himself just yet. He was determined to make the program work, so he was cooperating with everything they wanted him to do.

He moved up to the second level and could now go outside with the other kids, but nagging at him was the thought of seeing his father again. The fear and anxiety had been building all week, like a locomotive building up steam. In his counseling sessions, he was learning how to deal with his anger and how to disperse it in a good way; however, he was afraid he hadn't reached a point where he could control it, and his father was coming to visit.

He went downstairs to the dining room for breakfast, thankful to finally be off kitchen duty. Being Saturday, there would be no group therapy, although Chris would much rather sit in the sharing chair than deal with his father.

Across the table sat Amanda, who gave him a bright smile when he came into the room. They'd talked several times during the last few weeks and had become good friends. Next to him sat Keith, scarfing down his eggs and bacon. Chris wondered how a person could eat so much and stay so thin. Keith had become his new best friend. He could tell him anything without fear of being judged. Keith accepted him for who he was—a kid who just wanted to fit in. Keith confided in him about his father, his mother, and his girlfriend, whom he planned on marrying as soon as he turned eighteen.

Chris likewise confided in Keith about his father, but it took Chris by surprise when Keith told him how lucky he was to have a father who wanted a second chance to make things right. Chris, however, didn't feel lucky. He still harbored feelings of anger and resentment toward his father.

After breakfast, everyone went outside for some free time until the visitors arrived. Chris was sitting alone on the bench, his head in his hands, contemplating what the visit would bring. Would his father want him to talk about the drugs? About Katie? About mom? He wasn't ready to confront any of those issues.

"Think fast," Keith said, and threw the basketball at Chris. Luckily he looked up just in time to catch the basketball with his hands instead of his face. Keith sat down on the bench next to him, noticing the stressed look on his face. "Okay, what's up? Did Amanda finally realize what a loser you really are?" he said, laughing.

"Huh, you wish!" Chris said, smiling.

"Okay then, spill it."

Chris knew Keith wouldn't give up without an explanation. "My dad's coming for a visit. I just don't think I can deal with him right now."

"Why, does he make you feel like a horse's butt because you made some poor choices in your life?"

"No."

"Does he tell you you're always in the way, or treat you like you're not even there?"

"No, it's not like that. He just . . ."

"Oh, wait. I know. When nobody's watching he backhands you up side the head so hard it makes your ears ring," Keith said with animosity in his voice. Chris knew Keith was talking about his own father and decided he'd better back off.

"Sorry," Chris said sympathetically. "You're right. My father doesn't do any of that stuff. So why do I feel the way I do about him?"

"Adjustment is hard to get used to. Put your dad to the test and see if he's for real."

Chris gave him a confused look. "Okay, now you're scaring me. You sounded just like Ms. Holtz." Both of them laughed, knowing it was very true.

"What I mean is, ask your dad to do something he normally wouldn't have done in a million years. If he does it, you know he's for real. If he doesn't, well then, I guess you know where you stand."

"Have you done this with your dad?"

"Let's just say I know where I fall on his list of priorities!" He grabbed the basketball out of Chris's hands and stood up. "Looks like it's testing time," he said, smirking and pointing to the cars pulling through the gate.

"Is your dad coming?"

"Nah, he's having dinner with the mayor tonight. You know— *important* stuff." Chris could see the hurt in Keith's eyes, and he knew a visit from his father would mean more to Keith than he was letting on. "Let me know how it goes," Keith rattled as he ran off to the basketball court.

Chris watched as two cars pulled into the driveway and parked. Two girls ran over to the cars and were greeted with hugs and kisses. Chris kept his eyes on the gate, anxiously wondering if his father would even show up. Aside from his hard-core attitude, Chris really did want him to come, even if it was awkward.

A minivan pulled in and a boy about his age went to greet his overly happy parents. Chris laughed as he watched them. The way they were acting, you'd think they'd just discovered their long lost son instead of visiting their son, the drug addict.

Finally, a familiar truck pulled through the gate and headed toward

174

the house. Chris could feel his stomach churn. He swallowed hard, trying to keep down his bacon and eggs. When he stood up from the bench, his legs were like cement bricks. He wanted to move them, but they wouldn't budge. *What's the matter with me? It's only my dad*, he thought, trying to muster up some courage to move.

"Everything okay?" Ms. Holtz asked, suddenly standing beside him. He hadn't even noticed her. His mind was set on one thing and one thing only. "It's all right to be nervous, Chris. The first visit is always the hardest."

"I know. It's just . . . well, it wasn't a real good scene the last time I saw him. I guess that's probably why I'm so nervous," Chris said uneasily.

"Take it slow. Remember, one hour at a time, one day at a time. You can do this—I know you can. I've seen great improvement from you in the last week. You have a lot to be proud of, so go share your accomplishments with your father."

She patted him on the back as if she were sending him back into a baseball game. Bases are loaded, it's the bottom of the ninth, score is tied and you're up to bat. Now go in there and save the game! Little does she know when the going gets tough, he'd rather sit on the bench.

Larry was standing on the porch looking around when he saw Chris coming his way. He watched him, trying to anticipate his mood and fearful that Chris really meant what he said the last time they spoke. "Hi," Larry said, thinking how cheesy it sounded.

"Hi," Chris replied, keeping his eyes on the ground. "We can go inside to talk or we can go out back. They have some tables and chairs." Chris was antsy and swayed back and forth with his hands stuck in the pockets of his pants.

"It doesn't matter to me. You lead the way and I'll follow," Larry said, smiling. He was trying to stay positive and upbeat.

Chris turned to see if Ms. Holtz would come over and make the decision for him, but she was talking to another family who just pulled up. Chris led his father to the back yard where there were several chairs sitting under huge shade trees. They found a nice shady spot and sat down. Chris pulled his hands out of his pockets and silently chewed on a fingernail, one knee nervously bouncing up and down.

"This is a really nice place. Their brochure doesn't do it justice." Larry watched Chris's every move, noticing how nervous he was and feeling much the same. He wanted the visit to go well, but he felt like he was walking on cracked ice. At any minute it could give way, sending him plunging into the icy cold water.

"Yeah, it's pretty nice here."

"How are things going for you?"

"Fine, I guess," Chris muttered, avoiding eye contact.

"Is counseling going all right?"

"Yeah," Chris said, shrugging his shoulders. He didn't know why he felt so agitated being around his father. He knew he was where he needed to be, but at the same time, his father was the one who put him there without asking him how he felt about it. So he was caught somewhere in between "I hate you for it" and "I thank you for it." The silent pauses were almost unbearable for both of them. Chris was relieved when he noticed Ms. Holtz coming their way.

"Mr. Porter, how are you?" she asked holding out her hand to shake his.

"I'm fine, thank you," he said, standing to greet her.

"Is Christopher telling you about the program and how it's going?" she said, smiling at Chris who had finally stopped biting his nail.

"Well, actually, he's been rather quiet," Larry said with disappointment.

Ms. Holtz took a moment to go over a few details about Chris's progress over the last two weeks.

"He had a rough start, but he's made wonderful progress in the last week. He's advanced to level two and has set some really positive goals for himself. He gets along great with the other kids and has really come a long way," she said, smiling proudly. She then excused herself so Larry and Chris could talk in private.

"Chris, that's fantastic! I'm so proud of you!" Larry said with enthusiasm. "You'll be back home before you know it."

"And then what? Is it back to life as usual?" Chris asked harshly.

"No, things will be better. You'll be better." As soon as he said it he realized it came out all wrong.

"So everything's my fault?" Chris said angrily

"I didn't mean it like that. I just meant . . ."

"I know what you meant! You don't need to explain everything to me!"

"Come on, Chris! I'm really trying here. Cut me some slack, okay?" Larry asked with frustration.

"Sorry," Chris said in a calmer voice. He took a deep breath. "I'm trying too."

"I know you are. We'll take things slow. Jody and Katie can't wait to see you. Katie's been drawing you pictures and Jody's been writing you nearly every day."

"I know. I've been getting them. I even received one from Grandma Maggie." He had received three letters in the last week alone, telling him how much they missed him. There was a time not so long ago when he was close to both of his sisters, especially Jody. They were really more like twins, only fourteen months apart in age.

"Katie actually wanted me to give you her letter today." He pulled a white envelope out of his pocket. "She made me promise not to read it, so I hope you can figure out all the words," he said, laughing as he held out the letter. Chris just sat there, staring at it as if it were a snake ready to bite him. "What's the matter?" Larry asked, puzzled by Chris's reaction.

Chris reached out and took it from his hand. "Nothing," he said bluntly. It was covered in blue and pink colored hearts with the word love in the middle of each one. His name was written on the front in big bold letters and her name was written on the back. "It's definitely from Katie," he chuckled, and he stuffed it into the pocket of his Levi jeans. They were both silent, looking around the yard at the other families, wishing the tension between them would vanish. Chris hated this feeling and was ready for the visit to be over.

"Bishop Geary wants to come by next week, if that's okay," Larry spoke up, breaking the unbearable silence.

Actually, that's last thing Chris wanted right now, the bishop crying repentance. He felt like everything he said or did was being scrutinized. However, he wanted to try and make things work, so he reluctantly agreed to the visit.

"I want to ask you something," Chris said. He was thinking about what Keith had said about testing his father. He was ready to find out where exactly he stood with Larry. He remembered him talking about an important business trip coming up the third week of July, so Chris decided that would be an excellent time to ask his father to come for a visit. He took a deep breath, remembering the past and all the times his father had let him down. "I'll be able to have a day out with the family come the third week of July, so I was wondering . . . could you come up and take me somewhere?"

"Oh, well, I have meetings in Oregon all that week . . ."

"I knew it! Just forget it!" Chris snapped.

"Wait a minute, Chris. I wasn't through. What I was going to say was, I'll arrange it so I can fly home on that day and then fly back the next day for the rest of my meetings."

Chris was taken back by his father's generosity. "You mean you would fly back and forth to Oregon? Won't that be really expensive?" Chris could hardly believe what he was hearing. His father would actually leave his business trip for him?

Larry smiled. He noticed the expression on Chris's face and knew he'd made an impression. "Don't worry about it. Just let me know when to be here."

As they walked back to the truck, Chris realized his father had passed the test. He wanted to believe he'd changed but silently wondered if he was just putting on a show for the facility, acting like the caring, involved parent.

"I'll see you on Thursday night then," his father said, starting the engine.

"Thursday night? I thought Saturdays were visiting day?"

"Ms. Holtz invited the whole family to come to family counseling. Didn't she tell you?" Larry asked.

"No! She didn't tell me anything about it!" Chris said, agitated. "I'm not ready to see Katie and Jody yet! She should've checked with me first!"

"Chris, they're your sisters and they miss you. Couldn't you just give them a few minutes?" Larry was getting a little upset himself.

"No! I'm not ready for that!" Chris yelled, making a scene in front of the other parents.

Ms. Holtz heard the commotion and came rushing over. "Is there a problem, Chris?" she asked calmly.

Chris swung around, his face red with anger. He was outraged that she would go behind his back. He felt manipulated and deceived. "Why did you tell my dad he could bring my sisters on Thursday? I don't want to see them!" he snapped.

"Chris, calm down. You're getting upset for no reason," she insisted briskly. "Every other Thursday is family night. That means that this Thursday they *will* be joining you for your counseling." She said it with such clarification that it left no room for discussion.

"I'm not going to some stupid counseling session with my family! It's my drug problem, not my sisters'!" Chris didn't look at his father. He headed for the house and didn't stop running until he made it to his room. He slammed the door and threw himself on the bed, feeling all control slipping from his fingers.

They didn't understand anything. Why couldn't everyone just leave him alone? He couldn't face his sisters after what he'd done. They wouldn't look at him the same. They would judge him for what he'd done. Drawing his fingers through his hair, he sat on the edge of the bed and looked out the window. It was Katie he was really thinking about. She would never forgive him for all the terrible things he'd done. He knew it was Katie he was afraid to see, not Jody. He'd let her down and almost killed her. He would never be able to look at her again without feeling the remorse and shame.

Chris pulled the letter from his pocket and sat it on the nightstand. He was afraid to even open it. He couldn't bear to read what she had to say. He couldn't blame her if she hated him and never wanted to see him again.

There was a knock at the door, but Chris remained silent, hoping they would just go away. A knock and then another knock filled the silent room until he could no longer ignore it and opened the door. It was Ms. Holtz.

Her face showed disappointment as she stood in the doorway. "Do you want to talk about it?" she asked annoyingly.

"No, not right now," Chris replied. His anger was gone, and he couldn't help but feel embarrassed for the way he'd acted. He looked down at the floor.

"I'll give you until dinner, and then I want an explanation." She turned and walked away, leaving Chris to wonder how he was going to tell her he'd almost killed his little sister and that's why he couldn't face her.

Chris stayed in his room most of the afternoon talking to Keith. He explained how he'd put his father to the test and surprisingly, he'd passed. His business trips had always been top priority. He couldn't understand why now he was willing to juggle things around and make it a point to be there for him.

"Well, if you want my opinion, I think he's rearranged his priorities since your mom passed away. Knowing he wasted all those years on work and then losing her. I think he's really sincere," Keith said, as he lay on his bed, throwing the basketball up in the air and catching it as it came down.

Chris nodded, not really wanting to say it out loud. "Well either that, or he really wants to rack up those frequent flyer miles." Keith laughed and chucked the basketball at Chris.

Chris sat for a long time looking at the letter lying on the nightstand. He wondered what she had to say, and if she blamed him for everything. He loved Katie and would never hurt her, but instead of watching her like his father had said, he was passed out from the pain pills.

He lay back on the bed, his head aching from all the questions. Would he ever fully be accepted back into the family after all he'd said and done? Would his sisters forgive him and give him a second chance? Or was all lost?

# Chapter 25

Chris was silent during dinner. Amanda kept smiling at him and tried her best to make him laugh. There was something about her that absolutely fascinated him. She was easy to talk to and fun to be around. He really wanted to talk to her, but Ms. Holtz cornered him right after dinner and led him down the hall to her office.

Chris felt a little antsy as he walked into her office and took a seat. She closed the door and sat down in front of him. "You've come a long way in a short time. I thought we were past these outbursts?" She said it like a teacher putting her pupil in their place.

Chris looked at the yellow and blue squares in the carpet and wished he was a small ant and could hide from her opposing stare. He knew she had a way of looking right down into his soul, knowing the answers even before the questions were asked. It was more than a little irritating at times.

"I don't feel like I'm ready to see my sisters yet," he said uneasily. "I'm ashamed of what I've done and how I've treated everybody over the last few months, especially Katie."

"You mean, because of the accident?"

Chris's head shot up. How did she know? Most likely his father told her what happened at the lake. Realizing there was nowhere to run this time, Chris just nodded his head.

"I haven't pushed the subject because I know how much it's bothered you, but don't you think you would feel better if you talked about it?"

"No!" Chris said abruptly. "I don't want to talk about it, and I don't want to see Katie! Why can't anybody understand that?" He looked into her eyes and saw understanding and compassion.

"All right then, we'll wait. I'll call your dad and tell him not to come on Thursday. But sooner or later it will need to be dealt with." She got up and opened the door for him to leave. "Can I count on you tomorrow in group therapy to take the chair?"

"Possibly," he smiled teasingly.

When he got back to the dining room the table was cleared off. Amanda and another girl were doing the dishes even though it was supposed to be his night. He walked up to the other girl and asked if he could take her place. She happily obliged, handing him the dish towel and leaving the kitchen.

Chris chuckled at Amanda who had a spot of soap on the end of her nose. "What's so funny?" she asked. He took the end of his towel and patted the end of her nose. "Oh," she laughed. "I thought I felt something wet."

"I didn't see your name on the clean-up sheet," Chris asked curiously.

"Yeah, Keith asked me if I would sub for him. I saw Ms. Holtz leading you off to her office. Is everything okay?"

"Just more stupid questions. How did your visit with your mom go?"

She put the stack of plates in the cupboard and paused for a moment. "Fine, I guess. She only flies in every other Saturday. How about you?"

"It was all right. I really don't care if he comes to see me or not," Chris said, shrugging his shoulders to hide the truth. Somewhere inside he really did care but was afraid of getting hurt again. So for now, it would all stay buried.

They finished the dishes and went out back to find a place to talk. It would be lights out before long, and Chris would say good night to her once again. He could sense that something was weighing heavily on her mind. "Okay, what's bugging you?" Chris asked, sitting down in one of the white plastic chairs on the back patio. "Is it your mom?" He watched her expression, wondering if she would open up and talk to him.

Amanda let out a long, heavy sigh. "We just can't seem to get along anymore. She doesn't understand the decisions kids our age are faced with every day. She thinks it's just so simple." She shook her head in despair and looked at the ground.

"Are you talking about drugs?"

"Among other things. My mom and dad split when I was ten. My mom remarried a man that I can't stand. He drinks all the time and treats me like I'm an inconvenience. I tried to live with my dad, but his new live-in girlfriend wouldn't hear of it. I feel so alone in a very dysfunctional family. That's why I turned to drugs," she said sadly.

"I understand right where you're coming from," Chris said, thinking about his own family.

"My mom thought it was my friends and forbade me to see any of them ever again. She isolated me from everyone and everything until I just couldn't take it any more, so I ran away. The cops found me and locked me up." She looked up with tears in her eyes. "Mom told me I was being selfish and was trying to break up her marriage. She told me I was a disgrace to my family. The next day, she bought a plane ticket, and here I am," she said softly, wiping a tear from her eye.

Chris reached over and put his arm around her shoulders, wishing he could ease her pain. "Sometimes adults think they know everything, when they really don't. They think taking away our privileges and friends will make a difference. But I didn't start because of peer pressure." Chris released his arm and sat back in his chair.

"How did you start using?"

Chris put his elbows on his knees and looked down at his hands, contemplating the phrase "start using." It made him sound like a back alley druggy, sitting around a table with bunch of other kids *using* drugs. Nevertheless, he was using, even if he wasn't doing it openly.

"Well, I was jumped at the skate park. They messed me up pretty bad, so the doctor prescribed pain pills. When it came time to quit taking them, I couldn't—or maybe I didn't want to. The truth is that they helped me with more than just the pain. They helped me cope with the attack and my mother's death," Chris said, being honest with himself for the first time.

"I felt the same way. When I was using drugs, it was like I didn't care about anything. No one could hurt me anymore. I was invincible. Or so I thought."

"I guess we'd better go in," Chris sighed, noticing how the darkness seemed to sneak up around them.

He stood up and offered Amanda his hand, and she graciously accepted. She stood up from her chair and came face to face with Chris.

Without much thought, Chris pulled her close and pressed his lips to hers. She wrapped her arms around his neck, and for a moment, both were lost in the comfort of each other's arms and the tenderness of the kiss.

"Excuse me!"

Startled, Chris and Amanda jumped away from each other and turned to find Keith grinning from ear to ear at them. "Ms. Holtz is looking for you, Amanda," he said, laughing.

"Thanks," she said and shot Chris a soft smile before running off to the house.

"You could be in a lot of trouble for that, you know?" Keith smiled as if to give his approval and at the same time issue a warning.

"I know. Is it time to go in?"

"Yeah, like fifteen minutes ago. Amanda will have some explaining to do."

"Is she in trouble?" Chris asked, worried that he'd caused more problems for her.

"I don't know. Ms. Holtz was just a little upset that she couldn't find her. I'm not completely certain about this, but I think she knew you two were together," he teased. "So, are you going to give me all the steamy details, or am I going to have to beat it out of you?"

Chris just smiled. "Let's get in the house before Ms. Holtz comes looking for us too."

Monday morning, after breakfast and chores, they gathered for group therapy to talk about their visits on Saturday. Mostly everyone was excited to share the details of their parental meetings. Everyone, that is, except Chris. He sat quietly in the back corner, silently hoping to be overlooked.

Ms. Holtz knew everything there was to know about him. Well, almost everything. He'd yet to talk about his suicide attempt. When Chris thought about that day and how close he came to losing his little sister because of his stupidity, it tortured his soul. Nonetheless, Chris knew it was a time bomb waiting to go off, and Ms. Holtz held the detonator.

"Christopher, we haven't heard from you since the day you started with us. Would you come sit in the chair and tell us about your visit on Saturday?" Ms. Holtz asked. Actually, the way she said it was more of an order and not an invitation.

Wondering what he was going to say, he apprehensively walked to the front of the room. Sharing his feelings didn't come easy for him, especially in a room full of people. When he sat down in the chair, he felt as if all he needed was a dunce hat and a sign bearing the word "idiot" pinned to his chest. All eyes were on him, and it was almost as bad as having that dream where you show up at school in your underwear. He nervously bit his lower lip and took a deep breath. Amanda was sitting in the front row for moral support, and she shot him one of her award-winning smiles that put his mind at ease.

"Well, I wasn't really looking forward to seeing my dad. I had done some pretty awful stuff and . . . thought maybe he would throw it back in my face. But he didn't. He just wanted to talk about how I was doing here and what he could do to help me." He looked over at Ms. Holtz to see if that was enough.

"How did you feel when you realized your father wasn't judging you on your faults, but instead he wanted to help you get better?" she asked, edging him on.

"Relieved, I guess. I worried all week about what he would say to me. Then when the time came, it took me by surprise. For the first time in a long time I felt his sincerity. He hasn't always been there . . . he's never been there for me. It was always my mom who helped me out and stood by me. Then she passed away."

Why was he saying all this? Where was all this coming from? He wasn't going to tell all of his personal stuff to a bunch of kids he didn't know. But it was like someone had opened the flood gate and it suddenly came pouring out.

"Do you think you can you forgive your father and give him another chance?" Ms. Holtz said softly and compassionately.

Chris could feel the tears welling up in his eyes as he thought about forgiving his father. He realized how much he missed his family and longed to be home. Maybe in the not-so-distant future he could answer that question truthfully, but for now, the scars were still too fresh and the resentment overpowering.

"I'm finished," he blurted out as he stood up from the chair and walked to the back of the room. He kept his eyes on the floor to hide the tears that were threatening to fall. The room was silent as he took his place on the couch next to Keith.

"Thanks for sharing with us, Christopher," Ms. Holtz said, smiling with approval. Then all the kids joined in on the thanks. Before long the spotlight was off of him and onto someone else.

Chris sank down in the couch and let out a huge sigh in relief. Keith bumped his elbow into Chris's side and gave him a mischievous smile. "Just tell them what they want to hear," he whispered.

After lunch and math class, they were released for free time outside. Chris saw Amanda talking to some other girls and decided to find Keith instead. He scanned the yard and the basketball court but didn't see him anywhere. It wasn't like Keith not to take advantage of being outside. Chris ran into the house and up to their room where he found Keith sitting on his bed, head in his hands, crying like a small child.

Chris was stunned. Keith was always like the class clown, putting a smile on for everyone. Chris walked in and sat on his bed across from Keith. "What's up?" he asked gently. Keith looked up with tear-drenched eyes and shook his head.

"I hate my dad! I hate him!" he yelled though clenched teeth. "He won't take me back. He's sending me away!"

"What do you mean? Can he do that?" Chris was shocked and confused.

"I just had a meeting with Ms. Holtz and my dad on a conference call. He said I couldn't be trusted and he didn't want me home. He's sending me to some military school in Vermont. He doesn't care what I think or how I feel!" Keith was crying so hard that Chris could barely make out the words.

"Can't Ms. Holtz do something?"

"It's not up to her. She has no control over it. It's a done deal. I start school in two weeks. That's the end of my girl. She'll never stay with me now."

Chris could see the hurt and disappointment on his face, but there was also something else that Chris couldn't quite put his finger on. It was more than just anger and frustration. It was like someone had taken the last bit of life out of Keith, leaving nothing but empty despair. He tried to comfort his friend and reassure him things would work out, but he really didn't believe it himself.

Finally Chris got him calmed down and talked him into coming outside to the stables for an hour of horseback riding. He hoped maybe the fresh air and the ride would take Keith's mind off things.

There were several instructors waiting at the stables for the eager group of kids. The horses were all beautiful, but one in particular caught Chris's eye. It was a young black stallion. He wasn't quite as pretty as all the others. His silky black coat had some flaws and he stood an inch smaller than the rest. He stood in the back, as if not wanting to be noticed. Chris knew that feeling all too well and immediately knew he was the horse for him.

Chris pulled himself up into the saddle and felt empowered by the enormous strength of the horse. He learned that the horse's name was Thunder and that he was three years old. Chris patted his neck and wondered if Thunder felt as caged as he did. After some instructions on how to ride, Chris was sent off on his own. He immediately caught on and felt comfortable in the saddle, as if he had ridden a horse his whole life.

As he rode Thunder around the ring, Chris felt the pressures of the world slowly start to lift off his shoulders. There was a remarkable sense of control and freedom that seemed to lift his spirits. If they would only open the gate and let him go, he would ride as fast as Thunder would take him, feeling the cool wind against his face and the adrenaline rush from the speed of the horse. But instead, the wood slates kept them both imprisoned.

The whistle blew to bring the horses in. Reluctantly, Chris slid off Thunder and handed the reins to the instructor. He petted Thunder's nose, telling him what a handsome horse he was and that he was just as good as the others. Thunder nodded his head, and Chris was certain he understood.

Amanda found Chris walking back to the house alone and caught up with him. She jabbed him in the back. "Why are you walking so fast?" she asked.

"I was worried about Keith. He disappeared on me."

"Is everything all right?"

"Yeah, I think so. What about you? Did you get into trouble last night?"

"Nah, but she was asking a lot of questions about where I was and what I was doing."

"What'd you tell her?"

"Nothing. I just said I was outside with the other kids."

As they approached the porch, Amanda grabbed Chris by the shirt and pulled him to the side of the house. "If you want to finish what we started, meet me tonight after everybody's gone to sleep, out back by the shed." Before he could respond, she gave him a quick kiss on the lips and took off around the corner.

Chris stood there motionless, barely able to breathe. He was astonished at how forward she was and wondered just what she meant. Before he could ponder it longer, however, the call was made for dinner. He put his thoughts aside and went in to wash up.

Dinner was extremely tense as Chris tried to avoid Amanda's flirtatious stares and make Keith crack a smile. There was definitely something going on inside of Keith's head, but Chris couldn't get him to talk about it.

After dinner, Chris cornered Ms. Holtz, determined to fix everything. "Isn't there anything you can do?" Chris asked irritably. "Can't you tell his father that military school would be the worst thing he could do right now?"

"Christopher, as much as I disagree with Keith's father, it's out of my hands. I've talked until I'm blue in the face, and he won't listen. He's a very stubborn man."

Chris left her office feeling more helpless and more discouraged than before. He knew the way Keith felt about drugs and was sure he would start using just as soon as he got out. But now with his father deserting him, there would be no telling how far he would go.

Chris went back to the room and tried to talk to Keith again but got nowhere. Keith told him not to worry, he had a plan. He could see the wall Keith had put up around him and he wasn't letting anyone in, including Chris.

After lights out, Chris laid in the dark thinking about Amanda and wondering what she was insinuating. He hadn't thought much about his religion in the last several months, but one thing was for certain, he believed in complete fidelity. His mother instilled that in him from an early age. Surely that's not what Amanda was thinking. After all, they'd only known each other for two weeks.

Still, his curiosity got the best of him, and he quietly slipped outside to the old wood shed in the back yard where he found Amanda anxiously waiting for him. Her red hair sparkled in the moonlight, and her eyes lit up like the stars in the sky when she saw him.

"I thought you weren't coming," she said breathlessly. She pulled him close and eagerly pressed her lips to his. For a moment Chris was lost in the touch of her soft, warm lips and the sweet aroma of her perfume. As the kiss became more passionate, he regained his composure. He took her by the shoulders and gently pushed her away.

"Hold on. Don't you think we should take things a little slower?" He asked, trying not to sound hypocritical. After all, he was the one who made the first move.

"I thought you liked me!"

"I do! I just want to get to know you better. Is there something wrong with that?" Chris was dumbfounded by her forwardness.

"Yeah . . . I mean . . . I thought this was what you wanted." Amanda got a funny look on her face and placed both hands on her hips. She stared at him through squinted eyes. "You have a girlfriend, don't you? I should have known." She threw her hand in the air and turned to leave.

"No! Wait! I don't have a girlfriend. In fact, you're the first girl I've really ever liked."

She stopped and turned around, looking very confused. "Then what is it?"

Chris didn't give much thought to what he said next. He just opened his mouth and it all came rolling out like a rockslide. "I want to wait until I get married. I've always believed in saving myself for the woman I'm going to spend the rest of my life with."

She looked at him as though he'd just told her something so preposterous that he couldn't possibly be telling the truth.

"Isn't that a little old fashioned?" she asked.

Realizing that there was no turning back now, Chris watched her reaction. "Well, you see, I'm a Mormon," he said, anticipating the laughing or ridicule that he thought was sure to come.

"What's a Mormon?"

"You've never heard of the Mormons? How far away is Arkansas?" he said, laughing. Amanda had a blank look on her face.

"Get real—Joseph Smith . . . The book of Mormon . . . Temples?" He paused between each one, waiting to see if anything rang a bell.

"Oh, those pretty castle-like buildings? They're gorgeous."

Chris could hardly believe that she knew nothing about the Church. Everyone he'd ever known had heard of the Church.

"Anyway, it's our belief that we should save ourselves for marriage. That way we can be morally clean to be sealed in the temple." As soon as he spoke the words a glow came over her face. She was now both curious and intrigued by his statement.

They sat down on the grass and talked for over an hour about Joseph Smith, the restoration of the Church, and the Book of Mormon. Chris hadn't realized until then that he still had a testimony. But surprisingly, he felt very comfortable talking about it. Amanda was fascinated to learn that the Book of Mormon was another testament of Jesus Christ. She went from thinking he was some weird alien from another planet to admiring him for standing up for his beliefs.

"The things you believe in contradict some of the religions I've studied. But they all lack something. I'm always left with an empty feeling inside," she said, shaking her head. "It makes sense though. If you're a family here on earth, then you should be able to be a family in heaven."

"That's why temples are so important. Families can be sealed together for time and eternity by a man who has been given the authority to seal them. But you have to be clean and pure and follow all of God's commandments," Chris stated with conviction. However, he was silently kicking himself for the mistakes he'd made.

Chris suggested that they continue their conversation the next day since it was obviously getting very late. He held her hand as they walked back to the house. When they reached the front door he stopped and gave her a kiss on the cheek.

"I just have one more question, Christopher Porter. How does your church feel about your drug abuse? Will they kick you out for that?" she asked sincerely.

"Well, I don't know. I guess I may have some repenting to do when I get back home." He hadn't really thought much about it, or about church for that matter.

They said good night and Chris quietly got back into bed without waking up Keith. He had never had to stand up for his beliefs before, nor had he spoken of his testimony, but he felt his soul bursting with joy. He hadn't felt this way since his mother got sick, and he wondered if she was giving him the extra strength he needed.

# Chapter 26

Chris woke up, startled by the loud clap of thunder that shook the entire house. He sat up in bed and looked out the window. The sky was filled with ugly grey clouds, making everything dark and gloomy.

The week had once again whizzed by, and it was Friday morning. That meant tomorrow was visiting day, and his father and bishop Geary would be coming to see him. For the first time he was actually excited for the visit. His father would be bringing a Book of Mormon for him to give to Amanda. She was full of questions about the gospel, and Chris could hardly wait to give it to her.

It was gratifying to be able to share something so important with someone he now cared deeply for. He had never been one to bear his testimony, but it seemed to come easily with Amanda. The only scripture Chris could find was the Bible, so he did his best to tell her about the Nephites and Lamanites. He was amazed at how open to the gospel she was, taking in everything he told her and wanting to know more.

Chris lay back down, listening to the heavy raindrops hit the roof and thinking over the last week. Keith had become even more withdrawn and distant from everyone. Whenever Chris would try to talk to him about it, he just brushed him off with a laugh, saying he had everything covered. Chris even went back to Ms. Holtz, but was assured they were doing everything they could to help him.

Chris wondered if he was the only one who could see the changes in Keith. He didn't smile or crack jokes anymore. He didn't want to eat or play basketball. He just wanted to sit in his room alone.

He looked over at Keith's bed and suddenly realized it was empty. Chris thought it was particularly odd, considering it was only six o'clock in the morning, way too early for breakfast. He sat up and looked around the room. The covers on Keith's bed were messy, and his clothes were lying on the floor. An icy, cold chill ran down Chris's spine, and an uneasy, eerie feeling settled in the pit of his stomach.

He crawled out of bed, pulled on his blue jeans, and headed for the door. The hallway was dark and quiet, making the uneasy feeling even stronger. He quietly walked down the hallway, checking the bathroom on the way, and then to the staircase. He rounded the corner and looked out over the banister to see if there were any lights on downstairs. What he saw instead brought Chris to his knees.

The sight of Keith's lifeless body hanging from the top of the oak stairway hit Chris with a hammering blow to the chest. He let out a blood-curdling scream for help and immediately slipped his arms through the posts, grabbing Keith under his shoulders, struggling to lift his limp body. As his heart raced faster and faster, he screamed for help again, the weight of Keith's body almost more than he could bear.

One of the boys in the next room heard the cries and raced downstairs to wake the counselors. The other boys gathered around in shock, not knowing what to do. Ms. Holtz and a male counselor came running to his aid.

The male counselor pulled Keith up and cut the thick rope with a pocket knife. He gently laid his motionless body on the floor. Chris recognized the rope from the stables and realized that Keith had been planning this all week. He could see how blue Keith's lips were and knew from health class that he'd been deprived of oxygen for too long. Memories of Katie's near drowning consumed his mind, making it hard to concentrate. It was like reliving the whole nightmare over again.

Chris watched in horror as Ms. Holtz and the male counselor performed CPR. The sight of Keith lying there with deep, red rope burns around his neck was almost too much to bear.

"Come on, Keith, breathe!" Chris shouted breathlessly, tears filling his eyes.

"Chris, go outside and watch for the paramedics," Ms. Holtz ordered, realizing things were not looking good. Chris could hear the panic in her voice and gave her a questioning look. "Go, Chris, right now!" she demanded.

He ran outside just as the ambulance was pulling in. He waved them over and escorted them to Keith. Chris was pushed aside as they desperately worked to save Keith's life. Everyone stood silently watching in disbelief as a feeling of death seemed to consume the atmosphere around them.

Chris backed away and slumped down on the floor, his whole body shaking from shock. Amanda sat down next to him, placing an arm around his trembling shoulders. Chris collapsed in her arms, sobbing uncontrollably.

"It's all right, Chris. I'm here," she said softly.

With a sober look on her face, Ms. Holtz instructed everyone to go to the living room for group. As the kids filed down the stairs, Chris grabbed her by the arm. "Ms. Holtz?"

"I'm so sorry, Chris," she said, gently shaking her head.

"Why! Why did he do this?" Chris said angrily.

"I don't have any answers."

"It was his father!" Chris yelled irrationally. "He drove him to this!"

"Chris, you don't know that."

"Yes, I do! I tried to tell you, and you wouldn't listen! Now it's too late!" He stormed off down the hall, briefly looking back as he reached the bedroom door. Keith's body was lying on the gurney and was covered with a sheet as the paramedics took him away. Chris entered the bedroom and violently slammed the door, shutting the whole world out.

The sight of Keith's unmade bed and his clothes lying on the floor left a haunting image in Chris's mind. He couldn't believe Keith was really gone. It was like a bad dream he couldn't wake up from.

Chris sat down on his bed and felt sick to his stomach. Could he have stopped Keith? He saw the signs. Why didn't he make him talk? Thoughts were running through Chris's head faster than he could process them, until suddenly, out of nowhere, they came to an abrupt halt—he had tried to commit suicide too.

It seemed like centuries ago, but it had only been weeks. He was no different than Keith, feeling alone, desperate, like the weight of the world was resting on his shoulders. He'd just wanted to make it all go away. Chris wondered if that's what Keith was feeling right before he wrapped the rope around his neck. But Chris realized now how stupid it was. He wished he would have shared that with Keith before it was too late.

Chris finally dozed off to sleep somewhere between his thoughts of Keith and his regrets from his own mistakes. He would have slept the whole day away if it hadn't been for Ms. Holtz. She told him if he wasn't dressed and at the breakfast table in ten minutes, she was bringing another bucket of water up to pour over his head. One was quite enough for him, so he pulled his weak body out of bed and got dressed.

They had all finished eating and were working on their chores when Chris finally got down to the kitchen. A covered plate was sitting at the end of the table. He sat down and took the cover off to find pancakes and sausage. He pushed the food around on his plate, wondering how everyone could go on with life as usual when Keith's life was over.

"Not too hungry?" Amanda said, as she sat down in the chair next to him.

"Not really. Where's Ms. Holtz? She was so determined to get me down here and now she's disappeared."

"She's talking with some of the kids about what happened. Keith's father is supposed to be flying in this afternoon."

"Well, that figures. The only time he comes to visit and his son's dead!" he exclaimed bitterly.

"Chris!"

"It's true! Keith wanted him to come visit, though he'd never admit it. I could see the disappointment in his face every time his father made up some lame excuse as to why he couldn't make it." Chris was getting angrier by the minute.

"It stopped raining. Do you want to go for a walk?"

"What about classes?"

"They've canceled them today so the kids can talk to the counselors." She hesitated for a moment. "Unless you want to talk to a counselor instead. I'd understand."

"No, you'll do just fine," he said, smiling.

The sky was still covered in with dark clouds, but the rain had let up, leaving everything fresh and clean. It was cool out, but neither one seemed to mind. The smell of fresh rain was exhilarating.

They walked out to the barn and watched the horses playfully running in the corral. Chris noticed how carefree they were as they galloped around. Even Thunder was playfully kicking his hind legs and seemed to enjoy being drenched with rain.

It was both painful and liberating to talk about Keith. Chris felt a sense of relief come over him, sharing his guilt and grievance with

Amanda. She was easy to talk to and gave him the reassurance he was desperately looking for.

They were lost in conversation when the call for lunch came. He took her in his arms and held her close, giving her a long kiss on the lips. They walked back to the house arm and arm, holding each other for comfort. They hadn't gotten far, however, when the rain started up again, sending them running for cover under the porch.

Lunch was painfully quiet. Looking across the table at Keith's vacant chair cut deeply into Chris's troubled heart. Everyone looked around the room, expecting to see Keith come bouncing in with some smart remark about the food. Instead, the silence brought a firm reality of the events of that morning. Chris tried to hide his emotions, but he felt the emptiness more than anyone there.

After lunch, Chris helped in the kitchen, trying to escape the thoughts that plagued his mind. He was having a difficult time coping with the fact that Keith's life was really over. He wanted so desperately to go back in time and talk to him. Maybe he could have made a difference.

Soon the dishes were done and there was nothing left to do but face the silent emptiness of the bedroom. Chris opened the door and found a tall, thin man with graying hair, dressed in a business suit, sitting on the edge on Keith's bed. He was holding Keith's pillow in his arms and sobbing. Keith's suitcase and a box of his things were sitting on the floor next to the bed. Chris realized it was Keith's father, who had come to collect his things.

On top of the box was the picture Keith drew of a broken heart with dripping blood, a picture of Keith's girlfriend, and a poster of *The Lord of the Rings*. They were all the things that were important to Keith.

*Packed away, removed from sight, like we're just supposed to forget him,* thought Chris furiously.

"Come in, please," Keith's father said, wiping away the tears. "Were you one of Keith's friends?" he asked tearfully.

Chris was silent, not knowing if he should answer or run the other direction. "I . . . I was his roommate," he stuttered.

"You must be Chris! I've heard so much about you. Please come in," he exclaimed with enthusiasm.

Chris walked over and sat down on his bed, facing Keith's father. "He talked about me?"

"Of course, he did. He said you'd become his best friend."

The words "best friend" stabbed at Chris like the cold, dull blade of a knife. He felt the same way about Keith and already missed him greatly.

"I'm so glad he had you to talk to." His eyes started filling up with tears again. "I'm sorry. This is the hardest thing I've ever had to do. I just can't understand why he would do something like this. Did he seem depressed to you?"

"Well, he was extremely upset about going away to military school. And then there was the fact that you never took the time to visit him. I would say that those two things together might have pushed him over the edge," Chris blurted out bitterly.

"I didn't know what else to do with him. I thought if he was at military school, he wouldn't be using drugs." He looked strained and frustrated as he spoke.

"As for the other thing you accused me of, I'm 100 percent guilty. I put my career before my son and I regret that deeply. Now he's gone and I'll have to live with that burden for the rest of my life. I should have told him every day that I loved him, but the last year has been so hard."

He looked at the floor, and Chris wasn't sure if he was sad or ashamed—maybe a little of both. Chris watched in silence, trying to read his body language and waiting for an explanation. Not that it mattered now that Keith was gone. Nothing he could say or do would ever change that.

"Keith became a different person when he started using meth. He wouldn't listen to anything I said. He was mean and belligerent with everyone around him. He would disappear for days, without so much as a phone call to let me know he was all right. Then his friends would come dragging him home in terrible condition. After a few weeks, it would start all over again. We've tried two drug rehabs in the last year as well as spending time in juvenile detention. Nothing seemed to help, and I was at the end of my rope."

Chris stared out the window, remembering the conversation he and Keith had about drugs. He wondered if Keith was using drugs, not to make his father angry, but rather to gain his attention. After spending the last two weeks getting to know him, Chris was able to see past Keith's hard outer shell, and he knew he was just a hurt kid who craved his father's love and understanding.

Chris quietly listened as Keith's father talked about his son's drug addiction and the heartbreaking devastation it left on their family. Chris discovered there were two sides to every story, and Keith's father had been hurt just as badly as Keith. There was a small part of Chris that felt sorry for Keith's father and recognized the similarities in his relationship with his own father.

Chris was almost positive that things would have turned out differently if Keith and his father had only taken the time to break down the walls between them. He then realized that he'd been slowly building his own lonesome barricade, adding a brick every time someone hurt or offended him. It had become so thick with anger and resentment that he wasn't sure if he could break through it or if he even wanted to.

"I'm sorry for rattling on like that. I'm sure Keith had his fair share of complaints about me. It's just too bad there's no more time to straighten all this out."

"Is everything all right in here?" Ms. Holtz asked, surprised to see Chris sitting there.

"Yes. Chris and I were just talking about what a good friend Keith was." He stood up and put his hand out to Chris, who stood up and gladly shook it. He was seeing him in a different light now.

Keith's father picked up the suitcase in one hand, threw the pillow on top of the box, and stuck the box under his other arm. Then, with one last sorrowful glance around the room and the empty bed where his son had slept for the last eighty-seven days, he turned and silently walked out.

Chris sat alone on his bed, looking at the bare room. All of a sudden it was like Keith never existed. There were no more pictures he'd drawn hanging on the walls, no more clothes lying around on the floor, no more . . . Keith.

His thoughts returned to his own father and the terrible fights they'd had. He remembered Mother's Day and how angry he was at his father. He replayed all the horrible images that were locked away in his mind, right down to the unmentionable and unforgivable act of letting his little sister almost drown.

He reached over to his nightstand and picked up the unopened envelope with the letter from Katie still tucked inside. He held it in his hands, lightly rubbing his fingers over her name, afraid to open it, frightened of the words that were sealed inside. He wondered if she knew how much he loved her. He never would have done anything to hurt her.

He pushed his skepticism aside and ripped open the envelope, finally ready to confront the worst. With a deep breath he began to read.

**Dear Chris,**

i told dad to take you this leter for me. i mis
you lots!!!!! i want you to no i dont blam you
for wat hapen to me. i saw a frog in the water
then sliped in it not you fault you puled me out
and saved me!!!!!!!! for that i will love you for
always please come home soon i love you!!!!!!

**LOVE KATIE**

Chris sat speechless on the edge of the bed, staring at the letter in
disbelief. How could she forgive him for what he'd done? There were no
hurtful words, no blame, and no anger. He folded up the letter and placed
it in his drawer, astonished at her forgiving nature. He loved Katie so
much, and yet he had treated her so badly. But through all of that, she
was willing to forgive.

*What happened to me?* he thought as he ran his fingers though his thick,
curly hair. Heart-rending memories of the last three months swarmed his
mind. He suddenly felt trapped in his tiny bedroom, suffocating from
humiliation and regret.

He had to get out of there! Right now! Somewhere! Anywhere! Just not
there with all his regrets furiously pounding him! He raced downstairs,
adrenaline pumping though his veins, and jolted out the front door,
running like an escaped prisoner with no one there to stop him.

Faster and faster he ran, down the flooded driveway, trying to outrun
the tormenting thoughts that ravaged is mind. He'd let them down, all of
them. They should never forgive him for all the terrible things he'd done.
The lies, the deceit, the stealing—it was all so agonizingly clear to him
now. He didn't deserve to be forgiven. He'd been a coward and took the
easy way out by turning to drugs.

He ran harder and faster, his feet pounding sharply against the
pavement, feeling the strain of the vigorous exercise through his once-
broken ribs. His escape soon came to a halt as he hit the gate at the end
of the long driveway. He reached out and grabbed hold of it, shaking it
fiercely with both hands as hard as he could, letting out the frustration
and anger trapped inside. Suddenly, the gate slipped from his hands and
swung open, revealing the road to freedom. He looked around and saw

that no one was in sight. No security guard, no counselors, not even Ms. Holtz. It was an easy getaway.

He stood there breathlessly looking at the road ahead of him and then at the road behind him. The road behind him would be hard. It meant going back and taking responsibility for his actions. The road ahead of him would be the easier of the two. It meant running away from everything and not dealing with his mistakes.

He hesitated, staring at the road ahead of him. Thoughts of the past and of the future flooded his mind. Exhausted and overwhelmed, he fell to the pavement, pulling his knees up close to his chest and tightly wrapping his arms around them. He buried his head in his knees and cried as hard as the rain that was coming down. He cried for the people he'd hurt, the ones he'd lost, and the fear he felt inside.

The fear wrapped around him like a boa constrictor, squeezing him so tightly that he could barely breathe. He feared for his future. He feared to face his family, and he feared to confront his drug addiction. But most of all, he feared that one day he might end up like Keith.

After three weeks he still thought about drugs and yearned for the sensation they gave him. To know that he still harbored these tendencies made him feel weak and like a failure. But he also knew that if he was going to stand a fighting chance, he would need to complete the program and stay in counseling.

He reached up with both hands and wiped the tears away. Then with utmost determination, he took in a deep cleansing breath and pulled himself up. His clothes were drenched and his hair was dripping from the rain, but he finally understood what he had to do. He reached out, grabbed a hold of the gate and pulled it closed. He turned around and slowly walked back to the house, taking all of his regrets with him. He was ready once and for all to face up to everything he'd done.

# Chapter 27

When Chris reached the porch, he found Ms. Holtz sitting in one of the wooden chairs, holding a large towel in her arms. He looked shamefully down at the ground, knowing how disappointed in him she must be. After all their talks and counseling sessions, he still cracked under pressure. He admired her, not only for battling her own drug addiction, but also for the compassion and understanding he felt each time they talked. She counseled without judgment, and now he'd let her down yet again. He leaned up against the post, keeping his eyes to the ground, sadly wondering if she had finally given up on him.

She walked over to him and held out the towel. "Looks like you could use this," she said compassionately.

Chris didn't hesitate. He wrapped it around his shivering shoulders, feeling the warmth against his cold, wet skin. "Thanks," he said quietly, unable to look her in the eye.

"Why don't you go and get out of your wet clothes and then come down to my office so we can talk?"

Chris nodded his head, knowing that she deserved an explanation.

As he put on some dry clothes, he again found himself staring at the empty bed on the other side of the room. He realized the road to recovery would be long and hard, but determination now ran freely through him. He was ready to do whatever it took to regain control of his life. He would not surrender to the drug's seductive traits and its enticing effects. He would not end up like Keith!

Chris entered Ms. Holtz's office feeling the butterflies dancing around in the pit of his stomach. He sat down in one of her burgundy leather chairs and sighed heavily. He hadn't noticed before that her office was filled with pictures of kids that had successfully completed the program. Below their pictures hung letters of appreciation, thanking her for changing their lives. As he looked around the room he realized they were all just normal kids like him—kids who had all fallen into the same detrimental trap.

She sat down in the chair next to his. "There was nothing you could have done to stop Keith," she stated affirmatively.

"I guess so. I guess . . . I just feel bad. I wish I could have helped him."

"I know you do. Believe me, I've been struggling all day with that very same thought. I wanted to help him change his life, but I failed him and his father." Her voice was filled with sadness and disappointment.

Chris wasn't about to let her take the blame for what had happened. He knew telling Keith's secret might be breaking the bonds of friendship, but then again, it was Keith who took his own life without any regard for the people he'd left behind.

"You couldn't have helped Keith, Ms. Holtz, because he didn't want to be helped. He told me he would continue to use meth no matter what. He just told everyone what they wanted to hear so he could get out and start using again. He never had any intention of quitting."

Ms. Holtz gently shook her head in despair. "I guess I'm not all that surprised. I always felt he was just playing the system. Nevertheless, I had hoped he'd come around. There was one thing I could never get him to do, and that was to take responsibility for his actions. It was always someone else's fault."

They sat quietly for a moment, listening to the rain coming down outside. "Well, aren't you going to ask me why I came back?" Chris asked.

"I know why you came back, Chris. Why don't you tell me the reason you ran off?"

Chris inhaled slowly as he tried to figure out where to begin. "I guess I've been doing a lot of soul searching today because of what happened to Keith. Suddenly, all of my mistakes and all of the terrible things I've done came crashing down on me like a ton of bricks. Just thinking about my life, my family, and my own suicide attempt, was too much. I've hurt so many people I care about and I just don't know if there's a way back."

"Well, you're talking about it, and that's a good start. Tell me about your suicide attempt."

He took another deep breath and exhaled slowly, knowing it was time to get it all out in the open.

"Well, after I ran out of pills, I realized I couldn't function without them, so I sunk to a new low and bought them off the street. Nothing else seemed to matter as long as I had those pills."

Chris looked down at the floor in disgust as he remembered all the lies and deceit. "One morning my father insisted I go with them to the lake. I really wanted no part in it, but he made me go, so I took a pill before we left the cabin. It made me feel spacey and tired. All I wanted to do was sleep, but my father cut his hand and had to go back to the cabin, leaving Katie in my care. If he never would have made me go in the first place, none of it would have happened," Chris said remorsefully.

"But it was you who took the pill. Your father wouldn't have left you in charge of Katie had he known you were still on drugs."

"I know, and that's what eats at me the most. My dad trusted me with my little sister, and I let him down. I let them both down."

Chris could feel the tears working their way to the surface and fought desperately to keep them from falling. He didn't want to turn into some weepy little schoolboy. He wanted to prove to Ms. Holtz that he was strong-willed and fully committed to achieving his goals.

"When I looked into my dad's eyes, I saw hurt and disappointment. I just couldn't take it. I knew I should have been the one in that lake, not Katie. I didn't want to live anymore knowing what I'd done. I felt I was a total disappointment to my dad, and I couldn't live with that either. So, I went to the deck and pulled up the loose board where I'd hid the pills. All I could think about was how I'd let everyone down and I didn't deserve to live. I felt like it was the only way out, the only choice left. So, without regard for anyone else, I took the rest of the pills."

Chris could no longer keep the tears from falling as he remembered holding the pills in his hand, desperately wanting release from the agonizing despair that consumed his soul.

"I understand those feelings, Chris. They devour you until you feel there is no way back. But what you may not realize is, from the first time you start taking the drugs, they impair your thinking. Not only did you have feelings of hopelessness and despair, but your feelings were also intensified by the drug abuse. Especially with the pills you were taking.

The Lortab and other pain pills are depressants. They may give you a calming effect, but they also cause depression. It's a dangerous cycle, and one that can become deadly if you don't stop it."

"That's why I ran off and why I came back. After talking to Keith's father, I saw my dad's side of things for the first time. I realized what terrible things I did and said, not only to my dad, but also to my sisters. The walls felt like they were closing in on me, and I just had to get out. When I reached the gate and found that it was open, I knew I had a choice. I could either run away . . . again, or I could come back and try to fix all the damage I'd done and all the people I'd hurt." He looked up from the ground and finally made eye contact with Ms. Holtz.

"I'm tired of running, and I don't want to end up like Keith. I want to take back my life. You said you could help me do that."

The moment the words left his lips, he felt a sense of relief. Asking for help and admitting he couldn't do it on his own was like cutting the heavy chains that were bound to his ankles. Finally free of the enormous burdens that had been holding him down, he no longer desired to be alone in his fight for redemption. He needed Ms. Holtz's strength and wisdom to help him through.

"Of course I will. But you have to trust me completely and do as I say. That means no more lip. You got it?" she said, laughing. Chris smiled and nodded his head, knowing he'd not been the most cooperative kid in the facility.

After dinner, Amanda caught up with Chris, worried after seeing him run out the door. "Hey you, do you run marathons too?" she joked cheerfully.

"What, you saw me leave and didn't come after me? Were you afraid you couldn't keep up or something?"

"I was ready to, but Ms. Holtz told me to shut the door and leave you alone."

"Ms. Holtz saw me leave and didn't call security?"

"She knew you'd be back. She trusts you."

"She must have more faith in me than I do. I almost kept going."

"You didn't though. You came back. I have faith in you. This last week you've shown me that there's more to this life than what meets the eye. There's something better waiting for us. If you have as much faith in yourself as you do in your religion, then I would dare say you'll make it just fine."

Chris just smiled. He realized that tomorrow would be the real test. It was time to work things out with his father and ask for his forgiveness. He had to find a way to finally break down the walls between them, to push his resentment aside and make amends. The only problem was, he had less than twenty-four hours to figure it all out.

# Chapter 28

The morning came not a minute too soon. Chris awoke several times during the night, looking across the room and expecting to see Keith sleeping in the next bed. He looked outside to find the rain had let up and the sun was shining. It was going to be a beautiful day.

He'd tried to come up with some wonderful thing to say to his father—some explanation as to why he continued using drugs, why he'd lied and deceived him, and why he wanted a second chance, but his mind was blank. He decided perhaps the best thing to do was to leave it to fate.

He went downstairs for breakfast, and to his surprise, he was the first one at the table. He picked up the morning newspaper and plopped down on the living room couch.

"You're up early," Ms. Holtz said as she entered the room.

"I couldn't sleep—too many things going through my head."

"Like seeing your father today?"

Chris nodded.

"Don't stress about it. A parent's love is unconditional. You could burn down the house and they'd still love you."

"Are you sure about that," he said, grinning.

"Positive!" she exclaimed. "Now, to move on to other subjects, how's your love life?" With a curious look on her face, she sat down and folded her arms.

"What love life?" Chris gulped.

"You know what I'm talking about! The rules state that boys and girls are not to be alone together."

"Well, then that leaves us out. We consider ourselves a man and a woman," Chris said, half smirking and half smiling.

"Christopher Porter, you know what I mean. I'm trying to help the both of you with your addictions. I don't have time to babysit the two of you."

"You don't need to worry, Ms. Holtz. We're just good friends," he said reassuringly. He patted her on the shoulder as he stood up and started for the breakfast table. The food was out and some of the other kids were already being seated.

"Let's keep it that way. You have more important things to worry about!" she called after him as he walked away, waving his hand in the air. She then made a silent note to herself to stay on her guard.

After breakfast was over and chores were through, they all went outside for free time. Chris noticed how empty the basketball court was without Keith there shooting hoops. He picked up the basketball and looked at the hoop and then at the ball. Keith was an excellent player. He beat Chris every time—except one, and Chris knew Keith blew that game just so Chris wouldn't feel bad.

He stared down at the basketball, suddenly feeling very angry with Keith. He wondered how someone could be so selfish that they would take their own life, leaving behind close friends and family to mourn their death. Now they were the ones left to pick up the pieces and try to move on. Chris was starting to see things from a different perspective, and he realized how much his own suicide attempt must have hurt his father.

"Are you going to throw it or eat it?" Amanda asked, her hands on her hips.

"What are you doing out here? I thought you had a phone visit today?"

"Let's just say it was short and sweet. I told my mom I met a *Mormon boy*," she said, emphasizing the words "mormon" and "boy."

"You didn't!"

"Oh, yes I did. I wanted to see what she would say."

"And?"

"She said, and I quote, 'You stay away from him. We don't need any more trouble.' Then I said, 'Well you better get used to it, because I'm reading the Book of Mormon.' "

"I hope I didn't start something between you and your mom," Chris sighed.

She took the ball from his hands, stood very close to him, and looked him in the eye. "You may have started it, but it has nothing to do with you now. When I listen to your stories, it's like there's a fire inside me burning out of control. I know what you say is true. I can't explain it, but I feel it."

As Chris looked into Amanda's eyes, he could see the intense passion she was feeling for the gospel.

"That's the Holy Ghost," he told her. "He testifies to you that what you've heard or read is true."

"Well, I like this feeling, and I'm going to go to church when I get home."

"What about your mom?"

"She'll have to get used to it. After all, she did send me to the Mormon state," she said, laughing. "Thanks to you, I know my life has a purpose."

The cars started to roll into the drive one by one. Amanda threw the basketball, making a perfect basket. Chris laughed at the fact that even Amanda was a better player than he was. Chris saw his father pull in and took a deep breath. "Here goes nothing," he said.

"Good Luck." Amanda gave him a kiss on the cheek and ran off to the house.

Chris walked over to the truck where his father and Bishop Geary were just getting out. "Chris, it's good to see you again," Bishop Geary said, shaking his hand.

"Good to see you too, Bishop," Chris responded.

"I want to give you and your dad a little time alone before we talk. Is that all right?"

"Sure," Chris said, shrugging his shoulders.

"Good then. I'll just find a shady spot and you can come get me when you're finished."

Chris and his father walked out back to the gazebo. Chris sat on one side and Larry on the other. Chris could feel his emotions bubbling over inside him. He had a lot on his mind but was having trouble putting it all into words.

"So how have you been, Chris?"

"Fine. How are Jody and Katie?"

Larry was shocked but excited to hear Chris ask about them. "They're doing all right. They miss you."

"I miss them too," Chris said sadly, looking down at his shoes.

"Does that mean you're ready to see them?"

"Yeah, they can come this Thursday. Ms. Holtz made an exception this week just for me.

"They'll be so excited. How are things going with your counseling?"

Chris stayed silent. He was overcome by remorse. He took a deep breath but didn't say a word. His eyes filled with tears and he could feel his heart beating with anticipation, wondering how his father would respond to him.

"Chris, what's wrong?" his father asked with concern.

Chris looked up at his father with sorrowful eyes. "I'm so sorry . . . for everything," he said tearfully.

Larry quickly stood up. He crossed the gazebo, sat down beside Chris, and took him into his arms. He was seeing a side of Chris that had been missing for far too long. Chris wrapped his arms around his father and sobbed.

"It's all right, son. Everything's going to be all right," Larry said gently, and he also began to cry. He had waited so long for this. They were finally breaking through the thick barrier that had separated them for the last several years.

Chris sat back and wiped the tears from his face. "Can you ever forgive me for all the awful things I've done?"

"Oh, Chris, of course I can. I love you, son, more than anything on this earth. There is nothing you could do that would ever change that."

Chris smiled. "Even if I burn down the house?"

Larry had a confused look on his face. "What does that mean?" he said, smiling back at his son.

"Oh nothing. Just a little inside joke."

"It's nice to see you smiling again. I've really missed that."

"Me too," Chris confessed.

"And I'm glad things are going well for you here."

"Well, they didn't start out that way, but I've met some really good people that have helped me along. One of them is the girl who wants to read the Book of Mormon. You did bring it, right?" Chris asked.

"Yeah, I brought it. In fact, I brought your set of scriptures as well. I thought maybe you'd like to read them. Or am I being too pushy again?"

"No, you were right. I realized just this last week how important the gospel is to me. I wasn't sure I still had a testimony, but I found out that it is still there. I just needed to use it a little more often."

"Sounds kind of familiar," Larry said with a laugh. "After your mom passed away, I thought my faith was gone for good. But then a very wise bishop told me not to give up, it was still there. So I started to pray again, which wasn't easy for me, and I started reading my scriptures. And when I needed my faith the most, it came through. Both you and Katie are all right. I finally got my miracle."

Chris sat quietly listening to his father pour out his heart to him, telling him some of his most personal feelings. He never knew his father had struggled so much after his mother died. He'd selfishly thought he was the only one having a hard time coping with her death.

"I guess we've all felt the emptiness mom left behind. I should have talked to you about my feelings instead of locking them all up inside until they exploded like fireworks on the fourth of July."

Larry chuckled at his son's sense of humor. He could see the old Chris shinning through. "I think now it's my turn to ask for forgiveness. I know I haven't been there for you and your sisters. I regret making my job the priority in my life. After losing your mother, I realized how short life is, and I don't want to waste any more time. I know you didn't want to give me a second chance before, but I'm asking again in hopes that you've changed your mind." He looked at his son with sincerity, pleading from his heart for forgiveness.

Chris looked into this father's eyes and for the first time saw love and compassion. He thought perhaps it had always been there, he just hadn't looked for it. "I've been so angry at you for so long that I'm not even sure of all the reasons why. All I know is that there were so many times I wanted you to come watch me skate, or take me to a football game. As the years went by, I got angrier and angrier. But you know, I'm tired of feeling angry inside. I just want to let it go and start over."

Chris paused for minute. His father sat in silence, hanging his head in shame for deserting his only son. Chris touched his shoulder. "Hey dad, it's okay. If you can forgive me for all the terrible things I said and did, then surely I can forgive you."

Larry looked up at his son, his brown eyes red from the tears and his brown curls blowing in the soft breeze. "Starting today we'll wipe the slate clean," he said with a smile. "Your mother did a great job raising you kids. I just hope I can live up to that and continue on."

"You will. I have faith in you."

They left the gazebo feeling happier than they'd been in a long time. The tension between them had lifted and they had finally set free all of their anger, resentments, and regrets.

"Dad, can I ask you one more question?"

"Anything."

"Why didn't you come after me that night I ran off?"

Larry looked softly into his son's eyes. "Because I realized you had to make that decision on your own. I stayed by the window waiting for you—scared, nervous, and confused, but knowing you would make the right decision."

Chris smiled with relief, knowing now it wasn't hate that had kept him away that night, but rather trusting in him to make the right decision.

Chris and Bishop Geary sat down at one of the picnic tables out back. Chris was a little uneasy, feeling the guilt weighing heavily on his mind. He reminded himself that this was not a judgment, but rather a friendly talk with the one man that could help him find his way back spiritually.

"Thank you, Chris, for seeing me. I just wanted to talk to you for a few minutes and see if there is anything I can help you with." Chris was quietly looking down at the table, feeling too ashamed to look him in the eye. "I've been thinking a lot about you, Chris, and I want to let you know that there is nothing you've done that can't be forgiven, so don't ever feel like there's no way back. Satan loves to use guilt against you. He tries to convince you that your mistakes are so terrible that you can never be forgiven, or that you've gone so far off the path of righteousness that there is no use in trying to come back. But Satan is a liar and a deceiver. He wants you to be miserable, just as he is miserable."

"I felt that way at first. I felt ashamed and worthless. Life didn't mean anything to me. I quit praying and going to church because I knew Heavenly Father was disappointed in me. I was disappointed in me too. I didn't feel like I should be in his house or even speak to him because of the things I was doing. It became easier and easier to slip farther away. Pretty soon, I just didn't think about it anymore, until I met Amanda. We started talking about the gospel and the Book of Mormon. I realized I still had a testimony and that it had never left me. It felt really good to talk about my beliefs again, and it gave me the confidence I needed to move forward."

"I'm glad to hear that, Christopher. Are you saying your prayers?"

"Not yet. I feel so ashamed, and I don't know where to begin or what to say." Chris shook his head in despair, knowing how terrified he was to pray. It wasn't so much the Lord he was fearful of, but rather himself. The fear of failure kept him bound so tightly that he'd been unable to get down on his knees. He had already disappointed so many people he cared about. What if he failed again and disappointed his Father in Heaven?

"Start slowly. You don't need to rush things. Just talk to him about your day, about your feelings. As time passes, you'll start feeling more at ease when you pray. Then you'll be able to tell him everything and ask for his forgiveness. When you're back home and feeling stronger, come in and see me. I have faith in you, Christopher. Your mother was a strong, faithful woman who taught you the gospel through her example. You have her strength and your father's determination. You'll have no problem finding your way back. It sounds like you're already on your way."

Chris nodded, feeling more strength than he had in months.

"Here is the Book of Mormon you requested, and also your set from home. I took the liberty of marking a few scriptures that might be of interest to both of you."

With a smile of confidence on his face, the bishop handed the books to Chris. Amanda's Book of Mormon had a sticky note attached to the front that simply read, "This book is your key to eternal happiness." Chris smiled with excitement, eager to share all the blessings the book held inside.

"Thank you, Bishop. She's really excited to read it," Chris said with enthusiasm.

"That's good, but I hope you are too. Chris, there's one more thing I would like to do before I leave. If it's all right with you, I'd like your father and me to give you a priesthood blessing."

Chris thought it was a little strange since he wasn't sick or anything. He agreed, anxiously wanting to present the book to Amanda.

Larry blessed his son with strength to overcome all his trials. He assured Chris that his Father in Heaven was mindful of his struggles and that he was there for him if he would but kneel in prayer. He blessed him with the wisdom to recognize right from wrong and to know the right path to take. Larry closed the prayer, feeling confident that his son would be all right.

"Well, I guess we better go now. We've taken up way too much time," Larry said. "I'm proud of you Chris. I love you." He leaned over and gave Chris a hug good-bye.

"I love you too, dad," Chris responded. He realized it had been a long time since he told his father that he loved him, and he noticed tears of joy filling his father's eyes.

Chris waved good-bye from the porch and watched as his father's truck passed through the gate and started down the road. Chris was ecstatic to find Amanda and give her the Book of Mormon but was delayed by Ms. Holtz, who was waiting for him just inside the doorway.

"I see things went well today," she smiled.

"Yeah, you could say that," Chris boasted, satisfied with the visit as well as with his progress. He knew he still had a long way to go but felt like he'd broken the ice.

"You missed lunch. Are you hungry?"

"No, I haven't even thought about food today. I haven't felt this good since my mom built me my first skate ramp in our driveway," he said, chuckling.

"I'm glad you're moving in the right direction, but you're a long way from beating your drug addiction. Today was a good day, but you'll still have your bad days too. Those days when all you can think about is how badly you want a pill."

"I think I'm past that now. Really, you don't need to worry about me anymore. I could go home tomorrow and know that I would never take another pill!" he said enthusiastically as if he'd just conquered Rome.

"Don't be overconfident, Christopher. That's when you fall," she lectured sternly.

Chris just smiled and took off to find Amanda. *She doesn't know as much as she thinks she does,* he thought, self-assured that he was home free.

# Chapter 29

hris found Amanda out by the stables. He caught her by the arm, swinging her around and planting a kiss on her.

"Gee, what did I do to deserve that?" she asked, caught off guard by his openness.

"I have the Book of Mormon for you," he said excitedly. Her eyes lit up as he handed her the book. "This one is for you, and my dad brought mine from home." Chris felt like a lovesick schoolboy who couldn't wait to study his homework with the girl next door. He wanted to share all of his favorite scriptures with her.

"Thank you. Who's the note from?"

"My Bishop. He's a great man. He marked some important scriptures for us to read."

"Great, I'll go to my room and start reading," she said anxiously.

"Wait! You mean to say you don't want to read with me?" Chris felt his white cloud of joy suddenly turn grey and burst into a downpour.

Amanda let out a laugh. "If I have questions, you're the first person I'll come too. But I'd really like to read it on my own—more of a personal experience, if you know what I mean."

Chris was more than a little heartbroken, but he didn't express his feelings to Amanda. He just nodded and watched her run off like a child on Christmas morning. He looked down at his own book in his hands. It had probably been at least a year since he had even cracked it open, and his heart pounded with anticipation.

He found a secluded area behind the stables next to a large maple tree. He sat down, cradled the book in his hands, and suddenly felt a bit awkward.

He pushed his feelings of self-doubt aside and flipped open to the first scripture written on the yellow sticky note. It was 1 Nephi 15:24.

> And I said unto them that it was the word of God; and whoso would hearken unto the word of God, and would hold fast unto it, they would never perish; neither could the temptations and the fiery darts of the adversary overpower them unto blindness, to lead them away to destruction.

He moved on to the next scripture, 3 Nephi 18:18.

> Behold, verily, verily, I say unto you, ye must watch and pray always lest ye enter into temptation; for Satan desireth to have you, that he may sift you as wheat.

Chris leaned back against the huge tree trunk. *Sift me like wheat*, he thought. *That's pretty strong.* He reread the scripture again, realizing that the bishop had picked that scripture as a warning to him. He was reminding him how easily Satan can weasel his way back in. He thought back over the last several months. He'd let Satan influence him many times—in his language, in his decisions, and in his anger. The progress was so slow and subtle that he'd not noticed how much he was changing until it was almost too late.

Chris hadn't felt the Spirit with him until just the last week when he talked to Amanda about the gospel. He was taught that the Holy Ghost couldn't dwell in an unclean place. He had driven the Holy Ghost away when he started using drugs, which had left Chris with emptiness and despair. He'd taken a wonderful gift and had just thrown it away. Hopelessness and discouragement started to creep up inside him, but he quickly pushed them aside, remembering what the Bishop had told him. He was no longer going to surrender to Satan's influence.

He shook his head and read the next scripture, which was Ether 12:27.

> And if men come unto me I will show unto them their weakness. I give unto men weakness that they may be humble; and my grace is sufficient for all men that humble themselves before me; for if they humble themselves before me, and have faith in me, then will I make weak things become strong unto them.

Chris felt his spirit suddenly surge with optimism as he read. He reread the last part again. "Have faith in me, then will I make weak things become strong unto them." Chris smiled softly, reassured that his weaknesses were indeed known and that the Lord would be there to guide him.

Chris continued on to Doctrine and Covenants 122:7.

> And if thou shouldest be cast into the pit, or into the hands of murderers, and the sentence of death passed upon thee; if thou be cast into the deep; if the billowing surge conspire against thee; if fierce winds become thine enemy; if the heavens gather blackness, and all the elements combine to hedge up the way; and above all, if the very jaws of hell shall gape open the mouth wide after thee, know thou, my son, that all these things shall give thee experience, and shall be for thy good.

Hearing the call for dinner, Chris reluctantly closed his scriptures. He sat mesmerized at the last verse, wondering how everything that had happened could possibly be for his own good. *How can losing my mother be a good experience?* he thought, troubled by the verse. *Why would the Lord give us such terrible trials in life?* Those thoughts weighed heavy on his mind as he slowly walked back to the house for dinner.

Chris sat quietly at the table, pondering what he'd just read. His optimism was slowing transforming into confusion. He looked across the table at Amanda. She was glowing brighter than he'd ever seen her before. She smiled brightly at him, like a child who had just learned a huge secret.

After dinner he caught Amanda running off to her room. "Hey, how's the reading coming along?" he asked with curiosity.

"Great! I'm already in second Nephi. I just can't seem to put it down," she exclaimed, grinning from ear to ear. "How about you?"

"It's going all right, I guess. Some of the scriptures are a little confusing to me."

"Keep reading. That's what I've found to be helpful. Well, I'll see you later," she said eagerly, wanting to get back to her newfound book.

Chris watched as she rushed back to her bedroom. He was amazed at how open she was to the gospel. She already held a unique kind of faith that he envied. He never would've thought it would go this far from simply stating he was Mormon. Now she could be well on her way to baptism and becoming a member of the Church. This would not have happened if hadn't started taking drugs to begin with.

Chris sat down on the side of his bed, recapping his last thought. If he'd never started taking drugs, then he wouldn't be here, and Amanda wouldn't be reading the Book of Mormon. He started thinking about it a little more. He wouldn't have started taking the drugs in the first place if he hadn't gotten in that terrible fight, which was all because he'd hit that kid for saying something about his mother . . . who died.

"That's it!" he gasped. Losing his mother was a horrible tragedy, but if Amanda gained a testimony and joined the Church, then something good would come out of all his misery. Suddenly it was making sense. There had been a string of events leading up to that one moment in time when he introduced Amanda to the gospel. But it wasn't just Amanda who had been affected. He too was learning something from all of this. He was learning to be unselfish and forgiving of others, as well as making amends with his father. Chris then realized everything does happen for a reason, even if we don't always understand why.

He eagerly picked up his Book of Mormon and read the Doctrine and Covenants 122:7 again, this time with more clarification and meaning.

> "And if thou shouldst be cast into the pit, or into the hands of murderers, and the sentence of death passed upon thee; if thou be cast into the deep; if the billowing surge conspire against thee; if fierce winds become thine enemy; if the heavens gather blackness, and all the elements combine to hedge up the way; and above all, if the very jaws of hell shall gape open the mouth wide after thee, know thou, my son that all these things shall give thee experience, and shall be for thy good."

His mind was at ease now that he understood the scripture and could see the bigger picture. He happily moved on to the next scripture, yearning for more information. In Moroni 6:8 he read,

> But as oft as they repented and sought forgiveness, with real intent, they were forgiven.

The words "real intent" caught his eye. It was the key to true repentance, the one thing he'd feared all along. He wanted to be sincerely ready for repentance, but at the same time, he didn't want to use that as an

216

excuse to delay the process. He let out a huge sigh of frustration, feeling suffocated with his cowardliness.

He continued with the next scripture, hoping for some relief from the burden he felt. It was Moroni 10:33.

> And again, if ye by the grace of God are perfect in Christ, and deny not his power, then are ye sanctified in Christ by the grace of God, through the shedding of the blood of Christ, which is in the covenant of the Father unto the remission of your sins, that ye become holy, without spot.

Chris realized after reading that scripture that Christ had already suffered for his sins. It was now on Chris's shoulders. He felt an overpowering sense of guilt at the thought of Christ bleeding from every pore, taking upon himself the sins of the whole world, and all Chris had to do was kneel down, with real intent, and ask for forgiveness. So why was he hesitating? *Our part seems too easy,* he thought as he continued to read in 2 Nephi 32:3.

> Angels speak by the power of the Holy Ghost; wherefore, they speak the words of Christ; Wherefore, I said unto you, feast upon the words of Christ; for behold, the words of Christ will tell you all things what ye should do.

And verses 8–9:

> And now, my beloved brethren, I perceive that ye ponder still in your hearts; and it grieveth me that I must speak concerning this thing. For if ye would hearken unto the Spirit which teacheth a man to pray ye would know that ye must pray; for the evil spirit teacheth not a man to pray, but teacheth him that he must not pray.

> But behold, I say unto you that ye must pray always, and not faint; that ye must not perform any thing unto the Lord save in the first place ye shall pray unto the Father in the name of Christ, that he will consecrate thy performance unto thee, that thy performance may be for the welfare of thy soul.

Pondering the last verses, Chris closed the book once more and laid it on the nightstand. Praying had always been a hard thing for him, especially after his mother passed away.

He'd prayed night and day for her to get well, but it seemed his prayers were left unanswered, so he eventually stopped praying altogether. His mother, however, was quick to see the changes in him and called him to her bedside. He told her he'd lost faith in prayer because she wasn't getting better.

He remembered how she struggled to pull herself up to a sitting position, looked him straight in the eye, and told him that he must not let the adversary win.

"Satan puts those thoughts in your head to confuse you and lead you astray," she said firmly. "I have something I need to do, but it's not on this earth. Your prayers help me get through the pain each day, so please don't stop praying for me."

Chris realized that he was praying for the wrong reasons—selfish reasons—and he began to pray for her pain to stop. Shortly after that, she passed away. He often wondered if his prayers had been answered, just not in the way he wanted them to be.

Chris sat silently staring out the window at the other kids playing basketball. He noticed there were two beautiful red and brown robins perched on the branch outside his window. They would chirp happily for a few moments and then stop to watch the kids beneath them. He studied their movements and their distinctive beauty and wondered how it would feel to be so free—free of rules, chaos, and life's complications. He laughed as they flew away, thinking that the only thing a bird has to worry about is staying away from the cat.

He lay back on his bed, placed his hands behind his head, and looked up at the ceiling. He thought about the birds again and wished he could fly away from all his problems. Of course, he knew eventually he would come to his senses and fly home again. Guilt and shame were once again weaseling their way back into his head, and thoughts of his future plummeted his weary mind. Seeing his father today was tough, but facing Katie on Thursday would be his greatest obstacle so far. Doubt filled him up inside, leaving him wondering what the future would hold.

As the sun slipped down behind the mountain and the room became dark, Chris knew the time was drawing near. He needed to ask for forgiveness from the Lord. He wanted to feel as free as the birds outside his window, and he knew that kind of self-found freedom could only come from one place.

He took a deep breath and exhaled slowly, releasing the skepticism he held inside. His heart pounded loudly with anticipation as he knelt down beside his bed. He started out slowly, thanking his Father in Heaven for the wonderful blessings he'd received, and for a loving family to help him through the hard times in life. He was silent for a moment. All was quiet, except the soft laughter of the two boys in the next room. He took another deep breath and started again.

"Heavenly Father . . . I probably don't deserve a second chance, but . . . I would really like one, so . . . please forgive me for all the terrible things I've done."

The words were slow in coming as he fought off feelings of shame and embarrassment. "Please forgive me for the lies . . . the anger . . . the drinking, smoking, and using drugs that were all for my own selfish reasons. I know what I did was wrong, but Father, if thou wilt only forgive me, I promise to always live up to my baptismal covenants and never stray off the path again."

Tears welled up in his eyes as he was suddenly filled with an overwhelming feeling of peace and comfort. The guilt and shame he'd felt had vanished, and he knew without a doubt that the Lord was listening to his prayers. He didn't feel judged or persecuted for his mistakes, just loved. A thought came into his mind so strongly that it was like someone was kneeling right beside him, talking to him in the flesh. *You are my child. I will always love you and never desert you.*

Chris knelt there on the floor, overcome by the Spirit and basking in the love he felt from his Heavenly Father. The tears streamed down his face as he whispered a soft "thank you" before ending his prayer and climbing back into bed.

Chris lay awake in the darkness of the room, thinking about all he'd read and all he'd felt that day. His life was once again moving in the right direction. He was comforted to know that Heavenly Father had heard his prayer. He knew that from then on he would never again feel alone.

# Chapter 30

Thursday came along sooner than Chris had hoped. He still wanted to see his sisters, but he felt nervous and anxious at the same time. He wanted them to see him the way he used to be, before the drugs.

The week had been a frustrating one for him. First, he missed Keith terribly and wished he could talk to him about all that had happened with his father. Second, he had a new roommate, Carlos. Carlos moved in on Tuesday, but it didn't seem right letting someone move in so soon after Keith's death. He argued that fact with Ms. Holtz but was told that there were a lot of kids out there who needed help, and she wasn't going to turn them away. Chris couldn't stand that she was always right.

Carlos didn't speak to Chris much, and Chris couldn't decide if he was shy or just plain rude. It would take some time to find out. He saw Carlos going through the same symptoms that he'd gone through—the shakes, the cold sweats, and the anger. It was amazing how obvious it was standing from the outside looking in. He tried to be supportive, giving him advice on Dr. Quack and Ms. Holtz, but he didn't seem to care.

Carlos was from St. George, Utah, and a freshman at school. Chris came to understand that Carlos had been using drugs a long time, but he couldn't find out just what it was he had been using.

Amanda had finished the Book of Mormon and was excited to meet the Mormon missionaries who were coming to talk to her that Saturday. It had been enlightening to watch her progress spiritually. They talked often about the gospel, which strengthened Chris's testimony a great deal.

She once told him that he'd saved her, but she did not realize that it was she who had saved him. Without her enthusiasm for the Church, Chris realized that he might not have started thinking about his own faith. It was her strength that had set up the vital stepping-stones he needed to turn his life around.

Amanda would be leaving in just two weeks. They had talked it over and decided to keep in touch by writing at least twice a month. Still, Chris treasured their priceless friendship and didn't want to let her go. They were both dreading the day when they would have to say good-bye.

After breakfast and chores were finished, everyone gathered in the living room for group. They talked for a while about responsibility and accountability and then went around the room to see if anyone wanted to share anything.

Chris slowly got up and walked to the front of the room. "I know it's been hard on all of us, losing Keith like that, but I just wanted to share some of my feelings with you." He looked around the room and all eyes were focused on him. For a moment he wished he'd stayed quiet.

"When I was using pain pills, it seemed like life didn't mean anything. I couldn't function. I couldn't interact with anybody without blowing up at them. I felt terrible about myself. I was in a downward spiral with no way to stop. I finally hit rock bottom the day I tried to kill myself," he said softly, looking down at the floor.

"I was supposed to be watching over my eight-year-old sister at the lake, but instead, I'd taken more pills and couldn't stay focused on anything. Because of my carelessness and stupidity, she fell in the lake . . . and almost drowned. That day when I looked into my father's eyes, I saw nothing but disappointment. I didn't want to live knowing that I'd let them both down, so I went back to the cabin and took the rest of the pain pills. I remember thinking how everyone would be better off without me, and that I didn't deserve to live after what I'd done. I even thought about trying it again when I got back home. But seeing Keith take his own life changed mine forever. I realized that life is a wonderful gift, and we have no right to throw that gift away."

"Sure, life is going to have its potholes and rainy days, but I can now honestly tell you this: There will be sunny days too. Our potholes in life are only as big as we make them, and if life keeps giving you buckets of rain, well, then, buy a rain barrel and wait for the sun, because it will shine again. I know that more than anything now. I guess that's all I wanted to say."

Chris stood up and started back to his seat. Ms. Holtz stood up and started clapping her hands, and then others joined in. Chris looked around the room in surprise. He smiled, hoping that he'd gotten through to someone and made a difference in their life. He didn't want anyone to experience the satanic darkness he'd been lost in.

"Chris, thank you. That was wonderful. Thank you for sharing your feelings with us," Ms. Holtz said, grinning from ear to ear.

Chris went outside to clear his head and prepare for seeing his sisters in just a few hours. The day had whizzed by, and the time was growing near. He sat down on the bench and felt the warmth of the sun on his face. With all the tension of seeing his sisters again, the feeling of needing a pain pill was suddenly overwhelming. It consumed his thoughts, and he realized that he was still very vulnerable to the cravings inside.

He was angry and agitated by the way he was feeling. He knew it wasn't the pill in itself he craved, but rather the feeling of needing to stay in control. That was how the weak Chris dealt with things, turning to the drugs to help him cope. As he tried to fight back the desire, a powerful thought came barreling into his mind. Watching to make sure no one saw him, he got up from the bench and went behind the barn.

Realizing he couldn't fight this feeling on his own, he knelt down and began to pray. "Heavenly Father, please give me the strength I need to fight my desire for the pills and overcome my addiction."

As he ended his prayer and started back toward the house, he suddenly felt a calming sensation come over him as he regained control of himself. It was liberating and refreshing to know that help was just a prayer away, and that through faith and prayer, anything was possible.

Chris was just finishing up his math assignment when Ms. Holtz came in to let him know his family had arrived. He stood up and took a deep breath.

"You're ready for this Christopher," she said with confidence.

"Tell that to my shaking knees," he said, laughing, but he was very serious.

As he walked down the staircase, he could see Katie checking out everything in the room. Then he saw Jody, dressed in her favorite red-striped T-shirt and her designer blue jeans, sitting patiently on the couch next to their father. His heart leapt with joy at the sight of his family. Even though he missed his mother greatly, he knew she was where she needed to be, and his family would be there for him to lean on—especially his father.

"Chris!" Katie exclaimed, and she ran to give him a big bear hug. Chris dropped to his knees and took her in his arms. Katie squeezed him as tightly as she could and said, "I missed you soooooo much!"

Chris's emotions overcame him and his eyes filled with tears. He could feel Katie's love for him, and he instantly knew that she would never hold him responsible for what had happened.

"I've missed you too, short stuff," he said tearfully.

"Katie, let the poor boy breathe, for heaven's sake," Larry said, approaching them.

"She's all right," Chris said, standing up to greet his father.

"Hi, Dad," he said as he put his arms around him and gave him a hug. Chris was now finding it much easier to show his affections.

Jody sat quietly on the couch, not sure if she should move. She was shocked and relieved to see the two of them embrace. She knew then that they were a family again.

Chris walked over and stood beside her. "Hi, Jody," he said nervously.

"How are you?" she asked timidly.

Chris laughed. "Couldn't be better. How are you?" He didn't want this to turn into small talk. He was ready to move on.

"I'm fine," she smiled. Katie came running over, pleading for Chris to show her the horses.

"Why don't I take Katie to see the horses while you two talk?" Larry said, wanting them to have some time alone. He took Katie by the hand and led her out the front door.

"How is it here?" Jody asked, looking around at how beautiful everything was.

"It's all right. I've gotten a lot of things straightened out. Best of all, I'm off the drugs." Trying to shake the awkwardness, he sat down on the couch beside her.

"So, were you taking them for a long time?"

"It started right after the attack. At first I used them for the pain, but then . . . I just couldn't stop. I thought I could do it on my own, but . . . I can see now I wouldn't have been able to."

"I'm sorry, Chris. I wish I could have helped you. I just didn't . . ."

"It's okay, Jody. I tried my best to hide it from everyone—not that you couldn't tell something was wrong with me. I just hope you can forgive me for all the rotten things I said and did."

"Chris, you're my brother and I love you. Nothing can change that."

"You mean that?"

Jody smiled. "Of course I mean that. I've missed you." She leaned over and threw her arms around his neck, giving him a gigantic hug.

"I've missed you too."

"Have you made lots of friends here?"

"Yeah, a couple of good ones. Keith was my roommate and my best friend here. We talked about everything from girls to parents." He smiled at the thought of Keith advising him on parents and warning him about girls. "He killed himself last week, right before he was to go home."

"I'm sorry, Chris. Are you all right?"

"I am now. His suicide forced me to look at my own life, and I realized how wrong I was about our family . . . Dad . . . a lot of things. But I've put that all behind me, and I'm starting over. We all are."

"I'm glad to hear you say that. I was scared we'd never be a family again."

"Well, you don't need to worry anymore. Anyway, I also met the most wonderful girl," he exclaimed.

"A *girl*? Do you want to elaborate on that?" She smiled curiously and poked him in the rib.

"She's fifteen with silky red hair, beautiful green eyes, and her smile . . ."

"You like her!"

"She's been with me through everything. We've become really close."

"Have you kissed her?"

"Gentlemen never kiss and tell," he teased. "I'd really like to introduce her to you."

"Maybe some other time," she said, disappointed. "Here come dad and Katie back from the barn."

For over an hour they talked and laughed together as a family. Larry could see they were finally bonding together.

Their visit ended with lots of hugs and kisses. Chris took Katie by the hand and knelt down on both knees so he could look into her eyes. "Katie, I want to tell you something," he said gently. "I'm sorry I didn't watch you better that day at the lake. It's my fault you fell in, not yours."

"But, Chris, I . . ."

"No, Katie. What I did was very wrong. I was putting bad stuff into my body and it impaired my thinking. It wasn't your fault, it was mine, and it will never happen again, okay?" he said firmly.

"Okay," Katie replied.

"I love you, Katie!"

"I love you too, Chris," Katie said, smiling as she gave her big brother one last hug.

"I'm so proud of you, Christopher. You're going to be okay. I love you, son," Larry said, giving Chris a hug.

"I love you too, Dad. You know, I'll be home in just five weeks," Chris said, smiling.

"I know! Does that mean I have to kick out the boarder I'm renting your room to?" Larry remarked, laughing. Chris shot his father a smile. "I'm kidding," he added quickly. "We're all looking forward to having you back."

As Chris watched them drive away, he was thankful for such a loving and understanding family. He'd put them through so much, and yet they were all so quick to forgive. He made a solemn promise to himself and to the Lord that from that day on, he would treat them all with love and respect and never let them down again.

Chris knew he had the Lord to thank for the strength he was feeling. Remembering what Ms. Holtz had said, he knew he was still a long way from recovery. But with Heavenly Father's help, he had no doubt that he could do it. However, he would always need to be on his guard against the adversary, who he knew would never give up.

Larry watched Chris in the rearview mirror until he could no longer see him. *I'm indeed blessed,* he thought. *Jody's opened up, giving me a second chance, Katie survived her near drowning, and Chris found his way back from his drug addiction, becoming stronger than I ever thought he could.*

They were building a strong relationship as father and son, and Larry couldn't help but wonder if Barbara was pushing things along from the other side. Four months ago he thought that all was lost, but now things couldn't be looking more positive. Sure they would still have their trials and rough times ahead, but they were together again as a family, and with that strength, they could conquer anything.

*Thank heaven for miracles,* Larry thought as he happily drove away from the Sunrise Youth Center. *And second chances!*

# Discussion Questions

1. How did their mother's death affect Jody, Chris, and Katie?

2. How did their father's absence affect each of them?

3. How did Barbara's death affect Larry?

4. Did Chris's drug addiction affect the members of his family? If so, how?

5. What were the consequences of Chris's actions?

6. How did Chris's testimony change?

7. How did Amanda and Keith alter Chris's future?

# About the Author

Linda was born and raised in Providence, Utah. She attended Cache County schools and graduated from Mountain Crest High School in 1988. She married the love of her life on November 28, 1987. Their marriage was later solemnized in the Logan Temple on June 3, 1989. They have five wonderful children, including a set of twins.

Linda and her family moved to Ogden, Utah, in 1994 where she continued her education at Certified Careers Institute. She graduated in 1995 with a degree in data entry. She has also taken classes in poetry and creative writing.

The Chadwicks moved back to Cache Valley in 1997 and have made their home in Providence. Linda is currently employed at the Cache Valley Youth Center, where she has worked as a cook for the last seven years.

Linda is a member of the Providence Third Ward and has had many callings in the Primary. When she's not attached to her computer writing, she enjoys spending time with her family camping, boating, and just hanging out with them.